POSSE WHIPPED 2: TRIAL BY FAR

by Paul K. Metheney

This is a work of fiction. Names, characters, places, and incidents are products of the author's imagination or used fictitiously. Any resemblance to actual persons (living or dead), events, entities, products, or locations is entirely coincidental.

Copyright © 2023 Paul K. Metheney
5753 Highway 85 North #6092 Crestview, FL 32536
All rights reserved. First Edition
ISBN Print Paperback: 978-1-949241-42-6
ISBN epub: 978-1-949241-43-3
ISBN Hard Cover: 978-1-949241-44-0

https://PaulMetheney.com
Twitter.com/PaulMetheney
Facebook.com/PaulKMetheney
Cover design by Paul Metheney, pmetheney@gmail.com

TABLE OF CONTENTS

The Raccoons Are Coming 1
   All the News That's Fit to Eat 2
WWTD 9
   35 Years Ago: 9
   Present: 10
Divide & Conquer 12
Major Developments 16
Love at The Hole 19
   Know When to Fold 'Em 21
A Horse is a Horse Unless Of Course 25
Sharper Knives 27
Lake View Included 30
Surely She's Surly 33
Brotherly Love 36
Break-Ins & Stake-Outs 41
No Such Thing as a Free Lunch 50
Forty Percent & White Hands 53
Same Trick, New Day 58
Chainsaw Bandits & Cut Scenes 61
   Not Just Another Day 62
Ice Cream & Community Service 69
   Work Outs & Work Days 70
Maximum Penalty 74
Any Port in a Shit Storm 76
   The Only Good Lawyer 81
Cool Heads & Councils 85
Back In Business 89
Jacob, Get Out! 91
News & Views 96
Say Hey 99
Friends in Low Places 101
Plea Deals & Prints 103
Fire: Steady, Stable Work 107
Trial: Opening Statements 110
Fire: Blazing Saddles 112
Trial: Distasteful Testimony 114
Fire: Dante's Inferno 118
Trial: With Friends Like These 119
Fire: The Roof is On Far! 126
Trial: No Free Will of His Own 130
Fire: Great Barns of Fire 136
Trial & Fire: Motives, Men's Rooms, & Molestation 138

Fire: Bronco Bust In 142
Fire: Smokin' Hot Wife 146
Trial: One Day Earlier 148
Fire: Childhood's End...154
Flip The Script 161
Trial: Resting Guilt Face...164
Follow The Money...166
Yard Work of the Heart 170
F.N.G. 173
No News is No News 177
Reading & Revelations...183
When It Rains 188
Shock & Aw 191
Necessity is the Mother Of Intervention..195
Heaven Help Us 200
Losing at Legalized Gambling..203
   Three Days Earlier:.. 203
   Present:... 204
Affordable Advice 206
Toys in the Attic 209
Supply the Pie...213
Relatively Family 219
   We Don't Need No Steenken Warrants... 221
Burying The Lede Under Lard 225
Dishes & Deities...229
Two Bits & A Shave...231
Sibling Rivalry 235
Photos & Phone Calls..237
   Far From Evidence.. 238
Picking Up the Trash 240
Ghost, Busters & Break Downs...244
Darlene for the Defense 252
Trial: A New Sheriff in Town...254
Leading Lessons Learned 265
Trial: He Got Better...267
Trial: Phone Tagged 273
Trial: Evidently Inadmissible 276
No Allowance For Crime..287
Phones, Faults, And Follow-Up...291
Epilogue 294
Special Thanks 298
More from Paul K. Metheney..299

The Raccoons Are Coming

Jacob and Hannah MacDowell thought life was as good as it could get. Their son, Jeb, and seven-year-old granddaughter, Naomi, had moved back in with them. True, the murder of Jeb's wife, Beth, last year, instigated the move, but that was a path everyone avoided treading. Because of their outdoor and active lifestyle, the MacDowells were in better shape than most people half their age, minus the joy of dieting or going to the gym.

A large portion of their happiness could be linked directly back to the amount of time they got to play and spend with their granddaughter. Watching Naomi grow into a beautiful and intelligent child was one of their lasting joys. Mac doted on the child like no other.

The MacDowell ranch in northern Kentucky was doing quite well. Besides the income from being a working farm, the MacDowells had resumed Hannah's grandfather's horse breeding, training, and boarding business. Thanks to the reputation of her family's name and fair pricing, they had all the business they could handle. The family enjoyed dividends from a co-op sharing program the town had instituted in support of a new tourism development plan. There was some small profit from a buckboard wagon/tourist-ride side venture Hannah had invested in with a former employee. Add Mac's salary as the sheriff of Mounton County and they were doing well financially, lived in one of the nicest spreads in the area, and had their family with them. Yepper, the MacDowells were living the dream.

Until the troubles started.

The first of their problems snuck up on them like a raccoon in the garbage. And was just about as welcome.

#

All the News That's Fit to Eat

"Sheriff. Jeb. How do The Boys MacDowell fare this fine day?" Ginny asked as the father-and-son team entered his diner with a jangle of the bell above the door.

Ginny was constantly reminded how much the two men looked like brothers, sharing lean frames, and dressed in identical jeans, boots, and tan sheriff's department short-sleeve shirts. Mac sported more than a bit of gray in his crew-cut hair years away from his son's thicker brown hair. Instead of Mac's worn, brown Stetson, Jeb wore a Louisville Cardinals' baseball cap. Truth be told, Jeb, while slightly shorter than his dad was a bit more muscular than Mac, although his father loathed to admit it. The other major difference: Jeb wore a side arm and a Sam Brown police belt, whereas Mac wore a tooled leather belt and silver rodeo buckle. In a town with a population of a biscuit over six hundred, he simply didn't see the point. He just didn't feel the need to wear a handgun. More importantly, Hannah didn't.

Ginny was the current proprietor and senior chef of *Ginny's Diner*. Ginny was not his real name. His mother didn't saddle him with that. She did much, much worse. He kept his first name a secret known exclusively to Mac, Adrian Stemple, and a few others in the nearly-impossible-to-keep-a-secret community of Mounton. There was a great deal about the enormous biker-looking diner owner's past the town did not know. His propensity for flowery vocabulary, where he had learned his extraordinary culinary skills, and why Mac was one of the few people who knew both his real name and the answers to all those questions still baffled much of the back-woods town. These were still well-kept secrets in a village where everyone knew everything about everybody else. The bitties down at *Darlene's Beauty Emporium/Barbershop/Tanning Salon* were practically apoplectic over the mysteries that surrounded the man who looked more like a body-building Hell's Angel than a restaurant chef. They knew he inherited the diner from his mother, Virginia, who inherited it from a long line of *Ginnys*. But other than that, the town knew very little about him. Well, other than the obvious. Ginny was the biggest man in Mounton. With arms like knotted oak trees covered in tattoos, he kept his long hair in a plastic hair bonnet while preparing his culinary masterpieces. Stubble adorned the face only a mother bear could love, which sat above the thick neck typically protruding out of a slightly too-tight classic rock tee shirt. When on duty, the giant wore an apron with stains dating back to before Virginia gave birth to him. The fact of the matter was: Ginny was Mac's best friend. How the two had met and bonded was as much an enigma as his vocabulary.

The diner itself looked like an oversized Airstream trailer with a polished aluminum exterior and curved walls straight out of the 1940s. The interior featured the original black and white checkered flooring, red vinyl bench seats in the booths, and a counter down the length of the diner. No matter what was on the menu for the day, the diner carried the aroma of crisp bacon and freshly brewed coffee.

"Ginny," Jeb acknowledged, as Mac removed his brown Stetson. Ginny was well aware Mac was the town's stoic and usually let Jeb do most of his talking. With a lifetime of translating Dad-Speak, it was as natural to the father-son team as breathing.

"Ginny, is it my imagination, or have you changed your hair?" asked Jeb.

"Indeed. I observed I was getting some awkward gazes from you and decided to reduce the temptation in your path," Ginny joked.

"I would think a guy your age would be happy for any attention he got," Jeb laughed.

"I'll have you know young MacDowell," Ginny said with a faux smile, "I am but a half-score years older than yourself."

Mac and Jeb joined Duncan at the MacDowell's regular table. It was an unspoken fact Ginny typically kept it empty when he thought the MacDowell buys might come in, but Duncan was the exception. As one of Mac's closest friends, he had an open invitation to sit at their private table. Good thing. He would sit anywhere he liked anyway.

"Aye, ifn' it ain't the Tourist an' his better-lookin' offspring!" Duncan greeted them in his thick Scottish brogue.

"Duncan," Mac replied as he sat his Stetson aside and placed it crown down on the seat next to him.

"I assume it will be the Lunch Special?" Ginny inquired.

"Depends. Was it four-legged or two, before it became the Special?" Jeb joked.

"Ha! Neither. It slithered." Ginny smiled as he returned to the kitchen. Ginny insisted he be the one who waited on the MacDowell family when they ate at his establishment. Partially because he never charged them for their meals and it wouldn't be fair to his waitress, Peggy, to wait on them, and to some extent because it was one of the few chances he had to socialize with his friends. Ginny was the second closest thing Mounton had to Google. Hannah's Church Ladies were the closest.

While Duncan and the two MacDowells sat in their usual booth with the cracked red vinyl seats and waited for their lunch, Ginny brought Jeb's sweet tea and Mac's coffee.

"Here you go," Ginny said when he sat plates in front of the two men. "What do you stalwart lads have on your agenda for the nonce?"

"You're getting as hard to understand as Duncan. If you mean 'what are we doing today?'" Jeb smirked, "This afternoon, I go pick up Naomi from school. We'll probably feed and water the animals until dinner. Now that Jesse's a full-time deputy, Dad was able to change the schedule to enable us all to work five days and get two days off in a row. I opted not to so Dad and I could patrol on Saturday mornings. What would Saturday be without eating here and your awesome company?"

"I will grant you fellows, when it's not a pulse-pounding frenzy around here, it has an astounding tendency to be dishrag dull," Ginny commented.

"Yepper," Mac said.

"In our business, dull is good," Jeb reluctantly agreed. It was clear to Ginny Jeb yearned for a more action-packed lifestyle. Another victim of cop-cinema.

"Well, permit me to be the first to energize your day," Ginny began. "It appears Syrus and Spencer Stamper were discharged back into what we laughingly refer to as civilized society."

"How did that happen?" Jeb asked. Mac listened as he worked on his lunch. It didn't taste like slithering anything. In fact, it tasted like chicken. But then, what didn't?

"An enormous miscarriage of justice it seems," Ginny explained. "Despite my testimony of my attempted kidnapping, there was no physical proof other than my word. Some high-priced Lexington law firm by the name of Beacon, Hill, and Hollister pleaded it down to a lesser charge for which they received a less than adequate penalty of 'time served' and got them retroactively paroled for previous indiscretions." The plot last year that ended with Beth's death involved the three Stamper brothers among others. Ginny turned toward Duncan. "Duncan didn't technically witness them commit any crimes, they were just in the vicinity of the detained victims. A lack of fingerprints, DNA, or other physical evidence assisted in throwing out their case. The prosecutors disregarded former mayor Jarvis's statement about their participation as an attempt to plea bargain his own involvement."

Besides being one of Mac's closest and oldest friends, Alistair Duncan was a local store owner of proud Scottish descent. He aided in the apprehension of all the criminals involved including former mayor Jarvis. The mastermind behind it all, Commonwealth Attorney Devlin Douvez, previously arranged for Jarvis's release after Mac arrested him earlier for murder.

"What about Sonny?" Jeb asked Ginny. Mac stopped eating. Sonny Stamper was the youngest of the three Stamper brothers andthe second largest man in Mounton County, but a little on the 'simple' side. Sonny privately expressed his regrets and helped Mac learn more about his enemies. He and Hannah had taken a special interest in the young man and helped him literally clean up his act, get a job as a bouncer at the local watering hole, and find a new life on the straight and narrow. Mac vouched for the man during his trial when Sonny testified to not only his brothers' criminal activities but his own. The judge released Sonny into Mac's custody and for the last year, the bear-like man-child had been nothing but a saint.

"As it happens, the aforementioned barristers conjured up some psychologists who asserted Sonny was too mentally incompetent to testify against his siblings," Ginny continued. "Ironic, given, as of the three of them, he is, without question, the best of the bunch."

"An' what does it say about our judicial, psychiatric, an' educational systems that an inbred simpleton with nae education is the best of the three of them an' they can't recognize the fact?" Duncan asked.

"Barristers spin reality the way they desire the courts to visualize it," Ginny lamented with a shake of his head.

"So, the eidjits Stampers are oot and aboot? Any idea what they be planning now?" Duncan asked.

"Not as such. Released from incarceration but yesterday. I suspect they have not yet had time to reach their full potential for mayhem. Given their past history and inclinations, I would allow them until at least this afternoon before they commence with a new scheme."

"I'll go check on Sonny as soon as I can," Mac spoke up.

"Yeah, knowing those miscreants, it seems likely their first priority would be to get the band back together," Ginny smiled grimly. "Besides, he was their muscle. Without him, they are simply *conniving* and *mean-spirited*."

"I take it Syrus stars as *conniving* and Spencer plays *mean-spirited*?" Jeb smiled.

"It could go either way, but while Sonny is no Stephen Hawking, he was the brawn of the triumvirate, if not the exclusively good-hearted one."

"Ye need to be careful, lad," Duncan said to Mac. "Those inbreds are eidjits, but they can be *vicious* eidjits if'n they're a mind to. Ye need to be watchin' your own back a wee bit more. Ya spend all your time lookin' out for others when sometimes, it's your neck on the line. Just because you're a good man, you know, for a tourist, doesn't mean God won't find ye guilty and yank yer halo away. Mac me boy, I worry Heaven won't have ye, and it'd be exactly like ye to run for the office of the sheriff of Hell."

Mac shook his head slightly. Duncan, well known for his frugality, pride in his heritage, and his caution, did not exhibit much of a sense of humor. Regardless, Mac needed to make sure Sonny was okay now that his brothers were out of jail.

"What do we owe you for lunch?" Mac asked Ginny, just as he did every day.

Ginny gave Mac a look that would have chilled his coffee, just as he did every day.

Ginny watched as the three men stood and Mac tipped his worn, brown Stetson at the ancient woman knitting at the cash register as old as she was. After a moment, Jeb snatched his Cardinals baseball cap from his head and nodded.

"Shirley," Mac acknowledged.

"Susie," Shirley responded. She poked fun of Mac's tendency to find peaceful resolutions, but all ninety-four pounds of her had stood up and been counted last year when Mac's friends and family were taken. Mac eyed the knitting bag that Ginny knew contained one of the largest .44 Magnums ever made. *If every business had a security system like that, there would be no robberies,* Ginny thought. *Then again, if every diner had a Shirley at the front, there would be no business.*

#

As the three men stepped into the bright Kentucky sunshine, they walked a few blocks down and over to The Side Street toward the clapboard Mounton County Sheriff's Department, where Jeb and Mac parked their trucks. Duncan continued on to his store on Main Street.

The MacDowells walked past Jeb's truck parked next to the new white Chevy SUV the county commissioners had provided after the department broke up Devin Douvez's drug cartel and his corrupt plans to become governor of Kentucky. Both men continued on and Mac opened the door to the office.

"What do you think the Stampers are up to?" Jeb asked his father.
"About their fifth strike."

#

WWTD

On the walk back to the station from the diner, Mac thought about what Duncan had said about looking after others. His eyes hardened as his mind drifted decades into the past.

35 Years Ago:
   Jacob was barely into his teens and his mother had succumbed several years earlier to an unwinnable battle with ovarian cancer. His father retired from the Army after her death to take care of his sons and the three of them had moved to a small, one-story house in Wilson, North Carolina. It was a big change from their postings worldwide, especially the latest in Korea. His father was never much of a talker and practically became a stone after Jacob's mother passed away. The few people who did speak with him, mostly old Army buddies checking in, called him "Top," short for Top Kick. He pensioned out as a first sergeant and despite years of half-heartedly trying, at his late wife's request, was never able to get promoted past that. Jacob believed his father's superiors didn't think he was a team player. So, on a first sergeant's retirement and a VA loan, the three MacDowells settled into Wilson. Jacob felt his father had picked the backwoods village as it was one of the most remote and hard-to-reach towns in the state. He thought it a perfect metaphor for his father's personality. Their father retreated more and more into himself as the years passed. He just didn't recover from the loss of his wife.
   A particularly vivid moment for Jacob was when Mrs. Tanner, an

elderly woman who lived next door, struggled to lift a ladder to paint some trim around a window. She couldn't afford a professional painter on a school teacher's retirement. Top and his boys were unloading bags of mulch from the back of his truck when Jacob noticed the woman and pointed it out to his dad. His dad shrugged and told the boys to pick up the pace. When Jacob set down his bag of mulch and started toward Mrs. Tanner, his father yelled at him to get back and help him and his brother. Jacob hesitated, looked at the old woman, who had heard the yelling, and reluctantly returned to his father's truck. He never looked at his father the same way again.

His father died of congenital heart failure years later during Jacob's first hitch. He had purposely joined the Marines, instead of the Army, because his dad hated them. Jacob attended the military funeral in his dress greens and showed no shock at how few people showed up. Top's old Army buddies had eventually faded out of his life years earlier. His brother did not make the trip. Jacob said he understood, but deep down never really forgave him for that.

Jacob believed the low attendance at the funeral was a direct result of Top's strict adherence to looking out for Number One. Jacob didn't fully realize until he was around other Marines, that his father had closed himself off from even his own sons. His refusal to put anyone before his own needs had earned him few mourners and fewer friends. Which is how Top probably preferred it.

Jacob formerly decided a number of things standing over the grave by himself. He would never go by the name 'Jacob' again. He could remember how his father had barked it and it left him feeling three years old. And he would not live as Top had lived: self-centered and unsupportive. Years later, he would joke he wanted to get a bracelet that had "WWTD" inscribed on it. "What Would Top Do," and then do the opposite.

Present:

Mac and his son reached the sheriff's station and Mac opened the door for his son. Mac looked back at the last thirty-five years and felt an uncharacteristic swell of pride. He had broken his programming. If he had followed his father's lead, by this point, he would be a self-centered curmudgeon. Instead, he was a loving and affectionate husband, father, and grandfather with a town full of friends who had proven they would have his back in any situation.

He went out of his way to take care of those friends and to keep them safe and protected, always putting their needs first. He wanted nothing more in life than for his friends, family, and town to be safe and happy. He thought of it as his job, no, his *personal duty*, to protect them from everything. Mac's obsession with taking care of everyone else had been an occasional issue between he and Hannah. Even though the Bible said to care for others more than yourself, she felt he took it too far. She wanted him to take care of himself better and he simply never seemed to find the time.

As he and his son stepped into the station, he silently renewed his vow to put everyone else's needs in front of the few he had. Mac's funeral would NOT go unattended. Hannah would make sure of that.

#

Divide & Conquer

The sheriff's station had remained virtually unmanned for the hour they ate lunch, but Jeb had forwarded the station's phones to both their cell phones and radios.

"What's on the list?" Mac asked Jeb as they entered the office.

"So much we may need to hire more help," Jeb joked, looking down at some papers. "Pretty much the usual. A couple of steers loose in the road out by the lake, the Morris's cat is out again, and Bernie called from *The New Texaco*.

"Someone broke into the station through the little window in his storeroom. They stole $37 from the register, a case of two-stroke motor oil, some candy, and a few energy drinks. The funny part is the box with the motor oil wouldn't fit through the window frame. They stole the plastic bottles of oil inside and left the box on a shelf inside the window."

"Must have been a small window," Mac smiled.

Jeb checked his notes. "About one foot tall by two feet wide. Bernie said it happened sometime in the middle of the night and there was no hurry about getting over there. He boarded the window up and replaced the cash in the till with money from his wallet. Not exactly CSI-worthy. All these were the calls from this morning, but I figured they'd wait until after lunch."

"Excellent. I'll take the steers. I need to go out to *Digger's Hole* anyway," Mac said, not knowing it would be days before he could get out to the honky-tonk. "It's close to the end of your shift. Have Jesse retrieve the Morris's cat and you can go over to *The New Texaco* and take Bernie's statement."

"I'll go out and round up the usual suspects and get someone to confess," Jeb said.

"Hold up there, son," Mac chided. "Have a little patience. Take some time. Line up all the evidence, then go out and pick up the *actual* perpetrators."

"But–"

"Take it easy, Jeb," Mac said. "A big part of this job is patiently waiting, methodical thinking, mixed with a little compassion, and self-sacrifice."

"Alright, Dad," Jeb said. "I still think going out and scooping up the local hooligans is the fastest play, but I'll try it your way."

"If we ever catch 'em, more than likely it will have been kids that robbed him," Mac said. "Probably known locals and it will involve a conversation with their parents. I can handle it if you want me to."

"No. If I want people to recognize me as your senior deputy, then I need to earn the respect of the county. I should talk to them. When, and if, we ever catch these desperadoes, my guess is: it won't be a heated gun battle."

Mac couldn't have been prouder of his son. Mac had been telling Jeb for decades, "It was better for people to respect the man, than the badge, or the gun." Telling parents older than you that their child has embarked on a lifetime, or evening, of crime, wouldn't be easy. Stepping up to the hard chores was a sign of becoming a real sheriff, and better yet, a real man.

"Keep the phones forwarded and I will see you before end of watch."

"Yessir," Jeb said as both men left the office.

#

On the way to the Morris's, a car-hauling semi blew past Jesse down State Road 55 way over the speed limit. He was sitting at a stop sign intersection when the truck blasted past him. Turning on the light bar on top of the other SUV the sheriff's department maintained, he pursued the truck for about another mile until it found a safe place to pull over.

"Can I help you, officer?" The trucker asked out his window before getting a good look at Jesse. He pushed back his ballcap as a grin broke out on his tan, but stubbled, face when he noticed how young the deputy was. Clean-shaven, skinny, and dimpled like his momma, Jesse wasn't the most imposing of law enforcement officers. He knew his lean frame bordered on skinny and hardly filled out his deputy's uniform.

Jesse, having recently turned twenty years old, was Mac's newest hire. He brought him on last year after the boy had proven himself by helping out when Mac's family was in trouble. While one of the best sharpshooters in the county with a rifle, the kid had shown remarkable restraint and common sense. Attributes Mac treasured in a deputy. The young man had worked as a trainee for a long time while continuing online studies in criminal science and law enforcement. His father, Eaton, was ecstatic. Jesse was the first Henderson to choose to not be a farmer and find a job in civil service. It didn't hurt that working at the sheriff's office kept him living at home as well as opposed to running off to college out of state.

"I'll need to see your license, registration, and proof of insurance, sir," Jesse asked from slightly behind the driver's window. He had already radioed in the stop and the truck's plates to Mac, who was on his way to his car, across the county, getting ready to head in the other direction. Jesse tried to run the plates via his in-car laptop, but the computer used a cellular signal for its Internet connection and there was no signal in most of the county. Jeb was out of the office. There was no one to verify the information on the ID or the truck's plates.

"Do you need any backup?" Mac had asked his newest deputy. Jeb was closer, but still about fifteen minutes out. If there was a problem, Mac wanted to make sure it was him in the line of fire, not Jesse.

Jesse smiled. Leave it to the sheriff to offer to drive all the way across the county to make sure he was okay.

"No, sir. It's a simple speeding ticket. He pulled over without any hesitancy. I'll write him up and head over to the Morris's," Jesse had replied.

"Sir, you were driving above the posted speed limit," Jesse handed back 'Mark Calhoun' his driver's license.

"Really? I guess I wasn't paying any attention."

"Yes, sir. I'm going to have to issue you a citation. You can follow the instructions on the back to pay it."

"Well, if you absolutely have to," Calhoun complained. "It will kind of get me in Dutch with my boss."

"I'm sorry about that, but unfortunately, you were going fast enough I can't give you a warning."

"Okay. I guess if you have to," he responded.

Jesse wrote up the citation and handed a carbon copy to Calhoun, glancing up at the load of previously owned vans stacked two rows high. "Nice cars. Where are you taking them?"

"I take 'em to Cincinnati," Calhoun replied. "Where they go from there, who knows?"

"Yeah, who knows where anyone goes after Cincinnati."

#

Major Developments

Mac's phone rang immediately after he signed off on Jesse's radio call and before he got all the way to his patchwork-colored Bronco. While reaching for his phone, Mac admired the old truck. He had bought it barely used back in the 90s before he and Hannah had married and he babied it like a child. In the last several years, he had sanded out all the rust spots, Bondo'd them, and applied a new coat of primer over the repairs. His hope was: if this year was good to the ranch, he could splurge and have the paint job restored to its original green and tan. Probably not. He knew Naomi had her eye on a new saddle for her pony and if he got ahead at all, he would more than likely spend the money on her.

"Sheriff's office."

"Mac? It's Dave," his friend from the FBI started. "How ya doin', jarhead?"

It was a running joke between the two men. Mac received an honorable discharge from the Marines as an MP and Dave Smathers retired as a major from the Army before joining the FBI.

"Got no majors to complain to. What would be the point?" Mac smiled into the phone.

"They wouldn't listen anyway," Smathers replied laughing. "Listen, I got a couple of updates on the Douvez thing from last year. Thought you might want to be kept in the loop."

"Yepper. It would surprise you at how much that thing is still haunting us around here."

"You want the bad news or the bad news?"

"Let me ponder for a second," Mac said. "Hmmm. Let's go with the bad news."

"It seems the young Mason Wheeler is no longer a ward of the state. I guess being a former law enforcement officer-turned-rat was not extraordinarily popular at Big Sandy." Douvez had placed Wheeler as a mole in the sheriff's office. Big Sandy Penitentiary in Inez, Kentucky was not a place for the faint of heart.

"What happened?" Mac asked as he settled into the Bronco and fired it up.

"Same ole cliché. Toothbrush sharpened into a shank. Goodnight sweet prince. Nobody saw anything."

"I hate to hear that, but he did shoot Beth. I reckon there won't be a lot of tears shed for him at my house tonight," Mac said grimly. "Though, if I know Hannah, she'll probably pray for his soul anyway. Or bake a cake. It could go either way. What's the other bad news?"

"Turns out your buddy, Douvez, was trickier than we figured. We thought we had found all his hidey holes for money, but the forensic accounting dweebs told me the money he made from his illegal enterprises should be much more than the money we found in the various offshore banks. We thought we had it all when the amounts from those accounts matched up with what he was paying his minions. Turns out he had a truckload of cash stashed somewhere earmarked for retirement or to continue financing his way to the governorship."

"No chance of him getting out, is there?" Mac asked.

"No. We have him secured away from gen pop because he was once the Commonwealth's attorney and we would hate to see him get his teeth brushed the same way Mason did," Smathers said. "His cellmate is ratting to us on a regular basis and Douvez, at most, talks to his lawyer. No other visitors. According to his cellmate, they're talking about Douvez's appeal. With everything we have on him, he will never see the light of day. More than likely his money won't either. Damn shame about that, though. Sounds like it would be a pretty penny to forfeiture."

"I'm sure Uncle Sam will survive without his ill-gotten gains. How *is* life in the federal arena?"

"Good. You know from our last talk Mike and I got a bump in position and more importantly, pay, from the Douvez case. Things have been nowhere near as exciting, but we remain ever vigilant in America's ongoing war against crime."

"So," Mac translated, "boring as all get out."

"Like watching paint dry," Dave laughed. "Can't you boys dig up another big criminal mastermind to make us look good?"

"I'll keep on the lookout. When you coming down from Lexington for dinner?"

"Next time we get a big break in the upswing of criminal activity," Smathers smiled through the phone. "Hannah making fried chicken?"

"Probably steaks. You know we own a ranch, right?"

"A horse ranch. And with you, I never know where the steaks came from. Uh, is Hannah making a pie?"

"Probably," Mac said.

"Er, I'll get back to you. I suddenly feel a crime wave coming on."

Mac laughed out loud as his friend disconnected.

#

Love at The Hole

"Why, thank you Sonny," Peggy Clay said as Sonny Stamper moved to take the cardboard case of red candle globes from her. Peggy was the regular waitress at *Ginny's Diner*, but Mac had asked the manager of *The Digger's Hole* to hire her on the weekends. She could use the money to help support her two boys after former mine official, Mayor Neville Jarvis, killed her abusive husband in response to blackmail.

Mac had gotten Sonny a job at *The Hole* as a bouncer, instead of sending him to prison. After helping Mac recover his family, and despite his minor part in their attack last year, Hannah and Mac had practically adopted the good-natured behemoth. *The Hole's* business had increased dramatically since Sonny started as the bouncer. His mere presence discouraged ne'er-do-wells from starting trouble and local families started to re-frequent the watering hole. With the increased business, Peggy had picked up some extra nights while her mother moved back in and helped with her boys.

Years ago, Peggy had been one of the prettiest girls in Mounton County. Then she met Wilbur Clay in high school. At first, he had been charming in a drunken-senior-football-player sort of way. It didn't take long for him to transition to drunken-miner after graduation and then to drunken-abuser once the boys arrived. When the mines closed, Peggy was the sole breadwinner with her waitressing job at *Ginny's*. Wilbur's fragile male ego and tendency to drink focused his bulk, anger, and abuse on her and the boys on a regular basis. The community watched as Peggy's spirit and appearance declined, but life in Mounton had programmed her too long as a miner's wife to complain or run away with the boys. After Wilbur's death, the old Peggy blossomed and she and the boys seemed to come alive again.

Sonny followed Peggy around the honky-tonk with the case of candles like a puppy as she inspected the ones sitting on the table and replaced them when needed. The bar wouldn't be busy for another hour or two, but Peggy showed up early to help prepare the place for business. Sonny lived in the small room above the bar and came down to help her.

"Thank you again, Sonny, you didn't have to do that," Peggy smiled at the big man. Sonny was a couple of years her junior, but more than made up for it in size. Like her late husband, the youngest Stamper was a giant of a man. While both men weighed in at well over three hundred pounds, Wilbur was mostly hard knuckles and beer gut, whereas Sonny was thick with solid muscle. Unlike Wilbur, he was quiet, unassuming, and one of the gentlest men Peggy had ever met. Him asking to hold the case of candles was the most she had ever heard him say. Between waiting tables, she had watched him. He never started any trouble and did everything he could to stop it without resorting to violence. Another big difference between Sonny and Wilbur. Her late husband was quick to lash out for any reason and many a time, she and her boys were the recipients of his rage. Wilbur enjoyed being vicious. When Sonny did have to get physical to stop a problem in the bar, he usually did it with one punch and a look of sadness on his face because he had to resort to it.

Peggy was aware that Sonny knew all about her husband and his murder after Wilbur started walking home from *The Hole* over a year ago. Sonny also knew that Wilbur used to beat her and the kids in drunken stupors. What she didn't know was Sonny was alternately glad Wilbur was dead but often wished he was still alive. He was secretly happy Peggy was now a free woman and glad Wilbur was gone and that Peggy didn't have to live through those beatings anymore. At other times, Sonny was sad Wilbur was no longer available to learn how *real* abuse felt. Sonny's own pa had been quick to drink and swing a switch or his fists and unknowingly. Sonny had some unresolved issues he needed to work out. Sonny didn't have the words for it, but anyone who abused Peggy was as good a place as any to start some therapy.

For his part, Peggy often caught Sonny watching her from his spot at the door. She didn't know that he admired how she smiled at everyone despite how rough her past was. He marveled that she was strong enough to make a new life for both herself and her boys.

Peggy was serving a table and was just close enough to overhear:

"Aye, an' she's a handsome filly, eh me boyo?" Howdy Barnes, the manager of *The Digger's Hole,* had slipped up behind Sonny while he looked at Peggy.

"If'n you say so, Mr. Howdy," Sonny whispered.

"You know what I find dearest about yon Peg?" Howdy asked. "She's smart and strong enough to not need a man."

"Really?" Sonny answered, sounding dejected.

"Aye. She's strong enough not to NEED a man," Howdy smiled as he walked back toward the bar. "But maybe a really strong man might need her."

#

Know When to Fold 'Em

It was seven fifty-seven p.m. when Alistair Duncan pulled up to *The New Texaco* in his '71 Oldsmobile Cutlass. He parked as far away from the assorted trucks and cars outside as he could. Not because he was anti-social, but he didn't want any of the others to accidentally ding his doors. The Olds was in mint condition. Except for buying two fan belts and a water pump from *The New Texaco* in the last few decades, he did all the work on the car himself, including the Bondo and bodywork. Despite the care he lavished on the car, Kentucky still salted the roads in the winter. He had taken the Olds to Louisville ten years ago to get it repainted the original olive green after he babied the body back into new condition. He kept it waxed and well-protected inside his small garage, covered by a smooth tarp. Duncan loved the car like he had never loved a woman and felt he might be able to keep the beautiful antique until the day he died. He paid three grand for it brand new in 1971 and felt like he finally got his money's worth out of it.

The owner of *Duncan's Mercantile and General Store* walked through the gas station to the dimly lit storage room in the back.

"Ladies and gentlemen," Darlene, the owner of *Darlene's Beauty Emporium/Barbershop/Tanning Salon*, announced from the green felt table in the center of the storage room, "this meeting of the Mounton Chamber of Commerce Officers Committee can now commence."

Bernie, the owner/operator of *The New Texaco*, kicked a seat out at the poker table to allow Duncan to sit. "Have a seat, ya old skinflint. The seat's free, but the poker ain't."

Duncan pulled out the seat and ten dollars in one-dollar bills and coins out of his various overall pockets. The store owner was a contradiction in styles. He looked like Central Casting's idea of a hillbilly with his rotund figure, reddish-blond beard (going gray), plaid shirt, and bib overalls. Contrary to his appearance, his red hair alone hinted at Duncan's Scottish roots.

The backroom to the gas station hadn't changed much in the thirty years it had been there. The people of Mounton still called it *The New Texaco*. Duncan did notice the plywood covering the outside of the one-foot by two-foot window near the ceiling.

"Redecorating, I see," Duncan commented.

"Yep, figured it'd be better for business if nobody saw me having you come by," Bernie said without looking up from his cards. "People might think I was lowering my standards or something."

"Ten dollars?" Ginny asked incredulously. "Duncan, you do realize this particular game of chance is no-limit hold'em? Week after week you bring singles and change for your stake. Ten dollars is barely enough to buy-in."

"Dinnae ye be worryin' yourself, lad," Duncan groused, "Tis more than enough spoondoolies to do what needs doing."

"You're wasting' your breath, Ginny," Bernie laughed. "Old Duncan there is so tight he does his own oil changes on that classic beauty outside to save ten dollars."

"Aye, and I'll continue to do such as long as a dighted choop like yourself pretends to know anything aboot mechanics," Duncan said, changing his one-dollar bills and change for chips.

"I am gonna assume for the sake of our friendship 'dighted choop' means 'good looking and intelligent fellow,'" Bernie smiled with teeth too white and perfect to be natural.

"An' that's exactly what a dighted choop *would* think," Duncan snorted seriously as he counted his chips again.

The store room was barely wide enough for a small poker table and chairs and smelled like old oil and tires. Longer than it was wide, the dark room featured a bench seat long ago pulled from some vehicle, where Mr. Darlene sat quietly reading the Mounton Gazette while his wife played cards. Not due to social politeness, but because of the gas and oil fumes, Bernie never let anyone smoke at the poker games. Ironic, since Bernie was the only one who smoked among them.

"You know, if you spoke proper English," Darlene growled, "people would more likely enjoy your company."

"Ye say that like it's a good thing," Duncan smirked.

Besides Ginny, Duncan, Darlene, Bernie, Rufus Moss (the publisher of the *Mounton Gazette* and part-time court reporter), Ephraim Emerson (owner of the old-time photo shop), District Judge Brown sat at the table. There were more members of the Mounton Chamber of Commerce, but these were the ones who played poker. The rest were Baptists. Though admittedly, Rufus Moss was a C&E (Christmas and Easter only).

The game proceeded as it usually did. This week, Bernie lost a bit, Ginny and Ephraim won a little, Judge Brown kept pulling more money out of his pocket, Darlene was cleaning up, and Duncan hovered at $10.25.

"You know, Dunc," Rufus poked, "If you weren't so tight a player, everybody wouldn't fold as soon as you made a bet."

"Ye play yer game, ya bloody tourist, and I'll play mine."

"Hey, I saw the durndest thing out to the lake today," Bernie changed the subject. Everyone knew he was talking about winding Lake Mounton, the largest serious body of water between the Ship River in Louisville and Campbellsville, sixty-eight miles south. "I was out fishing on my *yacht*" (his 12-foot rowboat) "and I seen two youngun's skinny-dippin' and fooling' around, neckid as jaybirds."

"Who was it?" Darlene asked interested. Gossip at the *Beauty Emporium/Barbershop/Tanning Salon* was a liquid commodity. It was the second hottest spot for 'news' in the county, but since half the women in the Church Ladies got their hair done there, with the other half eating at *Ginny's*, it may have been a tie.

"Couldn't tell," Bernie remembered. "I was too far away, but they was young. You could tell by the way they was scamperin' around quick-like. I hauled anchor and moved on down the lake. I ain't no prevert."

"Did you see what they were drivin'?" Duncan asked.

"Nah. I seen a flash of yeller in the trees. They musta parked it back in the woods. They was up by them shallows at the north end of the lake. Up towards where Highway 44 and 248 split off."

Duncan thought about what Bernie relayed for a few moments. 248 was a rural road connected to Highway 44 for a few miles and then turned southeast, deeper into Kentucky, while 44 twisted northeast toward Interstate 64 and Frankfort. The section of the lake Bernie described was merely a few miles long where it was close to 44.

Ginny looked at the Scottish store owner curiously. "Pray tell, Duncan, what deviousness are you cogitating?"

"I am of a mind that I've taken all the money from you eidjits there is to take," Duncan said counting his $10.25 in chips. "Cash me out."

#

A Horse is a Horse Unless Of Course...

Hannah watched from the barn as Naomi led her pony, Bob, from the training arena. Naomi was big enough to undo the horse's saddle cinch and barely big enough to drag the big Western saddle off the horse. She dragged the well-worn saddle to the split rail fence around the arena and flopped it over the bottom rail. Grabbing a bucket and a step stool from near the fence, she carried it to Bob and pulled a brush out. She could reach up about three-quarters of the way up without the stool, but that didn't stop her from brushing the whole horse like a show pony.

Hannah watched with some concern. Many horses shy away from the brush and get anxious, but Bob stood like a trooper and nuzzled Naomi as she rubbed his sides. After she brushed him thoroughly, she pulled some carrots from the bucket and petted the pony as she fed him. She smiled at the fact Naomi had probably snagged the carrots from their own refrigerator, remembering when she had done the exact same thing decades before.

Hannah and Mac had given Bob to Naomi for her sixth birthday, on the condition Jeb could break him enough for the girl to safely ride him.

The young gelding was barely above the age of a pony. Hannah normally didn't castrate her ponies in order to breed them later, but this one showed an 'overabundance of spirit.' The original owner believed its bloodline would inherit the trait. Once 'fixed,' the young stallion calmed down and became extraordinarily gentle and Hannah reluctantly succumbed to Naomi's pleas to let her have the gelding. As soon as Jeb had finished breaking the horse and was sure it was safe, Naomi had jumped in the saddle and was riding around the training ring like she and the pony had been doing it for decades, despite their ages. Hannah had tried for days to talk the then six-year-old out of the horse, but along with her and Jeb's green eyes, good looks, and dimples, Naomi had inherited Mac's stubborn streak. Months later, despite Hannah's misgivings, Naomi was still mucking the pony's stall, using a step stool to brush him, and feeding him. Bob, in turn, had developed an unexplainable devotion, loyalty, and gentleness to the little girl.

   She watched as Naomi led Bob to the stable. Last year, her granddaughter had suffered the greatest loss a little girl could and it took a six-hundred-pound pony to help her heal. That act alone made Hannah love the animal more than any she had ever owned.

#

Sharper Knives

Peggy Clay wrapped both her arms around herself and stared at the small pickup truck.

"Sonny me boyo," Howdy told his friend as he looked into the back of his pickup, "I jes' don't know how we are going to get these monsters out of the back of the truck."

The two men had climbed out of the front of Howdy's truck at Peggy Clay's mobile home. She had purchased a used washer and dryer set for $75 from a family moving out of Mounton and had reluctantly asked Sonny and Howdy to help her move them. The family who had sold them helped get them into Howdy's little truck, but now it was up to Sonny and Howdy to get them down and move them.

Sonny looked at Peggy as she stood helplessly to the side. "Miz Peggy, reckon where you want 'em?"

"Well," the pretty waitress frowned, "if we could get them down, there are hook-ups in the hall closet."

"Mr. Howdy, could you get the door?" Sonny asked as he wrapped his bear-like arms around the washer in the back of the truck. With a grunt, he lifted the appliance up, and without lowering it to the ground, carried straight it into the mobile home. Both Peggy and Howdy stood with their mouths wide open. After setting it down, Sonny came back outside for the dryer.

"D'ye not want to take a break, lad?" Howdy asked.

"Why?"

After Sonny placed the dryer next to the washer, Howdy hooked up the appliances and tested both.

"Wow. The least I can do is fix both you boys lunch," Peggy smiled at her new appliances and the heroes who made it happen.

"I'm wishing I could, lass, but I've got a shipment of liquor coming in and we would be a poor excuse of a drinking establishment without alcohol," Howdy said. Looking at Sonny, "But if you would be kind enough to bring Sonny into work with you tonight, perhaps you could persuade him to stay."

"Sonny? What about it? Would you like to stay for lunch?" Peggy asked.

Sonny looked at Howdy, then at Peggy.

"That'd be right nice, Miz Peggy," Sonny swallowed.

"It's just 'Peggy,' Sonny. I'm afraid it won't be much, some warmed-up meatloaf and potatoes. Might be able to round up some biscuits if you don't mind the canned ones. Okay by you?"

"Biscuits?" Sonny grinned. He warmed most of his meals on the hotplate in his room above the bar. "Biscuits'd be wonnerful."

"Fine. I'll be seein' you two at work later," Howdy said as he headed to the front door.

"Sonny, if you like, I think the boys are playing out back," Peggy pointed at the back door.

"Really?" Sonny's face broke out in a big beaming smile that stretched his beard wide. Then, as if he remembered his manners, "You jes' let me know if'n I can do anything to help."

"Thank you, but I think Mom and I have it under control. Go have some fun."

The big bear of a man stared at her one last moment and then turned toward the back door and the yard outside. Peggy's boys, five and six years old, cheered as Sonny joined them in the backyard.

"You know he's not the sharpest knife in the rack, right," her mother asked, coming up from behind her in the kitchen area of the small mobile home.

"You know Mom, that's a good thing," Peggy said as she looked out the kitchen window while preparing lunch. "Sharp knives are the ones that can cut you."

#

Lake View Included

Alistair Duncan finally gave in to his curiosity. He couldn't sleep a big chunk of the night of the poker game because of what Bernie had told them. He rose early the next morning. He had some ideas he needed to follow up on. Ideas that wouldn't let him get back to sleep.

"Here, McTavish! Let's go fer a ride, ye wee duggie," Duncan called, after getting dressed.

A seven-pound Shitzu ripped through the small house and skidded to a stop at the garage door. Many of the Mounton residents snickered at the fact this red-headed bull of a man walked such a tiny dog. Everyone, including Mac, gave his friend some grief due to the fact McTavish was a Shitzu and not a Scottish Terrier. "He's got the heart of a Scot!" Duncan fired back. What he didn't admit, especially to himself, was the Scottish heart the dog had, was his own.

Dressed in his usual bib overalls and flannel shirt, Duncan grabbed the Shitzu's leash and opened the kitchen door to the garage for the small dog to run to the driver's door of his Cutlass. Duncan gently pulled the cover off the Oldsmobile. Once opened, McTavish leapt in, dashed across the bench seat, and sat impatiently on the Tartan blanket Duncan had spread over the passenger side to protect it.

Duncan drove the exact speed limit north on Highway 55 till he turned east on Highway 44. In his whole life, there had never been room for a speeding ticket in the Duncan budget and at his current age, where did he have to go in a hurry? He stayed on the four-lane highway for a while and got off on County Road 248. He followed

248 until he parked in an empty cul de sac not far from the lake.

Carrying the leash in case they stumbled across someone, Duncan and McTavish wandered through the woods toward the lake. He intended to use the excuse of walking the dog as his reason for being in this part of the woods. The dog chased after an occasional butterfly or leaf, but never strayed more than fifteen feet from his red-headed pet's side. Once they hit the edge of the lake, they turned northeast to parallel the water's edge. It didn't take long to come across ruts in the overgrown brush leading to the sandbar at the lake. Duncan followed the old logging trail, or whatever it was, back toward Highway 44 and away from Lake Mounton. In order to preserve its paint job it would never occur to him to drive his cherished Oldsmobile down the trail, but someone had, and recently. The weeds and brush, newly broken, showed signs of a vehicle recently coming through.

Duncan in his bib overalls, wet with morning dew and his work boots filthy, cradled the soggy little McTavish, covered in mud and nettles. Man and dog had skipped breakfast and felt damp, tired, and hungry. He made a mental note to take off his boots before getting into the Cutlass and to spread McTavish's blanket over his portion of the seat as well.

The trail came out at Highway 44 and Duncan decided he had had enough of playing Nancy Drew for the morning. McTavish quit frolicking and stayed close to Duncan, a sure sign of his weariness.

"McTavish me lad, I am fair puckled meself." Duncan, unused to the exercise, had hiked several miles through the woods.

There were at most a few buildings scattered around on their walk back to the Oldsmobile. A tackle and bait shop based out of someone's garage. A smattering of houses spread few and far between. And as they got closer to the intersection of 248 and 44 where they had parked the car, he spied a ratty-looking motel. As he glanced at the parking lot of the motel, he spotted a year-old Dodge Challenger in the motel lot. The yellow color of the car was practically blinding in contrast to the few cars parked there. It definitely stood out.

"McTavish me wee yin, I'm thinkin' I'll be needing to be back here soon."

As he walked past the motel, despite the distance, Duncan could see the scratches down the side of the car.

#

Surely She's Surly

"You're the new one, huh?" Shirley asked from her perpetual perch on the stool at the cash register of *Ginny's Diner*.

The pretty girl paying for her breakfast looked up from her wallet and then had to look back down again since Shirley didn't quite reach five feet tall and was considerably shorter sitting on her stool. The girl was quite stunning. Long, curly, reddish hair, a pornstar's figure, and unusually tall for a woman. She could have been a model except for her imperceptibly thicker wrists and slightly enlarged knuckles. Those were not the first of her features most men noticed.

Shirley, on the other hand, could have easily played one of the crone witches from Macbeth without makeup. The beauty was: Shirley didn't care. Either due to her age or award-winning personality, she cared less than spit for what other people thought of her.

"I guess," the young woman said. "How did you know?"

"Everybody in town comes to *Ginny's*. I know everybody who lives here and I don't know you. So, you're new," Shirley rasped in a voice ravaged by years of cigarettes and age.

"Makes sense," the woman held out her hand. "Heaven Carlysle."

Shirley looked at the hand without taking it.

"I go by Shirley," Shirley croaked. "Heaven, huh? Your folks musta had a pretty high opinion of you. They musta known you was grow inta that rack."

Heaven dropped her hand after realizing Shirley wasn't going to shake it. "Nope. Mom named me after a perfume she liked. My dad told me she trapped him with her perfume long before he saw her."

"What brings you to Mounton, girlie?"

"I needed to move out of New Jersey and this was where my car ran out of electricity. It seems like a good place to settle for a while and here I am," the young woman explained.

"Seems pretty similar to how they founded Mounton, except no one came from Jersey, old or new, no one ever named their kid Heaven, and they sure as hell weren't no electrical cars involved. Come to think of it, it ain't much like how this place started at all."

"Are there any charging stations in town?"

"No 'charging stations.' We got a gas station, *The New Texaco*, but Bernie probably don't know nothing about no electrical cars and I doubt he ever will. My guess is: you got yourself a 900-pound flower planter."

"Well, everything seems to be within walking distance. I rented a part of one of the newly renovated homes abandoned in the last year or so. A nice Mr. Stemple leased it to me a week or so ago. Do you know him?"

Shirley snorted. "I've known 'Stinky' Stemple since he were in short pants. His daddy done run this town and mines into the ground if you don't mind the pun. Stinky's okay. I reckon he's trying a might too hard to make up for his daddy's sins. Ain't nobody got enough time on this planet to make up for that much sin."

"You don't know if anybody's looking for some help, would you? I have some savings, but if I want to keep it, I guess I'll need to find a job. A good gym wouldn't hurt either," Heaven said.

"We ain't got no gym. Folks 'round here mostly stay in shape by working for a living. We got a community center where the new deputy's wife teaches some stuff. I know she does some yogi stuff and bow and arrows. Never been there, but it's a bunch a new-age horse feathers if'n you ask me." Having given the girl her change, Shirley returned to her knitting, signaling she had ended the conversation.

Heaven, a little taken aback by the bruskness of the old woman, said, "It was good talking to you, I guess." As she opened the door and the bell above it jangled, she mumbled, "Good luck with your jobs at the Chamber of Commerce and Welcome Wagon."

Shirley looked out the glass door at the woman as she walked toward downtown Mounton.

"How'd she know'd I was in the Chamber of Commerce?"

#

Brotherly Love

"Sonny, you don't understand, boy. We got us a primo opportunity here to make some real foldin' money," Syrus explained to his youngest brother.

Syrus, Spencer, and their youngest brother, Sonny, were sitting at a table at *The Digger's Hole*.

"No matter what you told them federals," Syrus told him, his voice sugary-sweet, "we ain't holdin' a grudge. You was jes' doin' what you needed to keep out of jail. Any of us woulda done the same. No harm done."

Sonny looked at one brother, then the other. Syrus, the oldest, was short and lean and the schemer of the three since he had the benefit of a fifth grade education. Spencer had a slight limp after being dragged by the RV used in the kidnappings while trying to escape last year. The two older brothers were already dirty and smelly despite just getting out of jail. Sonny noted their bushy hair, unshaved faces, and ragged clothes; attributes he used to share until Mac's wife, Hannah, literally helped him clean up his act in order to get the job as bouncer. The main difference between he and his brothers was his size. The youngest Stamper was a bear of a man, easily twice the size and maybe three times the strength, of either of his brothers. Another difference was his IQ. Sonny was a man of simple thoughts and easily led.

"Brother, this is a good deal," Spencer, the second oldest said.

"We got someone actually paying us to rob someone. We get to sell most of what we get and we get paid to do it! I bet yore thinkin' 'It cain't get no better.' It can. I'll tell you how. We get to rob the Sheriff! Ain't it a stitch?" Syrus was practically giggling.

"That sunnuvabitch tried to send us to prison. Turned out our new employer hates him more than we do," Spencer chimed in. "They went and got us sprung from prison with some fancy-pants lawyer."

"What d'ya say, Sonny-boy?" Syrus asked. "We shore could use someone of your abilities, plus you is kin. The Stamper Brothers always work as a team."

Sonny looked at Syrus.

"Yore gonna rob Sheriff Mac?" he asked.

"Yep, ain't it something? A little payback for all he done to our family."

The brothers verbally bounced back and forth, putting pressure on the impressionable younger man. In the past, Sonny had always followed Syrus's lead and they had no reason to believe he would not now.

Sonny thought about it. He was a different man now thanks to Miz Hannah and Sheriff Mac. He greatly admired Mr. Ginny's look. He kept his full beard neatly trimmed instead of a wild bush crawling up to his eyes and down his neck. His beard grew much thicker and longer than Ginny's, but it he kept it clean and well-groomed. Sonny now washed his hair and pulled it back in a short ponytail. Clothes donated by Mr. Ginny barely fit the giant of a man, but Sonny really liked the tee shirts with the old rock bands on them. He had been working at *The Digger's Hole* for roughly a year and enjoyed his job. The bar manager let him stay in the tiny room above the bar for free. Sonny was cheaper than putting in a security system.

"No," was all the big man whispered. Sonny couldn't put it into words, but it turned out he liked the man he is now versus who he was then.

"What? You gonna turn your back on your own kin?" Syrus asked in shock. "I cain't believe it."

"Sheriff Mac and Miz Hannah been good to me. I ain't about to repay their kindness by stealing from them. 'Sides, Jeb and his little girl lives there now and it wouldn't be right," Sonny said dully.

"I never thought I'd see the day. A Stamper turned on his own," Syrus yelled. "What would Pa say? I'll tell you what he'd say. Any boy that'd turned his back on kin ain't a Stamper no more!"

"Syrus! Don't say that," Sonny was in tears. Tiny rivulets of moisture dripped down the face of the man who topped out well over three hundred pounds. "Syrus, you know I'd do anythin' you say, but Sheriff Mac and Miz Hannah, well, they been takin' real good care of me. They even had me over for supper a few times."

"There it is. Some fancy clothes and fried chicken and suddenly you don't know who yore real family is no more," Syrus spat, turning his back to the bear-like man.

It was then the bar manager came over. No more than five feet tall and less than a hundred pounds, Howdy Barnes looked for the world like a red-headed leprechaun. Behind him stood Peggy Clay, coming in for her evening waitress shift.

"Everything okay, Sonny?"

"Everything jes' fine, ya little runt!" Syrus barked. "You and your whore can jes' get back to wiping them glasses and leave this conversation to family afore you get a five-gallon keg of whoop ass."

"Laddie, you'll be taking a more civil tone or you'll have to leave," Howdy said, drying his hands with a bar towel.

"And reckon what happens if'n we don't?" Spencer stood quickly and knocked his chair over backward. You and this little whore enough'n to stop us?"

Syrus and Spencer didn't know it but they crossed a line with Sonny. Howdy was nice to him. And Peggy. They shouldn't talk about Peggy like that.

"Time to go, Syrus," the giant Stamper whispered.

Syrus and Spencer turned to look at their brother, now standing as well. It was one thing to pick a fight with a sawed-off shrimp like the barkeep, but taking on Sonny was a different matter.

"We're goin'," Syrus snarled as he and Spencer edged toward the front door, always facing Sonny and Howdy. "But you made a mistake

Sonny. Big mistake. From now on, you ain't no Stamper. You is out of this family. You mind me, Sonny-boy. You gonna remember the day you turned yore back on kin."

The two brothers tried to slam the door on their way out, but the hydraulic hinge kept it slow enough to close quietly.

"You're better off, lad," Howdy said, patting the bear-like bouncer on the shoulder blades.

"Yeah, but now I got no family," Sonny said quietly.

"Boyo, with family like yours, we'd all be better off orphans."

#

Mac drove through Mounton County on his way to *The Great Steer Stampede*. It would be the third one this month. It would take about thirty minutes to drive to the 'scene of the crime' through the winding roads. Despite its back-woods charm, Mac thought of this county as his responsibility. When the settlers' wagons broke down in the snow several hundred years ago, they founded the town of Mounton, which later became the county seat to Mounton County. Seemed like God's way of telling them this was a good place to live. Some of those settlers included Hannah's ancestors. The county was the second smallest in all of Kentucky even after a great deal of the population left to find work in Lexington, Louisville, or Frankfort when the mines shut down a year or so ago. There seems to be some disagreement as to why the original settlers spelled the town name *Mounton*.

Many blamed Mac for the mine closures, but in reality, he stumbled upon the lethal working conditions imposed by the mine owner, Judge Stemple, while trying to save his granddaughter from kidney failure. When Naomi witnessed the judge's grandchildren, Mandy and Jasper, involved in incestuous behavior while they babysat her, the situation became aggravated. The attention would have led to OSHA investigating the mines and their safety protocols. During a revealing confrontation, the judge ended up shot by Mac's friend Ginny, and Naomi ended up with the judge's kidneys.

Since then, mostly due to Mac's ideas and innovation, the town had reinvented itself as a turn-of-the-century mining attraction for tourists with bed and breakfast accommodations, a dedicated and gentrified Main Street, and ample entrepreneurial opportunities financed by the judge's far-from-the-tree son, Adrian Stemple. The town's population never really bounced back. Those who stayed and worked the plan shared in the town's new tourist attraction profits. Mac privately thought the ones who stayed still possessed the original settler's pioneer spirit, unlike those who fled for any kind of employment in large cities. Mac felt it made the town of Mounton a community of stronger character and easier to police.

#

Break-Ins & Stake-Outs

About seven miles out of town, two steers had busted through a fence on Highway 44 past Lake Mounton. A regular occurrence to be sure, but Mac was thankful the majority of his duties were as innocuous as this. He didn't know he was working but a few miles away from where Duncan parked his Cutlass. He had rounded up the last one and temporarily mended the fence when his radio squawked.

"Dad?" Jeb radioed in.

Mac found his mic near his collar and answered, "Yeah, Jeb, what's up?"

"I'm back to the station. Mom's on the line. Sounds important."

"Can you patch her through?" Mac asked, knowing Jeb had done it numerous times for various phone calls.

"Hannah? You there?" Mac clicked his mic.

"Mac? You need to come home right away." Hannah was on the edge of tears. He had seen her cry at funerals, reading mushy books, or watching sappy movies, but never during the middle of the day.

"Baby, what's the matter? Is it something with Naomi?"

"No, just come home right now. And don't bring Jeb."

"Okay. I am across the county, but I'm on my way." *Don't bring Jeb.* Hannah was implying he would need help, but she didn't want it to be Jeb. Mac had no idea why she would not want her son to come home, but he trusted Hannah's judgment. Jesse was across the county with a traffic stop. Dawe was working the eleven-to-seven shift later tonight. Davis was enjoying his day off, but if Mac needed help, Davis's years as a D.C. cop made him the most experienced deputy he had next to Jeb.

Mac drove until he had a few bars on his phone and then called Davis. He didn't want to radio Jeb to patch him through. His son would worry about why his mother called and didn't want him there.

"Davis?" Mac asked.

"Yeah, Sheriff. What's up?" Davis responded.

"I hate to bother you on your day off, but I need to. I don't want to use Jeb for this."

"It's all good," Davis said as he smiled at the phone. "I'm in the middle of some honey-do chores. Gabe will be out of school in a few hours, but Felicia is picking him up on her way home from the community center." Davis's wife, Felicia, taught archery, yoga, and a fitness boot-camp part-time at the community center, formerly known as the mining company cafeteria. "What do you need?"

"Meet me at my house as soon as you can," Mac commanded. "And wear your uniform. Your FULL uniform."

"My—okay, whatever you say, boss."

#

Hannah ran to meet their cars as Davis pulled into the drive at the front of their home and Mac pulled up behind him in his county SUV. She met them on the sidewalk to the circular drive.

"Baby, what's the matter?" Mac asked.

"Oh, Mac! Somebody…they…we've been robbed!" Hannah exclaimed.

Mac gently pushed Hannah to the side and signaled Davis to go around back. Mac mimed for Davis to pull his sidearm. Giving Davis a few seconds to get to the rear of the house, he walked in the open door and scanned the living room for intruders. After letting Davis in the back door of the kitchen, he moved toward their home office. He used it when he worked at home, and Hannah used it as the home office for the ranch and bill paying. With no one there or in the downstairs bedroom, the two men started upstairs. A thorough circuit of the upstairs and they declared the house clear.

It wasn't until they went downstairs, did it sink into Mac how trashed the house was. Furniture overturned, drawers dumped out, and lamps smashed to the floor. Hannah joined them as Mac and Davis walked back into the office. The burglars had tossed the desk.

"My laptop!" Hannah gasped.

Sure enough, her laptop was missing. The inkjet printer was still there, presumably too big to take quickly.

The gun safe sat wide open. "Looks like they hit the safe," Davis noted.

"Okay. Both of you. Don't touch anything. We are going to have to dust for prints," Mac said. "Hannah, sweetheart, I need you to put your hands in your pockets. Davis, you to stay with us and guarantee the sanctity of the crime scene."

The burglars had ransacked the downstairs bedroom similarly. The MacDowells and Williams walked upstairs and the first room on the left was Naomi's.

"This is where I came first; I didn't even notice the rest of the house. I wanted to gather her bed linens to wash them before she got home, and saw this," Hannah sobbed. "This is why I told you not to bring Jeb home. As soon as I saw this, I ran downstairs and out in the yard."

The burglars had destroyed the room. They had torn pictures from the walls and overturned the dresser with all of the drawers emptied onto the floor. With no reason or anything to steal, the perpetrators had defecated and urinated all over the broken furniture.

Mac clenched his jaw hard enough to hear his molars grinding.

"Okay, let's go through the whole house," Davis said gently. They had trashed the other rooms but not as much as Naomi's. It was as if the burglars had a vendetta against the child.

"Davis, you need to take the lead on this," Mac told his deputy. "Since Jeb and I live here, we can't be the lead investigators. If for no other reason, the insurance company will look at us as the prime suspects in a case of insurance fraud."

"They wouldn't!" Hannah quavered.

"Yes, baby, I'm afraid they would. To make matters worse, we filed a claim last year when someone in Douvez's crew trashed our tractor to put financial pressure on us. One major claim with no suspects might not be an issue, but two within the same year will raise red flags all over."

Davis called Dave Smathers at the FBI and then Kentucky State Police crime scene techs to process the scene. The FBI agreed to send someone as soon as possible to investigate a crime committed against a law enforcement officer.

Mac and Hannah were still working with Davis to assemble a list of items stolen and destroyed when Jeb burst into the house.

"What happened?" Jeb demanded.

"Looks like a break-in," Mac said calmly.

"Why didn't you call me?" Jeb demanded angrily. "Why did I have to hear about this on the radio?"

"Because we needed you to stay calm," Mac explained, knowing his son leaned toward impetuous.

"Jeb, they…Honey, they desecrated Naomi's room," Hannah said. "I told Mac not to bring you because I knew how you would react."

"Let me see," Jeb demanded, pushed past his parents and was suddenly stopped short by Davis's hand in the middle of his chest.

"Whoa there, cowboy," Davis said, holding Jeb back. "This is a crime scene. One you can't be anywhere near since you live here. You have a great alibi of being on duty at the station when this went down, but if you contaminate the scene, this gets muddy quickly."

Jeb looked up the stairs toward Naomi's room, then at his parents, and finally at Davis.

"You're right," Jeb conceded reluctantly. "I need to go get Naomi from school."

"Baby, don't bring her here," Hannah suggested. "Take her to Lexington overnight. She's been begging me to take her to the Children's Theater there. I don't know how long they will have the house locked down and then we have to get her room…clean."

"Okay." Jeb's tone of voice expressed his unwillingness to leave to his parents.

"I wouldn't tell her anything about all this, son," Mac said. "Little angel's been through a lot in the last year. We need to minimize the trauma in her life. We need to make her feel as safe as we can. It would be a shame if she didn't feel safe in her own home."

"Okay, Dad. Mom, can you grab a few things for her?" Jeb asked. "I've got everything I need in my go bag in the truck."

After Jeb left with Naomi's overnight bag and the crime scene techs from the FBI had departed, Davis walked Hannah and Mac through the house continuing to catalog the stolen items and photograph the damage more thoroughly.

The burglars took the flat-screen television. They had unplugged the power cord but cut the coaxial cable. Strangely, they had carefully removed it from the wall mount. Mac and Hannah never watched the thing except for the weather report on the news. Naomi watched some children's programming occasionally, and for some strange reason had taken a liking to the Hallmark channel. Both Mac and Hannah were happier their granddaughter enjoyed playing outdoors and riding horses more than sitting in front of a TV.

Though they stole her Apple laptop from the office, Hannah backed up most of her important files, including all her family pictures, to Dropbox or her iCloud account. She could recover any files of importance. Of immediate need was their insurance policy.

The safe was open and several weapons were missing, including Hannah's thirty-ought six deer rifle, its scope, and a few shotguns her father had handed down to her. The Pelican case for Mac's 1873 Colt Peacemaker Single Action Army revolver and holster still sat untouched, albeit covered in an unblemished layer of FBI's fingerprint dust. Seems the thieves didn't know what the case contained. Years ago, Mac had the Colt certified and the functioning antique, like the ranch, was worth a small fortune. And like the ranch, they would never sell it. Mac looked at the safe's door, covered in black fingerprint dust.

"You see anything strange here?" Mac asked Davis.

"Excuse me?"

"Well, there's gloved prints on the door and all over the inside of the safe, but not on the handgun case. Not one," Mac pointed out to his deputy. "And how did they get into the safe in the first place? Hannah, Jeb, and I alone know the combination, and I know we didn't leave it open. So, how did they get in? And what's this round spot where the dust shows glove prints all around it, but not there?"

Davis looked at the circle on the safe. Sure enough, there was a perfectly round circle of about two inches in diameter with smudged prints all around it, but none within the circle. He took photos with his phone and noted it on a pad he was carrying.

"Measure the circle. I don't know what it is, but it must mean something," Mac instructed as he locked the safe door and set the dial to zero.

"Let's check the rest of the house." As they walked through the trashed house, Davis took more photos with his phone. The techs would have taken crime scene photos, but Davis wanted a set for his records and for the MacDowell's insurance company.

The thieves had taken some sports equipment and old high school sports trophies from Jeb's room. Most importantly to Jeb, they stole a treasured keepsake, a Louisville Slugger his dad had gotten him from the Louisville Cardinals when he was a kid. A bat they dad had played ball with for years.

Hannah's jewelry box was missing from their bedroom, but there was nothing of any particular worth except the sentimental value of her father's old pocket watch. The list contained a few more items, but nothing of real note.

"No silverware?" Davis asked.

"Never saw the need," Hannah replied. "It's not like we throw fancy dinner parties. We got some as wedding presents, but we sold it close to thirty years ago. Think we used the cash to put down on a new baler."

"What about electronics?"

"We were both carrying our phones. We had a laptop. We never saw the need for an iPad or anything like that. Not like there are a whole lot of apps for breeding horses. Up in the attic, there are a few things, none of which are of any value: an electric typewriter, an old camera or two, a stereo I'm not sure works anymore, and maybe a few old, small kitchen appliances Mac said he was going to get around to fixing."

"Wait," Mac interjected. "Jeb installed a doorbell cam a week or two ago, but Hannah and I never got around to installing the app on our phones. Maybe Jeb did."

A quick call to Jeb confirmed it.

"Hang on a second Dad," Jeb said over the phone. "Let me pull over. Yeah, I've got it right here. I hadn't put the apps on your phones yet, so in my mind, it wasn't really live yet, but it works on a motion sensor and stores the video to the Cloud. Let me send it to your phone."

"Send it to Davis's as well. He's the lead on this."

"You got it yet?" Jeb asked.

A ding from both Davis's and Mac's phones rang out. The cell reception was poor in the county, but the MacDowells had a wireless router with Internet fed through a satellite dish. Jeb installed it inside a cabinet or the thieves would have likely stolen it as well.

"Yeah, Jeb. We got it. Looks like three men wearing masks came through the front door," Mac observed.

"I see it," Jeb replied. "Can't see their faces. The first one seemed pretty confident in what he was doing. The second guy was smaller and he and the third one looked a little nervous. The third one had a tad of a limp. On both of those two, you can see some greasy, long hair sticking out from under their ski masks. I guess they didn't see the doorbell cam. They must be idiots."

Jeb said it simultaneously over the phone as Mac stated it aloud, "The Stampers."

"Okay," Davis said. "I will write this all up and you can have a report to hand to the insurance company, probably by tomorrow."

"Thanks, Davis," Mac told his deputy.

"No worries, Sheriff. As you know, there are no pawn shops in Mounton. If your stuff did get pawned, it could be in Louisville, Lexington, or maybe even Frankfort. No telling where it landed, but we will put calls in to the detectives in those cities and see if they can find anything. It probably won't land there for a day or two, but it's worth a try."

"Davis," Hannah implored, "find my thirty ought-six and my daddy's shotguns."

#

Duncan came back to the motel on 44 later in the morning. Because of the heat of the upcoming day, he traded his long-sleeved flannel shirt for a tee shirt but still sported his trademarked bib overalls. He left McTavish at home since there was a possibility of danger in what he was doing. He drove past the cul de sac he parked in earlier and settled near the parking lot of the motel. He parked the dark green Cutlass in the shade of the forest nearby. This was northern Kentucky. It was ALL either horse pastures or trees. The shade provided him with enough respite from the Kentucky sunshine. He could sit in the car with the windows down now, not that Duncan would ever sit with the engine and air conditioning running, burning gas. The shadows provided some camouflage for the green Oldsmobile. It wasn't invisible, but the coloration and shade helped it blend into the background. Not like the bright yellow Challenger practically glowing in the noon sun.

The motel was one of those scabby, little, one-story outskirt affairs most small towns seeped like pus. The motel's poorly painted exterior doors all faced the gravel parking lot. The place's two selling points were: it was close to the highway and it was the lone fleabag motel for miles around. Very few vehicles parked in front of the rooms, despite those sterling qualities. Duncan assumed it might get slightly busier as night came on and drivers grew wearier. As frugal as he was, Duncan could never imagine needing a room where the resident insects outnumbered the guests to this degree.

Duncan sat there for several hours with no activity and was about to call it quits when a late-model, gray "mommy-van" pulled up next to the yellow Dodge. Duncan tried to imagine what would make a soccer mom desperate enough to stay at the squat, little motel. He had come to the conclusion the occupant was there for a clandestine rendezvous when the driver's side door opened and a tall man who appeared to be in his late twenties climbed out. *Definitely nae a soccer mom*, Duncan thought. When the man turned toward the door, Duncan caught a glimpse of a long ponytail hanging down the man's back, much longer than Sonny's. The man reached into the van and pulled out a gray, plastic grocery bag. The bag held something odd-shaped and heavy. Duncan grabbed the binoculars he had brought for his "stakeout" but was not fast enough to get a look at the man's face. Pony-Tail Man was wearing long sleeves, which was unusual for the temperature. While Duncan couldn't get a clear look at the man's face, he could see his long, brownish-blond hair and dark tan.

The man walked to the room right in front of the bright yellow Dodge and knocked. After a moment, he was let in and entered quickly, after glancing around to see if anyone was looking.

Duncan put the binoculars down. He was trying to put the pieces together but didn't have enough information. What he did have was the year-old, yellow Dodge and a tall, tan man with a ponytail who knocked on the motel door, carrying a heavy object in a plastic bag. When the man knocked on the door, Duncan saw the tan man's hands looked stark white.

#

No Such Thing as a Free Lunch

"Hey Mac! Long time, no see," Adrian Stemple beamed as he entered the diner for lunch with a jangle from the bell above the door.

"Howdy, Adrian," Mac said. "How's it going?"

"Can't complain. Besides, who would listen?" Adrian said, sitting down in Mac's booth.

Ginny came over with two glasses of water, silverware wrapped in napkins, and no menus. "Gentlemen. Coffee and sweet tea?"

Adrian nodded and turned to Mac as Ginny left. The diner was busier than usual today. "Does he ever give you a menu?"

"No, but on the other hand, he never charges me either. He always brings me the special and it's always a surprise."

"Same here," Adrian smiled. "Do you think he does that for everyone?"

"Probably the customers he likes. You don't want what he gives the people he doesn't like." Mac changed the subject. Nobody wanted to say anything bad about Ginny's cooking while he was in earshot. Talk about a sure way to get on the *not-liked list*. "How are the kids?"

"Can't say I know," Adrian said. His two children, Mandy and Jasper, were Naomi's babysitters up until their incestuous relationship brought to light their grandfather's illegal and unsafe mining operations. Once the situation came to a head, Adrian sent them to boarding schools on opposite sides of the country. When their litigious wrongful death suit regarding their grandfather against Mac and Ginny began, Adrian immediately cut them and their attorney off.

"Once I shut down their allowance, they no longer had any reason to call. I spoke with the administrators of their respective schools and once the kids turned eighteen and graduated, they more or less disappeared."

"The lawsuit must still be on," Mac said. "The process server finally found Ginny and me a while back but we haven't heard anything since."

"I'm shocked," Adrian said as Ginny brought their plates. "Seems I was the one paying for their damned lawyer." Ginny returned to the kitchen. "I feel bad I didn't catch it sooner and it went on for as long as it did. I thought for sure once they were cut off, the attorney would lose interest. The facts of the case make it such a loser no firm in their right mind would take it on a contingency. But I think you can safely say those kids just *love* you."

"Well, maybe they simply lost interest," Mac offered. "It's been months and we haven't heard anything. Ginny and I talked about it. He shot their grandfather while the judge was drawing down on me. Now granted, it was on my property and it was clearly in the course of his duties as a temporary deputy and in defense of my life. The grand jury didn't think it was worth a trial."

Ginny swung by their table long enough to drop off Mac's usual slice of pie and refill their drinks.

"Oh yeah. Evidently, you *specifically* are responsible for the allegedly unlawful death of their grandfather, the destruction of their family's empire, the loss of most the jobs in Mounton, the neutering of their grandfather's biggest failure—me, and even alienation of affection—theirs, for each other, as sick as it is. You are definitely the reason for everything bad that ever happened to those kids."

"Anything else for you gentlemen?" Ginny asked.

"We're good. Thanks," Adrian said. "As usual, everything was excellent."

Ginny didn't leave a check as he returned to the kitchen. He never charged Mac and it didn't seem right to charge Adrian since Ginny was the one who shot his father.

The gesture did not go unnoticed. "I'll get the tip," Adrian told Mac. "You know Shirley stills calls me' Stinky'?"

"Be thankful. She calls me 'Susie,'" Mac said as the two men got up to leave. "Don't worry too much, Adrian. Jasper and Mandy have always been big on living large and low on actual follow-through. I don't think you need to worry. They're eighteen years old. What could they possibly get into?"

#

Forty Percent & White Hands

Heaven hitched a ride out to *The Digger's Hole Saloon*. She would have called ahead but her cell phone barely had any bars and she wanted to see what there was to see around Mounton. She had met a number of people, and with the exception of the strange cashier at the diner, everyone was friendly and helpful. The owner of the gas station, while admitting he knew nothing about electric vehicles and had no way of charging her car, did say the bar out by the lake might be looking for an extra waitress. People were *really* friendly here. An older man in bib overalls with a classic Oldsmobile gave her a lift out to the saloon and Heaven felt completely at ease with him. Oh sure, he had given her the once-over, but as a pretty, young woman, Heaven almost expected appraising glances from men. *What's the harm? An admiring glance never hurt anyone.* He was old enough to be her grandfather, but she could tell he was a good man. He turned out to be the owner of the town's general store and was a perfect gentleman, wished her luck, and offered to hang around to offer her a lift back into town after her interview. *"Aye, an' I'd hate to see a bonny lass such as yourself stranded in these woods."* Certain he was harmless and had nothing but good intentions, Heaven thanked him and told him she would love to take him up on his offer. This lack of a functioning car thing may be a bigger issue than she had originally thought.

Climbing out of the Olds, she passed the second biggest man she had ever seen. His black hair was pulled tight back into a short ponytail *(at least it wasn't a man-bun!)* and his full beard trimmed neatly, he looked for the world like a well-groomed bear. Dressed in a snug, black tee-shirt featuring some band she had never heard of and a well-worn pair of jeans, he opened the door for her to let her in. *I could get used to this Southern gentleman thing,* she thought.

The bar was exactly what she expected: crowded, smokey, and a country band was playing something loud with a twangy guitar riff.

Heaven made her way through the crowd to get to the bar.

"I'm looking for the manager," she stated.

"Howdy," the little man behind the bar smiled, holding out his hand. He wasn't a midget, but he didn't top over five feet tall. His red hair and green outfit made him look like a real-life leprechaun.

"Hello to you too," shaking his hand, now shouting so he could hear her more clearly. "I AM LOOKING FOR THE MANAGER!"

"Howdy," the leprechaun said again.

"Uh, hello again. I said I am looking—"

"I know. I apologize. I'm the manager. My name is Howdy. Howdy Barnes. It's me one joke, and I hate to miss an opportunity to use it. We have damn few new people in town. How can I help you Miss...?"

"Heaven. Just Heaven."

"I bet you are," Howdy smiled.

"Cute. I've never heard *that* before."

"How did ye come by the name Heaven," Howdy asked.

"Mom loved Led Zeppelin's *Stairway to Heaven.*"

"I like her already. I can tell I'm not alone as someone who likes to have a wee bit of fun with a name. Let me guess, you've got a complaint about not getting your order in a timely manner. I apologize, but Peggy is doing the best she can," Howdy admitted. "We've gotten extremely busy in the last few months."

"That's why I'm here," Heaven explained. "I'm hoping you are in the market for an extra waitress."

Howdy arched a red eyebrow as he looked the beauty up and down. "Do you have any experience waiting tables?"

"Well, I got a degree in sports and health sciences and since there were no teaching jobs in Jersey...yes, I've waited plenty of tables."

Right then, a slurring voice called out to Heaven from behind. "Hey, schweetheart, how's about you come over here and have a drink with ush?"

"No, thank you," she replied. "I'm busy at the moment." She hadn't bothered to turn around.

"You too good to have a drink with us? You too pretty?"

Hannah never turned around and watched Howdy hang up the phone after a short conversation. "No, I'm too sober."

"Huh! Look what we got here! Another snotty broad who needs some lessons!"

The voice drew closer and louder. Heaven could tell from the sound of the voice the man was slightly taller than she was and much, much heavier. Talking to Howdy, she asked, "On a scale of Jerry Van Dyke to Jason Statham, how tough is this guy?"

Howdy looked around Heaven at the drunk behind her. "Oh, he's probably a solid Steven Seagal."

"Okay then," Heaven said exasperated. "Forty percent it is."

As the drunk put his big paw on her left shoulder, she swung around lifting her left arm up and around, trapping his hand between her torso and under her arm. In the same move, she jabbed her stiffened knuckles into his throat. Before he could choke, she completed her pivot by jerking her right knee up to where the legs of his jeans connected. It was all in one movement and took less than a second. The drunk fell to the floor one moment later, gasping for air and clutching his crotch.

His drunk buddies struggled to get up from the table they were sitting at in time to see Sonny come in the door and then promptly sat back down.

"Is there a problem, Mr. Howdy?" the bouncer asked.

"No, Sonny, I would like to introduce you to our new waitress, Heaven."

"How do, ma'am?"

"She does exceptionally well, Sonny," Howdy smiled. "She's going to help Peggy waitress a couple of nights a week and give you a couple of days off…with a pay bump for doorman duties, if that's okay with you, miss. Sonny, would you care to drag this ne'er-do-well outside where the sheriff's department will be along shortly to collect him?"

"You called the cops?" Heaven asked.

"Well, I didn't know you were going to go all Bruce Lee at the time," Howdy acknowledged. "Sonny could have handled him and his friends, but then there's the furniture damage and the insurance claims. It's easier to call the sheriff's department. They need something to do anyway."

"Think they need any part-time help?"

#

Duncan had decided his stakeout wasn't as dangerous as he originally thought, so for this evening's foray, he brought McTavish along for company. Stakeouts didn't seem this boring on TV. The Shitzu napped peacefully on his blanket on the bench seat of the Olds and occasionally let Duncan know he needed to walk. Duncan figured the trees and distance enabled him to walk the pup incognito.

It was during one of these walks he noticed the soccer mom van pull up next to the bright yellow Challenger. Duncan picked up McTavish to keep him quiet and carried him to the ice machine around the corner from the door where he could hear the conversation.

The tan man with the white hands and a long blond ponytail climbed out of the van and knocked on the door directly in front of his vehicle. The door opened, but from his angle, Duncan could not see inside. This time, the room occupants did not welcome the visitor inside. The occupant shoved White Hands a towel-wrapped bundle about a foot and a half long and several inches thick.

"Where's the bag?" White Hands demanded. "I gave it to you in a plastic bag."

"We lost it somewhere," a male voice inside the motel room snapped after he handed over the bundle. The voice sounded young, angry, and entitled. "Does it really matter?"

Right then, the compressor inside the ice machine decided to rattle and wheeze, as it dumped another load of ice into its storage bin.

White Hands glanced at the hastily wrapped white towel in his hand, looked left and right for anyone who might be watching, and shook his head. "No, but after this, forget you ever saw me."

"Dude, I don't wanna be seein' you now." And with that, he slammed the door.

White Hands tucked the bundle up under his arm and climbed back behind the wheel of the gray van.

Duncan lifted the Shitzu to his face and whispered as the dog licked at his red whiskers, "Aye, laddie, it's time for your supper, but fairst thing in the morning, I'll be needin' to find your Uncle Mac and havin' a fine conversation with him."

Turns out, Mac was busy. He didn't get to see Mac for a couple of days and in the flurry of current events, Duncan forgot to tell his friend about his 'stakeout' adventures.

#

Same Trick, New Day

"I'm sorry, Mrs. MacDowell, but Naomi said it wouldn't be a problem," the voice on the phone told Hannah. "It was her turn to bring snacks for the class. The school sent home a printed schedule a few weeks ago."

"Don't pay it no never mind," Hannah said into the landline phone hanging from the wall. "I'm sorry, I didn't get your name." An unknown caller, supposedly from Naomi's school, lured her to her own kidnapping last year. The voice on the phone sounded like a white male in his late twenties/early thirties.

"I apologize. My name is Dalton McGuire. I'm the new security officer here at the school. The principal asked me to call since she was getting ready to go into a meeting and Naomi's teacher's in class."

"Well, Mr. McGuire, Naomi is right, it's no problem. Everyone knows good grandmas keep a batch of freshly baked cookies at all times. Or they know where the closest store is to buy them. I can be there in about fifteen minutes." It was about a ten-minute drive to the school from the MacDowell farm.

"I'll let Mrs. Parton know. You can bring the cookies straight to Naomi's class. Her teacher will be expecting you."

Hannah hung up, thought about it for a minute, and then called the number for the school.

"Mounton School. This is Debra."

"Hello, Debra. This is Hannah MacDowell. Do you happen to have a new security guard there?" Hannah asked the school secretary.

"Oh, yes. Mr. McGuire. He's a godsend. Besides making sure the students and teachers are safe, he's helping out everyone. Your family's kidnapping out of the school parking lot was part of the reason we hired him."

"Thank you, Beth. I simply wanted to check," Hannah said.

She went to the kitchen and packed several dozen cookies in a Tupperware container. Grabbing her keys from the hook near the door, she carried the container out to her Jeep.

At the school, Beth wondered why Mrs. MacDowell was interested in the sixty-eight-year-old security guard.

As soon as Hannah's Jeep pulled down the road, a tall, tan man used a set of picks to unlock the back kitchen door and let himself into the MacDowell house. He knew there was no doorbell camera on this side of the house. It was a little more difficult with the white vinyl gloves on. Moving directly from the kitchen, he headed straight to the den and the safe sitting there. Kneeling down, he looked at a piece of paper he had written on a few days earlier and opened the safe's combination lock. Once he opened the safe, he grabbed the Colt case and opened it. Inside, the old-fashioned gunslinger belt lay coiled, along with a box of ammunition for the weapon. The foam outline for the Colt was empty. Pulling a sanitizer packet from his pocket, he opened the packet and used the sanitizer wipe to clean the weapon again. Before he replaced the case, he wiped it down again removing any DNA or smudge traces. He closed the safe door and spun the lock, eradicating any prints off the back door knob with the sanitizer wipe and re-locking it as he left. The whole operation took less than seven minutes.

Four minutes later, when Hannah walked the cookies into Naomi's class, the teacher looked at her in confusion.

"Mrs. MacDowell, I appreciate you bringing in treats for the kids, but it's Mrs. Emerson's turn. I can guess where the confusion started. We started putting the parent/student schedule online about a month ago instead of sending home notes. Naomi was supposed to tell you."

Hannah looked at the woman in confusion.

"Did you happen to ask a Mr. McGuire to call me?" Hannah asked.

"No. Did he? Well, no harm done. An extra cookie for their snack won't hurt anyone. Unless of course, there's nuts in them. You didn't put nuts in them, did you?" Naomi's teacher asked.

"No. There's something nuts going on, but it's not in the cookies," Hannah contemplated with a frown.

#

Chainsaw Bandits & Cut Scenes

Jeb was hanging up the phone as Mac walked in the station from his morning patrol.

"Hey, Dad. I barely got in myself when we got a call from the Mercer County Sheriff's Department down in Harrodsburg. Seems someone broke into a high-end tire store last night and robbed it. Sheriff's deputy says they scarcely got $200."

"Any descriptions or video?" Mac asked his son.

"Nope. No cameras in the store and it was the middle of the night. No one saw anything. The one possible witness they have was a guy walking his dog late at night, thought he heard a couple of chainsaws. Probably unrelated. No one used a chainsaw in the tire store break-in. Broke out a side window." Jeb re-read his notes to make sure. "Yep, broke a small window to get in and walked out the front door after they unlocked it from the inside."

"Great. Basically, we should be on the lookout for anyone carrying $200 in cash and chainsaws. Shouldn't be a hard case to crack." Jeb could practically smell the sarcasm coming from his father.

"I guess Mercer must have wanted us to know," Jeb said. "Maybe Paul Bunyan needed some cash. Guess he had all the tires he needed."

"Call the deputy back and ask if he could get a list of customers from the last week or two," Mac directed. "Addresses and car models."

"You think a former customer robbed the place?" Jeb asked.

"Noper. I have a sneaking suspicion whoever robbed the tire store never bought a tire there in their life. But get the list anyway."

#

Not Just Another Day

Adrian Stemple walked into his modest second-story office. The lower floor was a coffee/pastry shop a local had started up in the last year. Adrian could have afforded the nicest workspace in Mounton but chose an old building on Main Street the previous owners had abandoned when the mines closed. He had quietly picked up the title from the bank and was leasing the shop downstairs at a much lower rent than the state average. From there, he managed the business of *Stemple, Inc.* The company's primary focus was helping manage numerous businesses his family had acquired over the last two hundred years and to help the town of Mounton get back on its feet. As he let himself into the office, he passed his secretary, Hattie Vernon, the other half of *Stemple, Inc.*, working diligently at her desk. The aroma of freshly brewed coffee from the shop below filled the small offices.

"Mr. Stemple, you have several messages and the Emersons called and made an appointment to come by and speak with you in the next few minutes. I couldn't reach you but was expecting you back. I hope it was okay."

"It's fine, Hattie," Adrian smiled. "You know it's okay if people don't make an appointment. They can just drop by."

Adrian didn't really want or need a secretary, or 'administrative assistant' as is more politically correct, but Hattie lost her husband in a mining accident a few years ago and if she didn't find work in Mounton, she was going to have to move back with her folks down in Glasgow, Kentucky, and Adrian knew there were no jobs for an intelligent woman like Hattie there. So, as opposed to letting the young widow move to an area with no real prospects, he proposed she come work for him. It was one of the best decisions he had ever made. He believed Hattie worked diligently to earn his generosity of offering a job to an inexperienced single woman. In truth, she had proven herself invaluable a dozen times over.

"Mr. Stemple," Ephraim Emerson said as he and Laney sat in front of Adrian's desk fifteen minutes later, "like I was saying, we was wonderin' if you might have a word with Mr. Potter down at the bank. Laney and I are hardly a month or two behind on the house payment. We have kept the rent current on the photo shop, but the twins are way more expensive than we counted on. Much more so than our little Emmy."

Ephraim and Laney had stayed in Mounton when many others had fled for jobs in Louisville and Lexington after Adrian's father's mining infractions and criminal endeavors came to light and closed down the mines. The town reinvented itself as a destination to allow tourists to enjoy life a hundred years in the past. The Emersons, despite having recently birthed Mounton's newest citizens, loyally stayed and opened up a shop where tourists could have their picture taken dressed as they might have been in the last century. The Emersons' shop did well in its first two summers and Ephraim sold and delivered firewood from scraps at the lumberyard and did computer repair work in the winter when he could get it. Adrian had loaned them the money to buy the computers, cameras, equipment, and costumes to get the shop started and they paid him back in full in their first season.

Adrian looked down at the computer printout Ephraim had presented of their payment history.

"I will talk to old man Potter," Adrian comforted. "You two take a few months to get caught up and don't worry about it one bit."

"Mr. Stemple," Laney said, her eyes welling up. "You are a godsend. If it wasn't for you, this town would've dried up and blowed away."

"I wish that was the case, but the truth be told," Adrian said as he patted Ephraim on the shoulder as he led them to his office door, "it's the strong will, hard work, and determination of people like you who make Mounton what it is. I'm merely a guy who is trying to make up for the decades his family abused good folks like you. You two do the best you can and take care of those babies. They're young but once and I'm living proof you can screw it up if you don't love them enough."

After the Emersons left, Adrian spoke from his inner office door, "Hattie, cut a couple of checks. One to the bank for the Emersons' mortgage to cover three or four months and another for the same time period towards the lease on their shop. Let's buy them some time to get back on their feet."

"But didn't you say you would just *talk* to Mr. Potter?"

"And I will, as I hand him the check," Adrian smiled. "I will leave it to you to get the necessary account numbers and such. On second thought, do it tomorrow. I have a better idea for today. Why don't you take the rest of the afternoon off? You've been working like a dog and what's the point of making a living if you never get a life?"

"Well, if you really think it's okay, I could stand to go down to Darlene's and get something done with this rat's nest."

"Do it. And tell Darlene to put it on my tab. Consider it a little bonus you don't have to report to the IRS," Adrian said as he sorted through his messages.

"Mr. Stemple, you are the best boss I ever had."

"Hattie, if I'm not mistaken, I'm the ONLY boss you've ever had. No worries. Plus, I told you to call me Adrian. I'm going to make some of these calls and then I'm headed home myself. I'll see you tomorrow."

Turned out, he wouldn't.

#

"Hey, honey," Mac called out as he entered the farmhouse through the mudroom. He had finished his shift and was looking forward to a quiet evening of playing with Naomi and talking to his wife.

"Hey," Hannah replied a bit tersely.

"Everything okay?" Mac asked.

"Not so much," Hannah started. "I spoke with the manufacturer about the gun safe and they told me that as short-handed as they were, it would be six weeks before they could get someone out to change the combination."

"O-kay…means we have to lock up my Colt case somewhere else

to keep Naomi from being able to get to it. I can probably lock it up down at the station. Not a big deal. The other guns are still in the wind."

"I wish I didn't have any more bad news," Hannah said. "I talked to the insurance company about our claim. They are sending an investigator out. I spoke with a nice young lady on the phone and she confided she really shouldn't say this, but there was an excellent chance they may cancel our policy. They have already raised our premium once since the tractor claim and Jeb and Naomi moved in."

Mac thought back to the previous year to the Douvez case when someone had trashed their tractor to send a message to the MacDowells. He never caught he actual perpetrators, but Mac had a pretty good idea who it did it. The insurance company paid, albeit reluctantly. Someone had anonymously suggested because Mac was a law officer under investigation at the time, he knew how to make a crime more unsolvable. Mac believed Douvez called the insurance company anonymously. This seemed to make the insurance company more suspicious of fraud. Too many problems of late seemed to directly involve the Douvez case last year.

"Okay, let's start shopping for new insurance," Mac decided. "Two strikes against us in less than a year will make it more difficult and definitely more expensive, but the fact we have gone decades without a claim should work in our favor some."

"Well, it will take a few weeks for their investigator to get here. If we want any of this stuff replaced before then, it will have to be out of pocket."

"Let's replace the TV. Naomi needs something to watch and you needed a new laptop anyway. Keep receipts for everything. We'll hold off on the rifle and shotguns until we see what the insurance investigator has to say. I'm sure you can go a few weeks without your rifle," Mac smiled.

"Not if I find out who destroyed Naomi's room," Hannah said *without* a smile.

#

Mac came into the small sheriff's station from his afternoon patrol of Mounton. Jeb sat at the newer of the two computers in the office and typed his shift report.

"Dave called from the FBI office in Lexington," Jeb said, as he stopped typing. "Seems Jesse's truckload of SUVs wasn't quite what it seemed. The registration and driver's license weren't too awfully legitimate and Feds listed the cars on the truck as stolen. Dave and his team have been noticing an influx of stolen vans. Jesse tried to run the plate and license at the stop, but you know how spotty cell reception is out there. The driver convinced that he was going to get past Jesse, gave him the fake driver's license of a Mark Calhoun, aka William Grogan. The address was bogus by about three years." Jeb handed Mac an enlarged printout of the Calhoun driver's license. "Seems Grogan has a record a mile long for questioning about everything from B&E to now, it seems, grand theft auto. Georgia, Ohio, and most recently, Florida. You could best describe Grogan as 'morally ambiguous.'"

"Does Jesse know?" Mac asked.

"Oh, yeah. He was here when the call came in and is out patrolling in the hopes of catching a glimpse of Grogan in his truck again. He seemed...*eager* to speak to *Mr. Calhoun*. It's eating at him Grogan fooled him. He thinks if he had more experience, none of this would have happened."

As he finished, the office phone rang.

"Sheriff's office," Jeb answered.

After listening for a minute, he handed the phone to Mac. "It's Adrian. He wants to speak to 'Sheriff Jacob MacDowell,' and he sounds really weird."

"Hey, Adrian," Mac spoke into the receiver.

"Sheriff MacDowell, I need you to come out to my house. Alone. As soon as possible," Adrian said over the phone. Jeb was right. Something was strange about the way Adrian was speaking. Like he was reading from a script.

"Is everything okay?"

"Uh, yes. I want to finish our conversation we started at the diner. There is no need for Jebediah to come. Just you, Sheriff MacDowell. When can you come out?"

Mac thought about the call. *Jebediah?*

"I can be there in about thirty minutes. I'm about to finish my shift and it will take me a little less to get there."

"Excellent, Sheriff MacDowell. I look forward to concluding our diner conversation."

Mac looked at the disconnected phone. "You were right. Weird."

"You want me to come with you?" Jeb asked. "Jesse and Patricks have the three-to-eleven shift and Jesse came in early and is already out patrolling."

"Naw. You go pick up the angel. Adrian probably just needs to vent. I'll call Hannah on the way to his place and let her know I'll be home a little later."

As things worked out, it wasn't all that much later.

#

In about twenty minutes, Mac arrived at Adrian's estate. There was no other way to describe it. Mac had been here numerous times and still wasn't used to it. The Stemples had made a substantial fortune from land deals, investing in small businesses in Mounton County, and in the mining business. The Stemple property stretched for hundreds of acres in all directions, surrounded by an eye-popping white split-rail fence. People thought he and Hannah were well off due to the beautiful house and ranch her parents had left them. Hannah was particularly proud of the flowers planted around the flag pole in their circular drive. It took the better part of a year to revitalize them since Jeb had mowed them over with a snowblower. Mac knew for a fact living on a sheriff's salary, he couldn't afford the Stemples' fence, let alone the mansion and land it surrounded.

When he drove up the winding drive to get to the front door, he found an envelope taped to the door with a message on the outside.

Sheriff Jacob MacDowell, please secure this, unopened, in your personal safe until I call you. Sorry, I could not ask you

in person or meet with you. Regards, Adrian T. Stemple, Esq.

Mac looked at the outside of the sealed envelope and took it back to his truck. *This is getting weirder and weirder. Adrian's always been a stand-up guy. He must have some explanation for all this that makes sense.*

It bothered him all the way home. After staring at the combination dial for a moment, he dialed the combination to his gun safe, relayed the story to Hannah, and showed her the envelope. Tossing the sealed envelope inside, he looked at his beautiful wife as he set the dial to zero.

"Just about the darnedest thing I have ever heard in all my born days," she said. "It doesn't sound like Adrian a bit. And since when does he call you boys 'Jebediah' and 'Sheriff MacDowell'?"

#

Ice Cream & Community Service

Grogan walked down the Main Street in Mounton, licking on an ice cream cone. He had been keeping tabs on the MacDowell kid, making sure he kept his nose out of it. As instructed, Grogan had thrown some red herrings at the kid to keep him too busy to look into other things. His employer informed Grogan someone else was keeping old man MacDowell busy.

Man! There is nothing better than a hand-dipped pecan praline ice cream cone on a beautiful day.

He strolled through the small town, taking in the sights of the gentrified brick buildings which symbolized the village's turn-of-the-century tourism appeal. Mounton prohibited cars from Main Street, but the small town still enjoyed a busy retail section, despite its focus around life in Kentucky in the nineteenth century.

As he walked by a shop, he noticed it was also the post office. He looked up at the big wooden sign on the storefront. *Duncan's Mercantile & General Store.*

My nephew has a thing for commemorative stamps. I always thought it made him look like a bit of a sissy, but whatever makes him happy, he thought. After a few more licks, Grogan tossed the remainder of his sugar cone in a plastic-lined trash can inside a wooden barrel. *I guess they didn't have metal recycling trash cans back in the old days.*

He looked around the store a bit, finding everything from hardware to farm clothing to simple groceries. But the line to the single post office counter was five deep. After watching the line and how long it took, Grogan decided he didn't need to buy his nephew stamps bad enough to wait in line.

"Canna help ye?" A Scottish lilt came from behind him. A husky man with a reddish-gray beard, a full head of hair, wearing an old pair of bib overalls and a light flannel shirt, stood up from a seat behind the wooden checkout counter.

"Uh, I was going to buy some commemorative stamps for my nephew but the postmistress looks a little busy," Grogan explained.

"Aye, an' Mrs. Fisher is second in line. There'll be no end to the gossip when she gets to the front. Agnes took over the post office last year and she does a fine job of it, but she dinnae know when to cut some people off. The name's Duncan," the red-headed man said. "I can help ye here."

"As in *Duncan's Mercantile & General Store*?"

"Aye. Me family's owned this fine emporium for several generations. I come in these days to check on things mostly. Agnes does most of the real work," Duncan admitted. "We've got some excellent stamps the lad'll be likin'."

As Duncan made change for the him, Grogan noticed that the store owner was taking a mental photograph of him, noting his tan, height, and hair color. When he reached for his change, his tattoo, on his right forearm and wrist, escaped out of his rolled shirt sleeve. He was going to have to go much lower profile if all the residents were this nosy.

"Thanks, old-timer. Sure is a friendly town."

His hands weren't stark white. They were the same color as the rest of his deep tan, but when the man turned and headed for the door, Duncan knew for sure. Hanging halfway down the man's back was a long brownish-blond ponytail.

#

Work Outs & Work Days

Heaven jogged to the community center. It was a solid couple of miles out of town (*and uphill!*) at the former cafeteria of the now-defunct coal mines, but the fresh mountain air and run helped her feel healthier. She missed regular workouts at her gym in Jersey, but she thinks she may have come up with a solution.

She arrived at the big two-story building and looked it over. The lower story was a large open room converted into a yoga and exercise facility, while the second floor housed the few offices needed for the coal mine tour.

Heaven opened the door to the exercise studio to see a pretty black woman rolling up some yoga mats.

"Can I help you?" the woman asked. The gorgeous redhead looked at the woman of color in front of her who was wearing running shoes, yoga pants, and a midriff lycra top that displayed an impressive set of abs.

"I hope I can help *you*. I heard you run yoga and archery classes up here. My name is Heaven Carlysle."

"Oh, yeah. The new girl."

"Excuse me?" Heaven asked.

"Sorry. Mounton is a small town and everyone knows everyone else's business here. Between the Church Ladies and gossip down at *Ginny's Diner*, your exploits out at *Digger's Hole* are now legendary. My name is Felicia Harris-Williams. And yeah, we do have yoga, exercise, and archery workshops here a few days a week."

"Felicia Harris-Williams? There was a Felicia Harris a few years ago who was in the Olympics for archery. Was *that* you?"

"Alternate for the Olympic team, but yes. Impressive. Most people don't even know we have an archery team, much less who the alternates were, not to mention something in the ancient past."

"Not so long ago. I got my degree in sports and health sciences and was a bit of a reader and a geek."

"I'm trying to imagine you as a geek and am coming up short. But that's quite a memory you have. How'd you get a name like Heaven?"

"About fifteen years before my arrival, Dad loved the singer, Belinda Carlysle. You know, *Heaven is a Place on Earth*."

"Cute. What can I do for you, Heaven?"

"I hoped you could hire me. I wondered if you have any interest in offering some self-defense courses. I could also help teach some physical fitness classes," Heaven said.

"Wow. I never thought about offering self-defense courses. Do you have any experience? I mean besides your degree," Felicia said.

"I have three black belts: jiu-jitsu, Taekwondo, and Krav Maga. What can I say? I started young. In retrospect, I guess I really was a bit of a nerd."

"You are *way* overqualified. I'm afraid if we could fill those workshops, the pay would be next to nothing."

"Actually, I am okay with minimal pay. I don't mind because I am desperate for a regular workout and teaching would give me that, aside from the run up here and back. If you knew how much I was paying for a gym membership and sparring time in New Jersey, you would make me pay you!" Heaven said.

"Well, let's get some flyers printed and posted around town and see if we can get you some students. And call me Felicia, please. As a courtesy, I would like to get this approved by the guy who's letting me use this area in the first place, Adrian Stemple."

"Mr. Stemple! Shouldn't be a problem. He's my landlord. He'll just die, though, when he finds out I am earning money at *his* place to pay *to* him. Felicia, I do have to tell you upfront, I don't like teaching one specific discipline. I believe in teaching practical self-defense. Everyday tactics for real-world scenarios. If someone wants to go for a belt afterward, I'm fine with it, but first I want them to know how to live long enough to earn it."

"I am definitely taking your class. What do you suggest for a beginner?"

"Run away. The best way to end a fight is to avoid it," Heaven said without hesitation.

"What do you say we practice your first lesson now? On the days I don't haul extra equipment, I usually jog up here. You look like you could run back to town without breaking a sweat."

"If I don't run back, I would have to spend the night here and those yoga mats don't look too comfortable."

"If you're interested, on the days I don't jog up here, I usually run about 5:00 a.m.," Felicia offered.

"Sounds great, except four nights a week I will be working late down at *Digger's Hole*. 5:00 a.m. might be a little rough."

"I get it," Felicia said as she jogged down the hill, "but somehow, I get the feeling you are not someone worried about things getting a little rough."

#

Maximum Penalty

Mac was hiding. The sofa in his and Hannah's living room barely hid him. Dressed in his standard jeans and tan work shirt, he peered from behind the couch to check on his pursuer. The coast was clear.

From above him, he heard: "GOTCHA!"

His granddaughter, Naomi, jumped from the knitted afghan draped over the back of the couch to land on her Pappaw's back with a squeal.

Mac rolled over, grabbing the apple of his eye under her arms, extremely conscious of the healed scars on her lower torso. His smile was broad and genuine.

"You sure did, SweetPea. And here's your reward for catching such an ornery desperado." Naomi screamed laughter as he tickled her ribs.

"Pappaw! No!" Naomi gasped between sobs of laughter. "I'm gonna pee."

Mac lay on his back behind the sofa with Naomi suspended above him, giggling mercilessly.

"You better not. You know what's the penalty for peeing on Pappaw?" Mac laughed along. "The maximum sentence: more tickles!"

The doorbell rang and Hannah emerged from the kitchen, wiping her hands on a dish towel. "No, really. Don't bother. I'll get it." Her sarcasm muted by the smile on her face as she watched her husband and seven-year-old granddaughter play on the floor.

Mac tilted his wrist while holding Naomi to see his watch.

"SweetPea, it's gettin' on five-thirty. I better go help Mammaw with dinner or we'll both get the maximum penalty!"

"Mac? You need to come here." Hannah's voice from the front door sounded confused and strained.

"On my way," he said as he set Naomi down and rolled to his feet. *Not as quick as I used to,* he thought. "And you, young lady, can go set the table."

Four men stood on the front porch, two Kentucky State Police uniforms Mac didn't recognize, one man in an off-the-rack suit practically screaming FBI, and his friend Dave Smathers from the FBI's Lexington office. The agent Mac didn't recognize held several folded pieces of paper and extended his badge carrier to show his ID. Two KSP cruisers and a black SUV sat in the MacDowell circular drive.

"Jacob MacDowell?" asked the agent with the badge.

"Yepper."

"Sir, we have a warrant for your arrest for the murder of Adrian Stemple. As you may be aware, it's required if we arrest you in your home that we have a search warrant for your home and your office," he said as he handed Mac the warrants. "Patrolman, could you please read Sheriff MacDowell his rights?"

As one patrolman read from the Miranda card, one of the KSP troopers stepped up to cuff Mac's hands behind his back.

"Are you kidding? You want to cuff a decorated law officer? Mac, I'm truly sorry about this," Smathers apologized. "We just got handed the warrants and I couldn't even get a call to you to give you a heads up. I'm sure we can clear this up in no time."

"Sorry, Agent Smathers, we have orders to cuff him," the KSP trooper replied.

As Mac turned to be cuffed, he could see Naomi standing there in her little Wranglers and the shirt that matched his, her big, green eyes welling up with tears as she watched from the kitchen, forks and spoons clutched in her little hand.

#

Any Port in a Shit Storm

Mac sat on a bunk in an eight-foot by ten-foot cell in the Kentucky State Highway Patrol holding area. Because he was a law enforcement officer, the KSP arranged a private holding cell.

He tried to figure out what his situation was but didn't have enough facts. They dumped him in there and left him. No interrogation. No explanation. Took off the cuffs and left. The KSP troopers arrested him for the murder of Adrian Stemple. *Adrian was dead?* He had been one of the guiding hands in the county since his father died. *Would Mounton be the same without him?*

As he sat there, he worried about his town and family. *Were Hannah and Naomi okay?* He thought of the little girl's tears as they took him away. *Would she look at her Pappaw the same way again? Would Jeb be able to take care of things at the station? Would Dawe remember to check the doorknobs of all the shops in town to make the shop owners locked them? Would anybody do an occasional wellness check on old Ezekiel Thompson without him knowing what it was?*

Too many details regarding the care of his town nagged at him. He realized after last year's kidnappings he does not stand as the sole protector of Mounton, but feels as if he is negligent of his duty locked in this cell.

With an ironic smile, Mac realized incarceration in a cell hardly counted as *slacking off*. How could they implicate him in Adrian's death? How can he find the truth while locked in here? How does one go about fighting something like this? He had never been on this side of the law before. He had no idea how to proceed.

"Sheriff MacDowell?" the man on the outside of the chain-link cage asked with no trace of a Southern accent.

"Yepper."

"Sir, my name is Dayton Hollister, and I think I can help you."

The man was more than a little below average height, sported a dark Van Dyke beard around his mouth and chin, a shaved head, and had the saggy-faced look of a man who had recently, and quickly, lost a lot of weight. But well-tanned. *Maybe a spray-on tan or the kind of tan from a tanning booth, but definitely not outdoor work.* His nails were well-manicured. His expensive suit seemed one or two sizes too big. Someone had custom-tailored it for a larger man. The distressed leather satchel in his hand probably cost more than Mac's old Bronco did originally. He looked a little familiar, but Mac couldn't place him. He simply didn't know any short, skinny, tanned, rich, bald city-slickers. In northern Kentucky, they would kind of stand out.

"Well, Mr. Hollister, unless you can get me out of this cell and clear my name, I sincerely doubt it," Mac said.

"Then I guess that's just what I'll do," Dayton Hollister smiled, as he handed Mac a business card. "I'm a criminal defense attorney, Mr. MacDowell, and a damned good one. I've only lost one single case in the last fifteen years and it was nothing like yours. I believe I can help you. I heard about your situation and feel the State has committed a grave injustice. Are you interested in some assistance?"

Mac looked at Hollister's card. He did need help, and while the name sounded familiar, a single lost case in fifteen years was a pretty good record. He had given a lot of thought to his situation and had no idea where to start. Some professional help, especially in a murder case, seemed like a good idea.

"Mr. Hollister, may I ask how you happened to hear about my…situation?" Mac asked. "I've barely been here a few hours. My wife hasn't even come in yet."

"I have more than a few contacts in the court system and as soon as

I heard about your arrest, I knew you couldn't possibly have done it. They would let your attorney in to see you before they would your wife."

"I hope you don't take this wrong, but what's in it for you?"

"Well, Mr. MacDowell, I won't lie. I'm going to charge you for this, and charge you quite a bit. Fighting a murder charge is neither easy nor cheap. But you want the best on your case, not some discount attorney who'll plead you out."

At least he's honest about the profit motive. The 'contacts in the system' screams ambulance chaser, but it smacks of aggressive and right now I think I could stand to have a connected, aggressive lawyer.

"Okay, Mr. Hollister, if I were to hire you, what would be our first move?"

"Alrighty then. The first bit of business is to get a bail hearing and get you out of here. Given your background, I am hopeful it won't be hard, but bail for murder cases is unusual. Unfortunately, at this hour, it will likely be at least tomorrow morning before I can get us in front of a judge. The next step is to sit down and hear the entire story. Once I do, I will find out what the State has, and we can start to plan a defense. Don't think for a second this is going to go away quickly or easily. There's going to be a grand jury, some hearings, depositions, a handful of motions, jury selection, and if they have anything at all, most likely, a trial. Hopefully, you won't be in for the fight of your life, but I wouldn't bet on it."

#

In Carpenter's hurry to move on this case, his one mistake was: had they arrested him one day later, Mac would have sat in jail for a week, awaiting the next grand jury. As it was, they decided there was enough evidence for a trial.

Two mornings after his arrest, Hollister was able to squeeze him in front of Judge Brown to set bail. This wasn't an accident. Judge Brown was an old fishing buddy of Mac's. Extremely unusual for a murder case, Mac's attorney asked the court to release him ROR, without posting bail. The Commonwealth's attorney, Washington Carpenter, argued it was unheard of for a first-degree murder suspect to be released on his own recognizance. He requested the judge set the bail at one million dollars to prevent Mac's release and taking flight. Hollister cited Mac's ties to the community, his decades of service as both a sheriff and a Marine, and an established home and family. He called dozens of character witnesses who would have laughed at the idea of Mac running from a fight. The judge declared the absurdity of Mac jumping bail. Mac sighed in relief that the bail would not require a large chunk of a newly acquired line of credit to keep him out of jail until the trial.

On the downside, the Commonwealth's attorney used all those character witnesses from Mounton and Judge Brown's own personal prejudices to seek a motion that it would be impossible to seat an impartial jury in Mounton County. The circuit court judge reluctantly granted a change of venue. Lexington was not as close as Louisville, but a well-prepared Washington Carpenter anticipated that and pointed out that they had the next opening on the docket.

Several days later, Mac and Hollister sat in an office conference room while the Commonwealth's attorney deposed him. Mac had a chance to look at the search and arrest warrants, both signed by a judge at 9:12 a.m. on the day of his incarceration, but they didn't arrest him until 5:30 p.m. The Commonwealth's attorney's office had deliberately waited until he was with his granddaughter and not at work. The State's attorney wanted Naomi to see him in cuffs.

Mac's jaw tightened and wished he was holding Hannah's hand under the table. While this was his first deposition with Carpenter, it was his fourth meeting with Hollister since the arrest and Mac could practically feel the meter spinning.

As soon as the FBI and the KSP arrested Mac, he asked Hannah to go to the same bank her family had used her whole life and put the house and farm up as collateral for a line of credit to pay the criminal attorney, bail, and for a civil attorney for the lawsuit from the Stemple siblings. The house and farm had been in the family for generations and had never had a mortgage before. The Stemples' lawsuit had resurfaced immediately after KSP served the arrest warrant.

#

Mac's attorney earlier explained how Washington Carpenter employed a variety of tricks during a trial, all of them legal. One was to list anyone as a witness who remotely might have information about the events of the crimes. And there were A LOT of witnesses on the list. Carpenter had subpoenaed a good portion of the town of Mounton. The Commonwealth's attorney wouldn't call most of them to testify in court, but it made the defense team work much harder, cost Mac much more money, and kept the witnesses out of the courtroom, depriving Mac of any moral support.

Another tactic Carpenter often employed was to depose as many of the witnesses as he could. He was not answerable to the state of Kentucky for how much money he spent in the pursuit of his duties, but Mac and Hannah were paying for his attorney by the hour. Carpenter knew he could make the expense of the trial both excessively tiring and costly.

During those depositions, Carpenter had a reputation for asking a deluge of unrelated questions. The defense would not know which direction the prosecution may be following and have to spend more time and money investigating each line of questioning. He would not call most of the witnesses to the stand. He used the tactic to cloud the defense's focus and resources.

Mac's attorney explained at some point in the near future, but a hair before the discovery deadline, Carpenter would flood Hollister's office with all of the paperwork, whether relevant or not, from the FBI, the KSP investigation, Carpenter's own office, and public records. Any of this, if introduced in court, would then be admissible. Hollister and his office would have to sift through it all at the last minute. On Mac's nickel.

Carpenter had a perfect conviction rate and had assumed the top prosecution office in Kentucky after the arrest of Devin Douvez, the previous State's attorney and a personal friend of Carpenter's. Anytime he pursued a guilty verdict, he got one.

Mac's deposition went smoothly with Carpenter asking the questions and merely staring at the sheriff. His assistant took all the notes. The court reporter sat to the side typing furiously. Multiple video cameras captured the interview from numerous angles. The questions revolved mostly around the recent call from Adrian Stemple, and the visit to his house. Mac told them about the envelope on Adrian's door. Carpenter asked if he had touched the envelope. When asked about the whereabouts of the envelope, Mac told Carpenter and gave them the combination enabling them to get in to it without damaging the family safe.

After they left the State's attorney's office, Hannah joined them outside and Mac's attorney shook his head.

"What?" Hannah asked. "Mac told me it went well. Nothing discussed looked bad for him."

"That's just it," Mac's attorney said. "It went too well. Carpenter always asks a lot of questions. It was too short. Too easy. He asked about nothing pertaining to motive. He didn't ask about the Stemple kids' suit. As soon as he got the combination of your safe, he ended the interview. I have the feeling he has no intention of talking to Mac on the stand and already knows what's in the envelope. He wanted to get his hands on it to introduce it in court. Whatever's in that envelope is not good."

#

The Only Good Lawyer
"Do ye think ye can be trustin' him, laddie?" Alister Duncan asked Mac. The two men were in *Ginny's Diner* the morning after Mac's release. They sat in Mac's usual booth while Ginny stood by, coffee pot in hand. Duncan waved his pipe around to emphasize his points.

"A shyster appears out of nowhere, says he's going to cost you a truckload of money and ye hire him just like that?" Duncan said. "That's daft even for a bleedin' tourist like yourself."

Duncan's family had been some of the first to settle in Mounton centuries ago and to say the store owner embraced his Scottish heritage would be an understatement. He insisted anyone not born in Mounton or had lived here for at least fifty years was still a tourist. His brogue dialect, especially when excited, was thick enough that many had a hard time understanding him. The actual tourists thought it charming and part of the attraction of visiting his general store. Despite his ribbing of Mac's residency and status, Duncan was one of his oldest and dearest friends.

"I've barely had any time to check him out," Mac said. "He's not joking about an all but undefeated record. He handles exclusively criminal cases, everything from embezzlement to drug cases to murder. Based on who he has helped in the past, I definitely want him sitting right next to me. I trust him about as far as I can throw him, but I would say the same about any lawyer. The problem remains: I really need one. Nearly undefeated is as good as any."

"And ye don't find it queer some boggin' dobber appears right when ye need him?"

"He's a criminal attorney and I was in jail," Mac stated. "Seems pretty legitimate to me."

As the two enjoyed their breakfast, Mac said, "I'm sure glad Hannah was able to get a line of credit on the farm. We could have paid my bail if we had to."

"Nay worries, lad, ye were never gonna spend another night in the hoosegow," Duncan reassured.

"If she hadn't mortgaged the farm, I most likely would have. If they had set bail, where do you think it would have come from?" Mac asked.

Duncan sat for a moment or two, then said, "I've got a few spoondoolies tucked away for a rainy day."

"Duncan, I don't want to bust your bubble, but according to my attorney, my bail would probably have landed at least $250,000, which means I would have needed to post $25,000. That's more than a *few* 'spoondoolies'."

"Ha!" Ginny snorted.

"What's funny?" Mac asked.

"Mac," Ginny started, "I concede you and Duncan are brothers-in-arms, but there may be a considerable number of items you may not be privy to. His clan hasn't released a nickel they didn't have to since they relocated here two hundred years ago. Probably prior. With Adrian's passing, Mr. Duncan here is without question the richest man in Mounton."

"Nay, lad, t'is not true. And I am nae a tightwad. I bought a brand-new Oldsmobile, fresh off the lot," Duncan complained. "Nae miser would be doin' that."

Mac looked at his friend, "Duncan, you bought it in 1971."

"And a damned fine investment it was, too."

"Duncan, I would never ask you to post my bail," Mac said.

"Well, ye didn't have to. It's a shame, though. If I had done it, I would have only charged ye three percent interest."

#

Between his attorney, the FBI, Jeb, and the boys at the station, Mac was able to piece together a rough idea of the scene at Adrian's. The direction of the questioning from the Kentucky State Police detectives helped fill in some blanks as well.

Adrian was found by his housekeeper, Inez, a few hours after Mac left with the envelope taped to Adrian's door. It was her normal day off, but she had left her extra cleaning supplies there the day before and had used up her usual stores at another job. When Inez let herself in that evening, she discovered Adrian's body in his den with a single shot to the base of the skull. Or what remained of his head. Her alibi checked out. She was cleaning another house on her day off from Adrian's. The owners could attest to the fact Inez was there all day long and this was the same job where she had run out of cleaning supplies. After testing her for gunshot residue, the Kentucky State Police released her due to lack of motive, opportunity, or means.

The FBI found no unusual fingerprints, DNA, fibers, or unexplainable hair samples. Inez had cleaned the house the day before and it was immaculate. A single blank legal pad and pen lay on the desk next to a laptop.

Adrian was found face down on the hardwood floor of his den with a large portion of his skull blown off. KSP didn't recover a weapon and the shot came from directly behind him at close range. No possibility of suicide. The shot went clean through his skull. Mac wondered if 'clean' was subjective as the shot blew a large part of his brains all over the floor. They recovered a slug from the wall. While distorted from the dual impact of both skull and wall, the feds identified it as a large caliber and an extremely unusual type.

Lab testing considerably more sophisticated than rubbing a pencil over the legal pad showed the last thing written on it was a new will naming Mac both the new trustee and main beneficiary. Add the fact that one of the farmhands working the Stemple estate didn't see Mac's truck arrive but saw it pull out of the long drive, and Commonwealth Attorney Washington Carpenter figured he had enough to convict Sheriff MacDowell of first-degree murder. It was merely Day One of the investigation and he believed he could already nail MacDowell's coffin shut. Mostly because the bullet striations from the wall matched the barrel of Mac's Colt, on record from when he registered it.

#

Cool Heads & Councils

Mac got the word in the middle of the day. Two weeks after his grand jury appearance and the Mounton County Council called him in. They weren't scheduled to meet till later in the month, but nevertheless, he reported to the Courthouse/City Hall/Chamber of Commerce at quarter to 1:00.

Mac took off his hat and stood before eight of the nine council members seated at the several tables positioned in a U-shape. The council set up the room this way to see each other while discussing issues. Adrian Stemple's usual seat was conspicuously vacant. Hannah sat at the far end of one leg of the U, her lips pursed tightly together. She had served on the council for several years, more recently helping guide the county back from the economic disaster of the mines closing down. Mac looked at her, but she wouldn't meet his gaze. She folded her arms tightly over her chest. He could see the knots in her forearms.

Oh boy, that is NOT good for somebody!

"Mac, thank you for joining us in this emergency session on such short notice," Delbert Simmons, the council chairman, said. "We'll cut straight to it. We're going to have to ask you to step aside for the duration until this murder trial concludes. We can't have our sheriff accused of murdering one of our prominent citizens and fellow town council members. Obviously, we couldn't allow Hannah to vote, given her relationship with you, but rest assured, she voiced her displeasure with the discussion. Quite avidly."

I bet she did.

"But the decision was far from unanimous. Many felt this was a time when we should support you, but the majority felt it would be best if you stepped down for the time being, effective immediately. We'll inform Jeb he is our sheriff pro tem until the jury reaches a not guilty verdict or we can set up a special election for a new sheriff," Simmons continued. "I'm sure it won't be necessary and we'll cross that bridge when we come to it. Unfortunately, due to the circumstances, we have to make this suspension WITHOUT pay. We will need those funds to offset the overtime pay of the other officers to cover the slack. I hope you understand. Do you have any questions?"

Mac looked at the seven council members and Hannah.

"Noper." He reached up, unpinned his badge from his tan, short-sleeved shirt, carefully clipped the pin, and slipped it in his pants pocket. With a tip of his hat toward the ladies, he turned and left the courthouse.

#

Mac walked into the sheriff's office and toward his desk. As he moved behind it, Jeb asked,
"What's up with the council?"

"Quite a bit. I stand relieved of duty and you are the new acting sheriff."

"WHAT?"

"It makes sense. They can't keep me as sheriff while I'm on trial for murder. I'm surprised they got around to it this quickly, but not shocked they did it."

"But Mom...she's on the council. Surely, she didn't go along with this craziness," Jeb scoffed.

"No. I think your mother may have voiced a...dissenting opinion. Regardless, I'm out. You're in." Mac pulled his badge from his pocket and handed it to his son.

"But we're already short-handed!" Jeb complained.

"Talk to the new girl out at *Digger's*. Word around town is she can handle herself and has a cool head. If you like her for the job, she can start training part-time right away for a probationary period. She'll need some evenings free to work out at the *Hole*.

"You need to adjust the schedule and the council is allocating my salary to offset any overtime needed. Take care of business as usual. You got this. You've been training for it your whole life."

#

"I cannot believe those…cowards!" Hannah snapped as soon as Mac walked through their kitchen door.

"Honey—" Mac began.

"You've spent your whole life taking care of them, protecting them. All you do is look after them. And what do they do? The first sign of trouble and they kick you out like you were…guilty!"

"Hannah—"

"Mac, I swear, if it wasn't for the fact those idiots need a cool head to help keep this county afloat, I'd tell them where they could stuff their council seat."

"Yeah, *cool head*," Mac smiled. "Hannah. Stop. They had to do it. I could hardly be out there writing parking tickets while on trial for murder. They did what they had to do. I don't blame them a bit."

"Of course, you don't. You're a good man, Jacob Andrew Mac-Dowell. Not like those cowardly, disloyal…snakes. They suspended you without pay. After all you've done for them for all these years."

"Let's calm down a tad, baby. I hope to have those 'cowardly, disloyal snakes' pay my salary again someday. Let's not piss them off too much."

Hannah sighed a deep breath.

"I'm sorry I couldn't stop it, Jacob. I tried. A couple more voted against the suspension, but the rest of them were afraid of any liability for the county. I never stopped to ask how you're doing. What are you thinking?"

"Right this moment, I am almost glad whoever broke into the house stole your hunting rifle, you being the *cool head* on the council and all."

#

Word of Mac's suspension traveled the county like wildfire. Washington Carpenter and his team of state prosecutors were lightning-fast with their witness subpoenas. The process server cautioned each potential witness not to speak of the trial to anyone. This gag order, of course, meant the biggest topic of conversation in Mounton County was the upcoming trial and Sheriff MacDowell's arrest and suspension. In lieu of any real updates, word spread from The Church Ladies to *Ginny's* to eventually leak down to *Digger's Saloon*. It didn't take long for the latest news to enter the dirtiest of ears.

#

Back In Business

Syrus Stamper felt discombobulated. Part of him fumed that Sonny would not rejoin them and that *he went an' turned on his own kin. But on the other hand...*

"I'm telling you, Spence, this Stemple thing could be the best thing that's happened to us since gettin' out the hoosegow. Now, ole Adrian's dead as last week's road kill, which means he ain't no longer in charge of *Stamper Paint Thinner*." Mac had busted the Stampers last year trying to transport a semi-full of moonshine, but instead of incarcerating them, arranged to have Adrian oversee the marketing and sales of *Stamper Paint Thinner* on the condition no one EVER takes a sip of said paint thinner.

"And with the sheriff suspended 'cause he's on trial for murder, it's a whole new ball game," Syrus continued. "We can go back to sellin' 'shine for what God intended it to be used for and don't have to worry 'bout them two buttinskis messin' with us. We can get back to makin' some real money without ole Adrian or Uncle Sam takin' the lion's share. And we don't need to cut Sonny a piece."

His brother Spencer threw another stick of wood on the fire beneath the still. Syrus was the eldest, shortest, and wiliest of the three brothers, while Spencer was slightly taller, more vindictive, and less intelligent, if such a thing was possible. An alcoholic father raised the three brothers, including Sonny, in the hills, far from town. With fewer hygiene skills than a pack of wolves and about the same moral philosophy, the Stampers were voted throughout Mounton County as 'most likely to get caught stealing the wheels off of a moving truck.'

"I don't know who paid for them fancy-pants lawyers to spring us, but it shore was a gift from from God," Syrus beamed. "We weren't able to snatch that big ole Ginny no how last year, so they couldn't pin no kidnapping on us and we had nothing to do with the killin' of that boy's woman. We mighta run a bit Oxy in them garbage trucks Douvez set up, but cain't nobody prove it.

"Same feller we helped with breakin' into the sheriff's house got word to me he has another job for us. We can look forward to more money comin' in. He says we'll like this job as much as the first.

"Yep, I can see some sunny skies ahead for us. And speaking of Sonny, we gonna have to educate our little brother on the error of his ways. And I know jes' how to do it." Syrus glanced toward the newly acquired flat-screen TV hanging in the shack. "Now, if'n we could get cable up here in the holler."

#

Jacob, Get Out!

Mac was getting underfoot. Hannah didn't want to tell him, but if he didn't get out of the house soon, she was going to start shopping for a new deer rifle.

She could finally concede the town council *had* to temporarily suspend Mac while the trial was going on. Until a verdict came back, he couldn't work as sheriff. Mac looked at this as a forced vacation. He knew he didn't shoot Adrian, and firmly believed the truth would come out in court, but until then, he wanted to be helpful. His attorney had told him he wasn't allowed to leave the state and it would be better if he could stay close by in case something came up requiring his attendance. Both the prosecution and the defense attorneys were busy putting their cases together and it would be a little while before the case would try on the Lexington docket.

Due to his newly acquired free time and a desire to be helpful, Mac dutifully rose to make breakfast for Hannah, Naomi, Jeb, and himself. He played with Naomi before he took her to school, picked her up from school, and enjoyed his granddaughter in the evenings. But during the daytime, he got it into his head to help Hannah with the ranch. The problem was: he was terrible at it. He could ride well enough but didn't know a thing about training or breeding horses. Oddly, the horses seemed to shy away from him. Any crops he got close to seemed to die. Jeb, Hannah, and the few hands they had working for them took care of most of the work, leaving Mac to get in the way.

After two weeks, Hannah had had enough.

"Honey," she started over breakfast one morning, "you have two choices: get out of this house and find something useful to do with your time, or…nope. I take it back. You essentially have one choice. I love you, but you are a terrible rancher and are getting in the way of anyone else trying to get work done. With you suspended, this ranch needs to make all the money it can to make the mortgage payments we borrowed against it."

Mac pondered the thought. She knew he was well aware of his lack of abilities on the farm but was trying to help out in any way he could.

"Yepper. I reckon you're right as always. I'll take care of SweetPea in the mornings and after school. You and Jeb don't have to worry about her and I'll find something useful to busy myself with during the daytime. If you need anything, give a holler."

Hannah smiled, relieved her husband of twenty-nine years was taking this well.

"Maybe you could swing by the station and see if you could bother them," Hannah said with a smirk. "Just because you can't be sheriff doesn't mean you can't lend those boys the benefit of your years on the job."

"So, in other words, 'get out'?"

"I wouldn't put it quite *that* way," Hannah hugged him. "But yeah."

As she headed out to the barn, Hannah knew that Mac was considering where he might focus his time. The trial would start soon. All he had to do was find ways to occupy his time during the days until then. She knew he believed the trial would work itself out since he was innocent. *How would he take care of his town while he was suspended?*

#

The bell above the door jangled as Mac entered the diner.

"Shirley," Mac nodded as he tipped his hat at the ancient crone behind a cash register as old as he was.

"Hey, Susie," Shirley smiled with her best teeth. "Got some free advice for ya. Punch the biggest guy first and buy some soap-on-a-rope to take with ya."

"Good to know," Mac smiled.

"Don't ask me how I know. I wasn't always a cashier, ya know."

Ginny stepped up to Mac's table with a full coffee pot and a cup. Underneath his stained apron was today's tee shirt, a faded .38 Special tour shirt. Jeb and Jesse already sat in Mac's regular booth, finishing up their lunch.

"I was curious how long it would take Hannah to catapult you out of the house," Ginny said as the sheriff took his usual seat.

"Let's say she encouraged my absence," Mac acknowledged accepting a cup of coffee from the gigantic diner owner.

"Shot any millionaires lately?" Ginny asked.

"Nope. You?"

Ginny thought back to the incident with Judge Stemple the year before. "Not lately. The score is currently Ginny: one; millionaires: zero. But the season doesn't actually open for a few more months.

"Can I interest you in partaking of our special today? One of the former miners hit a muskrat with his truck today and I was dying to try out a new recipe of my own creation: *Muscascus Bourguignon*. Roadkill simmered in a rich red wine gravy. Très magnifique!"

"I think I'll pass on the muskrat," Mac laughed. "How about a piece of pie?"

"Philistine!"

"Hey, Dad," Already sitting in the booth, Jeb greeted Mac as Ginny left to fetch his pie.

"Boys."

"Jesse and I were discussing the music we listened to as kids," Jeb said smiling. "When you were a kid, what were your favorites? Bill Hailey? Tammy Wynette? Frank Sinatra? Maybe a little Patsy Cline?"

"Patsy Cline? How old do you think I am?" Mac asked in shock as Ginny set the pie plate and silverware/napkin roll in front of him. "I was more the Bruce Springsteen, Sawyer Brown, Meatloaf, Melissa Etheridge, Lynyrd Skynyrd type."

"Who's Leonard Skinnard?" Jesse asked.

Ginny and Mac looked at each other.

Ginny quietly said, "Badge or not, I am going to have to kill this boy."

"I've seen him do it, son," Mac smiled. "Full grown man...BANG!"

Jeb pushed Jesse from the booth forcefully. "Time to go."

"What?" Jesse asked. "I wasn't finished with my sweet tea."

"Yes, you are," Jeb said.

"Yes. You. Are," Ginny echoed between gritted teeth.

Ginny and Mac watched as the two younger deputies tipped their hats to Shirley as they made a hasty exit from the diner.

"You have to excuse him, Ginny," Mac smiled. "He probably grew up with Cold Play and Imagine Dragons. He doesn't know any better."

"No offense to Mr. and Mrs. Hendricks," Ginny said, cooling down, "but wolves probably reared the lad and the Hendricks more than likely adopted him late in life."

With a glance over his shoulder to make sure the kitchen wasn't burning down, Ginny squeezed his muscle-bound bulk into the booth seat across from Mac.

"You know the prosecution has me scheduled to be one of the first to testify, right?" Ginny asked Mac while his friend dug into the pie.

"The *prosecution*?"

"Indeed. I surmised the defense would utilize me as a character witness. If nothing else, but I never supposed Mr. Carpenter would call me as a witness for the prosecution. I know you and your attorney were there, but following the deposition, Carpenter made a considerable point advising me not to discuss the matter," Ginny whispered. "I walked away with the distinct impression Monsieur Carpenter is out for hemoglobin."

"Yepper. Wonder what I did to make him care this much?"

"I actually came by to see if you noticed any strangers in town," Mac asked his friend.

"Strangers?" Ginny asked. "Correct me if I am in error, but is Mounton now not a tourist destination? Our primary target market is persons-we-do-not-know."

"You know what I mean. Not the usual Prius-driving couples or too-cheap-to-go-to-Dollywood families." Mac frowned. "Probably single male, late twenties, early thirties, dark tan, long brown hair with some blond highlights, 180 to 190 pounds, six foot one or two, no mustache, but about half shaven, and a single large tat on his right forearm."

"That's a pretty specific stranger you are looking for. Aren't you suspended or something?" Ginny asked his friend.

"Yepper and yepper."

"Well, Mr. Single Tat has not been in here and the local grapevine hasn't remarked on anyone answering the description. An unattached young man fitting your depiction would stand out somewhat in Mounton. If nothing else, the Church Ladies would be bird-dogging him. What are you looking him up for? You think he had anything to do with Adrian's murder?"

"No," Mac replied, "but I would like to ask him what he knows about doorbells."

#

News & Views

Jeb arrived at the office earlier than usual. Since his dad's suspension, he was now the temporary acting sheriff. He wanted to get a jump on the day. He settled into the other deputy desk in front of his computer. He wasn't going to sit at his father's desk…yet. Those shoes were still a little bit big to fill.

"You catch yesterday's *Harrodsburg Herald*?" Dawe asked. "I read the e-edition online during my night shift. Looks like the smash-and-grab robbers are at it again."

Jeb fired up his computer and found the news online.

"Chainsaw Bandits Strike Again," the headline on the e-edition of the *Harrodsburg Herald* proclaimed.

Dawe summarized as Jeb read the article himself. Like *that* wasn't annoying.

"Seems these geniuses hit a closed, high-end liquor store and broke in through a back window with no alarm. The e-edition had a snippet of video of a blurry arm spraying paint over the video camera. We can't see anything. Despite no video, the camera still had audio. After some crashing around, you hear what for the world sounds like two chainsaws outside the store afterward and fading away. They got a little under $400 in cash and a couple six-packs of beer. The liquor alone could have been worth tens of thousands of dollars. They walked right by thousands of dollars in lottery tickets worth millions. The *Herald* came up with the 'Chainsaw Bandits' thing. Seems like it might sell some papers…or clicks…or whatever."

"You call Mercer County sheriffs?" Jeb asked.

"Yeah, I talked to a night deputy over there," Dawe said. "They don't have any more info than the paper does. Did you know they have like twenty-five deputies and support staff over there?"

"Dawe, we have *three* desks. Where would we put twenty-five deputies?"

"Hey, man, sharing is caring."

Jeb looked at the night deputy. "Brother, we have got to get you away from your kids' daytime TV."

#

Duncan and McTavish parked in their usual post on the edge of the woods by the motel. The bright yellow Challenger still sat parked in front of the room. That in itself was suspect. Nobody would stay in this rat-trap motel for more than a night if they could possibly help it.

A brand-new black Mercedes coupe parked next to the Dodge while Duncan and McTavish were trying to get comfortable. A silver-haired man with a matching mustache climbed out of the car carrying a leather satchel-style case. Duncan took notes with a stub of a pencil onto a piece of paper from his glove compartment. He couldn't see the license plate from this angle, but the man's suit probably cost more than Duncan's entire closet. At the last second, before the man stepped into the motel room, Duncan was able to get his flip phone out and snap a picture of the man. It was a bad angle and didn't show his face, but it did capture his appearance, height, and bearing.

Duncan was walking McTavish an hour later when the well-dressed man stepped out of the room to head back to his car. This time, a prepared Duncan pulled out his phone to snap several pictures of the man. Try as he might he could not remember having ever before seen the man with the thick, silver hair and matching mustache. He wasn't from Mounton as Duncan knew all the locals. As the man pulled away in his Mercedes, Duncan inconspicuously took a picture of his license plate.

"Aye, McTavish, me wee yin, this time tomorrow yore Uncle Mac will be knowin' who yon dobber is."

#

Grogan watched from his hiding spot as Jeb left the sheriff's office and climbed behind the wheel of a county SUV. The car headed south down The Side Street. Donning his white latex gloves, Grogan used the one working payphone in Mounton to call 911. He reported a burglary by three masked men in the south end of the county. Grogan knew Jeb would respond personally only to find it a false alarm. This was third time he had misdirected the acting sheriff since Mac had been arrested. Besides keeping tabs on the sheriff's son, he was keeping him so busy chasing his tail that he wouldn't have any time to investigate the murder or burglary. Little did either man know what was planned next for the MacDowell family.

#

Say Hey

Howdy Barnes finished cleaning the last of the mess from the night's revelries at *The Digger's Hole*. A last look around told him the place was ready for the next day's business. Howdy had taken over as bar manager a year ago when the previous manager lit out for the greener pastures of Louisville with both the weekend's receipts and the only waitress. The owner of record lived in Frankfort and saw *The Hole* as a minor investment. He was happy to have Howdy step up and take the reins. The bar's business continually increased which pleased him even more. He didn't know the improved profits were less from Howdy's savvy business acumen than three other factors: Howdy wasn't skimming from the profits as the previous manager had; Sonny started as the bouncer, reducing both the violence and damage to furnishings; the town of Mounton became a tourist destination, thanks to Sheriff MacDowell.

Sonny had retired to his small room above the bar and before Howdy finished cleaning, he could hear the snores of the big man vibrating through the ceiling. With a smile, he stepped out the back door and locked it behind him. Making his way to his little pickup, he thought about what a godsend the young giant had been. Taking Mac's suggestion to hire him had been one of the best decisions Howdy had made as the newly appointed manager. Townspeople and tourists were no longer afraid to come to *The Hole* because of the zero tolerance for violence. Troublemakers took one look at the colossal

Stamper and rethought their initial ideas. Furniture and glass replacement was down 800 percent.

After tossing a couple of garbage bags into the dumpster, Howdy turned to his truck when two shadows jumped from the shadows and began pummeling him with a baseball bat and a length of pipe. The little leprechaun of a barkeep went down in a heap. The two men wearing ski masks continued to swing.

As he was about to lose consciousness, he heard the shortest of his assailants say, "Say 'Hey' to Sonny."

#

Friends in Low Places

"Aye, laddie, I'm glad ye stopped in," Duncan told Mac. On his way home from court, the suspended sheriff stopped by *Duncan's Mercantile and General Store* to pick up some equipment parts for Hannah. It was often easier and cheaper to order them online, but Duncan gave them a ten percent discount. Duncan probably ordered them from the same place the MacDowells would have, but they went out of their way to support local businesses, especially those owned by their best friends.

"What's up?" Mac asked as he dug his credit card out to pay for the parts.

"I forgot to tell ye the other mornin'," Duncan said as he processed Mac's credit card. "I happened by *The Motel 44* a few times and think I may have spotted a couple of your friends."

"'Happened by,' huh? *A few times*? Kind of a drive from your place, isn't it?"

"Well, do ye wanna hear who it was or do ye wanna be bustin' me chops?" Duncan growled.

"Okay, I'll bite. Who was it? As far as I know, I don't have any friends at the Motel 44."

"Based on the bright yellow Dodge Challenger sittin' outside," now Duncan had Mac's attention, "and seein' the young dobbers meself, I'm happy to report I believe the wee ins Stemple are staying at the boggin roach motel."

"Really?" Mac rubbed his chin. Judge Stemple bought Jasper a brand-new, bright yellow Dodge Challenger last year before all the trouble started.

"Aye, and I watched a couple of visitors come by as well. I have some photies of 'em, including some license plates."

"Give me what you've got. This may add some of the missing pieces," Mac said.

Duncan spent the next fifteen minutes updating his friend.

"Great. More people in town who hate me," Mac shook his head. "I'm not sure what they are up to, but my guess is: it's not to join my fan club. As if I didn't have enough on my plate. Essentially, I have to find a way to stay out of prison in the next couple of days and now I have to find out what these yahoos are about. And take care of Mounton while I'm suspended. Boy howdy!"

#

Plea Deals & Prints

"Mac?"

"Yepper," Mac answered the voice on the phone.

"Dayton Hollister here. Carpenter called a moment ago. While we spoke, I tossed out the question: if you confessed, would they take the death penalty off the table?"

"YOU DID WHAT?" This incensed the normally unflappable Mac.

"Relax, relax," Hollister placated. "He didn't take it anyway. They still may not pursue it, but he didn't want to commit in case he gets lucky."

"Who told you to do something like that?"

"Mac, you need to start facing facts. You have no alibi for the time of Adrian's murder. Someone shot Adrian with *your* gun. You were at his house at the time of his murder and you were indirectly responsible for the killing of his father. There's a forced handwritten will giving you everything. I wish I sat on the prosecuting side of the aisle on this thing. We have next to no case."

"Except I didn't do it."

"Unless you can prove it in a court of law in the next few days, it sure looks like you did."

"What about innocent until proven guilty?" Mac demanded.

"Grow up, Mac," Hollister explained. "Innocence, in a court of law, needs to be proven beyond a shadow of a doubt. To the jury, the mere fact this has gone to court and past a grand jury means *guilty until proven otherwise.*"

"Then what am I paying you for?"

"You pay me for my expertise and advice. You pay me to tell you the truth. Speaking of which, the reason Carpenter didn't take the offer is: the FBI forensics report came back. The only prints found on your Colt and shell casings were yours."

#

Mac walked into the courtroom, Hannah's hand in his. His attorney, much more familiar with the setting, walked slightly in front of them. Mac paused and looked at the room that could quite possibly be the last new room he would ever see as a free man. In this space, twelve strangers would decide if he was a good man or bad. That jury would decide his and Hannah's future, right here, regardless of the reality. In his pre-trial meetings with his attorney, Mac decided Truth was the first victim of a trial, with presentation, partial facts, and technicalities the unrivaled true victors. Mac had been in this room before to testify on previous cases in his nearly three decades as sheriff, but because this was HIS trial, the room felt strange and hostile. Since Judge Brown had reluctantly agreed it would be impossible to get an impartial jury in Mounton County, he reluctantly relented to change the venue to Lexington.

Unlike the dark two-hundred-year-old woodwork, pillars, and single judge's bench in the Mounton County Courthouse, the Robert F. Stephens Circuit Courthouse was modern, open, and a study in light blonde wood and clean lines. Mac thought the room smelled of lemon Pledge and desperation. The judge would sit alone at the center of a large, slightly raised, seven-seat dais with chairs for the visual media tech and the clerk of courts below his left hand. The seven-seat dais took up the whole width of the room. These stations all had computer monitors. *Welcome to the new century,* Mac thought. The modern walnut veneer of the dais perfectly matched the paneling and reached halfway up the walls. The court reporter had a separate desk set perpendicular to the right of the space between the judge and attorneys. Hidden by the raised edges of their stations, the clerk of courts, AV tech, judge, and witness stand hosted computer monitors to view presented documents and evidence. The seal of the Commonwealth of Kentucky hung between an American flag and the Kentucky flag right behind the judge's seat. The designers placed off-white video cameras in discreet positions on the ceiling to capture the entire room. The two elongated, modern, conference tables for the defense and prosecutor sat separated by a microphoned podium. Fourteen comfortable-looking chairs, each with its own computer monitor, lined the right side of the room. *Probably where the jury sits*, Mac thought. Behind the defense and prosecution tables were rows of what looked to be modern church pews for the gallery. Unlike any Perry Mason show Mac had ever seen, there were no swinging doors or dividers. The ceiling was alternating fluorescent light panels and white acoustic drop-ceiling panels. The off-white walls, wall sconce lights, and large windows gave the room an eerie hospital-room brightness. Mac believed the designers of the space must have felt the brilliance would shine a light on the truth.

Sadly, the room looked more like a brightly lit surgical suite awaiting the amputation of the Truth, leaving behind the darkness to fester.

#

Prior to the trial date, Hollister had convinced Hannah they needed a jury consultant. With Mac's life on the line, Hannah hastily agreed. Mac was a little more dubious.

Sitting in Hollister's office, Mac turned to Hannah, "Baby, it's all well and good to get someone to help evaluate in jury selection, but what's the point of keeping me out of jail if you can't afford to eat afterward? What Mr. Hollister says makes good sense, but do you know how expensive this could get?"

"I don't care, Jacob," Hannah informed him. "If it will help find the right people to keep you free and prove you innocent, I don't care if it costs us every penny we have and all we can borrow. I am not going to lose you over money."

"Sheriff, I think Hannah has the right idea," Hollister chimed in. "Yes, these consultants are unbelievably expensive, but we are not talking about simply your freedom here. We could be talking about your life.

"As you are probably aware, but Hannah may not be, first-degree murder involves planning and malice of intent. Second-degree murder is when someone kills another but without planning or advance thought, such as a crazed husband killing his wife in a fit of rage. Murder one can involve the death penalty, but not murder two. Kentucky hasn't executed someone by lethal injection since 2008, but the first-degree murder charge puts it on the table. We could very well be talking about the end of your life. Definitely your freedom for the rest of your life."

Hannah had heard enough.

#

The first few days in the courtroom were about more motions and jury selection. Listed on the witness list, Hollister recommended Hannah not sit in court day-after-day and Mac had suggested she skip a few in order to keep everything running smoothly at home. Though there are protections for a wife testifying against her spouse, Hollister thought it best Hannah was not in the courtroom, to avoid any emotional demonstrations. Jury selection took longer than expected as the trial consultants instructed Hollister to use all of his challenges, as did Carpenter. Finally, both defense and prosecution seated a jury and the prosecution's witnesses would begin to testify the next day.

In the end, it was a jury that Carpenter was happier about despite the jury consultants and Hollter's challenges. Mac looked at the invoice for the trial consultants Hollister hired and wondered if maybe lethal injection wouldn't be a better route.

#

Fire: Steady, Stable Work

It was dark by the time Hannah had made her way to the stables. There never seemed to be enough time in the day. Granted, shooing Jacob away bought her an extra hour a day she didn't have to use to correct his mistakes or run interference between him and the business of running a ranch. Even without his *help*, the chores never seemed to end. Jeb and Naomi did as much as they could, but her son had taken the little angel in to get cleaned up, eat dinner, and put her to bed hours ago. After giving Jeb directions on how to heat up the leftovers from last night, Hannah had opted to postpone her own dinner and wait for Mac to get home. He had called to say he would be in court late and then walk around town a bit after he drove down from Lexington.

Throwing straw down for the horses' bedding and brushing a few of them out could wait till tomorrow, but Hannah wanted to get a jump on it. There would be something new tomorrow to eat up any extra time she saved tonight.

Her lithe body filled out her jeans and tee shirt well. For her age—hell, for any age, Hannah MacDowell knew she was a fine-looking woman. But, except for the fact she knew it made Mac happy, she simply didn't care. Farm chores kept her as trim as she had been in college and the steady outdoor work gave her face a healthy tan and glow. Her blonde-ish hair ponytailed out the snap-back of her John Deere baseball cap and bounced as she grabbed a partial bale of straw to scatter it throughout the horse stalls.

The stable contained forty stalls with twenty lining each wall. The upper story of the building held hay and straw for the horses. The MacDowells still baled hay and straw in rectangles versus the half-ton rolls everyone else seemed to favor. They were easier for Hannah to manage by herself and it was the way her family had always done it. The same baler and hay wagon her grandfather had used waited in the barn for next season's crop. Clients' horses filled most of the stalls.

Having finished with the straw, Hannah patted Bob on the neck with her leather-clad hands. Despite its natural energy, the gelding was as gentle as a giant teddy bear when it came to Naomi. This secretly pleased Hannah. She had her own horse growing up and except for her tenure as a wife and a grandmother, it was the happiest time of her life. She looked into the eye of the beast and thought she could see this horse would die before hurting Naomi. In the last few months, her granddaughter had developed the same love for the horse. And there was no doubt about it. This was Naomi's pony.

Hannah closed the stall behind her and started taking off her gloves as she moved to exit the stable. As she reached the halfway point, she saw the wooden entryway slam shut and she heard a heavy thunk behind it. She stopped at the sudden noise. The person-sized door of heavy wood had slammed closed next to a larger, garage-style, roll-down entry used for horses and farm equipment. This door was down, as it usually was.

"Miguel?" Hannah called out, thinking one of the hands had stayed late without telling her, didn't know she was still in the stable, and closed the door. "Frank?"

As she slowly moved toward the exits, a strange flickering light appeared through the cracks between the slats of the walls.

Hannah ran to the wooden door and pushed against it for all she was worth. Something jammed the door. She knew there was no lock or padlock on it for safety reasons. It was the sheriff's stable. What idiot would mess with it? But locked or not, it would not open. Hannah moved to the larger roll-down. She was unable to move this one as well. It was a pre-made aluminum entry they had purchased to fit the stable and Hannah knew there were rings for padlocks at the bottom. They never used them, but *something* kept it shut solidly to the ground.

As Hannah push upward against the metal, she could feel it heating up till it was unbearable to touch. She backed away and stared in shock.

Fire!

#

Trial: Opening Statements

"Ladies and gentlemen of the jury, my name is Washington Carpenter. I am the Commonwealth's attorney, essentially the district attorney for Kentucky. I am here to present evidence that Jacob MacDowell, without question, shot and murdered Adrian Stemple.

"Jacob MacDowell was at the Stemple residence during the time period the murder took place. He forced Adrian Stemple at gunpoint to handwrite a new will making him executor and heir to the Stemple estate. We will show he had other motives, including the dismissal of a wrongful death suit against him by Adrian's family. We will prove the gun and ammunition used belonged to Jacob MacDowell with solely his prints, his DNA, and Adrian's blood on them.

"We will prove beyond any reasonable doubt Jacob MacDowell had motive, means, and opportunity to murder Adrian Stemple. There is no question that the defendant shot and killed the victim with forethought and planning."

Carpenter made eye contact with each of the jury members and then sat down.

Mac watched as his attorney delivered his opening remarks.

"Ladies and gentlemen, I am Dayton Hollister. I am the defense attorney for Jacob MacDowell. All of the evidence presented by the prosecution is circumstantial. We will show there is no financial motive. There was no gunshot residue on my client, no eyewitnesses, and no blood splatter evidence. His DNA or fingerprints were not found at the scene of the crime. The day before the murder, burglars broke into the gun safe where Mac stored his Colt, as the police documented. In essence, we will disprove the prosecution's means, motive, and opportunity. We will disprove anything other than Sheriff MacDowell, a decorated veteran and respected law enforcement officer for over thirty years, did NOT kill Adrian Stemple."

Mac wondered why Hollister did not get up and approach the jury in order to establish a rapport. He noted all of Hollister's points were reactive and defensive, designed to counter the prosecution's case, but didn't offer any alternatives to Mac's guilt. Mac wondered:

Who would benefit from Adrian's death?

#

Fire: Blazing Saddles

Stay calm.

Hannah always had what she considered a perfectly rational fear of fire. Fire could burn you up. You could die. Painfully. If you were burned and survived, your scarred body would live in pain for the rest of your life. Hannah had a great aunt who burned her arms in a grease fire and Hannah couldn't bear to look at them.

A violet thump from one of the stalls snapped her out of her own head. *The horses.* If she was afraid, they must be on the verge of panic. *I have got to get the horses out of here.*

She ran the length of the stable and saw the lights of the fire were starting to shine through the board slats there. *Okay, no way out the back. Or was there?* At the back of the stable, leading to the training paddock, was an older, horizontally sliding, wooden door, unlike the metal roll-down at the front. She gripped the door with her re-gloved hands and pulled as hard as she could, but something was blocking the rollers from sliding. While she couldn't slide it aside, it was still just made of old wood. And she had plenty of power at her disposal. Horsepower.

Hannah ran to a stall where she housed a customer's horse, Dante. She forced herself to calm down to place the bit and bridle. Dante, still on the wild side, was a one-year-old whom the owner brought to the MacDowell farm to be trained. He convinced Hannah she could channel all that aggression into speed.

Hannah positioned the stallion away from the rear sliding door and tied the reins firmly to one of the stall frames. The horse was already near panic with the sound, smell, and heat of the fire coming through the walls of the stable. Smoke was choking both the woman and the horses. She moved behind and to the side of Dante, grabbed a loose set of reins from a hook on the wall. She waited until the panicked equine lost track of her, slipped up behind it, and slapped the rear haunches of the animal as hard as she could with the leather reins. She knew it was risky. The terrified horse wouldn't be able to see or smell her because of the smoke. A horse's kick moves at about 200 miles per hour and can contain over 2,000 pounds per square inch of force. It's the equivalent of being hit by a car at 20 miles per hour. Hannah was deliberately trying to get the meanest horse in her stable to kick at her.

The kick rattled the back door hard enough the vibrations could be felt all over the stable. Saddles fell from racks and tack shook loose from wooden pegs on the wall. Bales of hay and straw shifted in the loft above. The other horses' anxiety grew. Their eyes were starting to show whites all around the pupils. Hannah looked behind the horse to check out the sliding door. Other than two scuff marks and small cracks where the hooves hit the solid wooden entryway, Dante had not managed to damage the door.

#

Trial: Distasteful Testimony

Deputy Davis Williams dreaded the next part. He knew it was coming and unavoidable.

"Deputy Williams, how long have you been a deputy with the Mounton Sheriff's Department?" Commonwealth Attorney Washington Carpenter asked Davis from his podium between the defense and prosecution tables.

"About a year."

"In your entire career, have you ever been the lead investigator on a capital crime?"

"No."

"Have you ever been the lead investigator of any major crime during your tenure in Mounton County?" Carpenter asked without looking at any notes.

"Haven't seen a great deal of major crimes in Mounton in the last year," Davis replied.

"Would you consider yourself an expert in burglary or breaking and entering crimes?"

"An expert? Probably not. I assisted in a number of investigations as a uniformed officer when I lived in D.C."

"But as a uniformed officer, not as a detective?" Carpenter pointed out.

"Yes."

"Did Sheriff MacDowell know of your inexperience and limitations?"

Davis bridled at the inexperience comment. "I imagine he did. He read my resume and hired me."

"So, it's safe to say Sheriff MacDowell deliberately put an unqualified deputy under his employ in charge of the break-in of his house and safe, as well as his murder of Adrian Stemple?" Carpenter inquired.

"Objection," Mac's attorney didn't bother to stand up for this one. "Calls for speculation, implies prejudice, and is leading the witness." They jury was sure to have heard the words: *deliberately, unqualified* and *murder*.

"Sustained," the judge said. To the jury he said, "Please disregard the prosecutor's last question. Would you like to take another swing at it, Mr. Carpenter?"

"Thank you, Your Honor. I apologize." Then he turned back to Williams. "Deputy Williams, knowing your experience, or lack thereof, did Sheriff MacDowell put you in charge of the break-in at his home and the murder of Adrian Stemple?"

"Yes."

"Did you find any definite fingerprints or DNA evidence in or around Mr. MacDowell's gun safe?" the prosecutor asked.

Davis Williams hesitated for a second. *How did this go so pear-shaped?* "Just the sheriff's."

"Does Jacob MacDowell have the power to fire you without cause?"

"No, he is not the sheriff of Mounton County at this time," Davis glared at the prosecutor. "No one but the acting sheriff can fire me."

"Currently, his son. Alright, Deputy, when he assigned you these cases and while you were investigating them, did Sheriff MacDowell have the ability to fire you for any reason?"

Davis looked at Mac, sighed, and shook his head.

"Kentucky is an at-will state. Any employer can fire any employee without stating a cause."

"Thank you, Deputy Williams." Carpenter turned to Hollister, "Your witness."

"Deputy Williams, did you happen to speak with the FBI upon their arrival at the scene of the break-in?" Hollister started with Davis.

"Yes."

"What did they say?"

Carpenter didn't object because he knew the defense could present the same information by simply putting the FBI agents on the stand, which would add more credibility to William's story.

"They asked about what I did and what facts I had gathered thus far about the case."

"Anything else?" Hollister asked, knowing the answer already.

"Yes. They told me I did a 'great job' and thanked me for my help."

"So, you did a 'great job' with your investigation according to the FBI?"

"Yes."

"No further questions at this time. Thank you, Deputy Williams."

Washington Carpenter popped up from his seat. "Your Honor, if I may, I would like to clarify a point or two with Deputy Williams about his testimony?"

"Go on," Judge Gibson said.

"Deputy Williams," Carpenter started, "according to your testimony just now, you spoke with the FBI when they arrived at the scene of the break-in at the MacDowell house. Is this true?"

"Yes."

"How long after you called them did they arrive?"

"I don't know, I guess about forty minutes."

"Please just answer yes or no to this next question. Just you and the man who hired you, the same man who had the power to fire you at will, and his wife, were alone at the scene for more than forty minutes?"

The judge cleared his throat quietly, glancing at the defense table.

"Excuse me, Your Honor?" Carpenter asked.

"Nothing," the judge replied taking a sip of water. "Just something caught in my throat."

Davis's lips formed a tight line. "Could you repeat the question?"

"It was just you and the man who hired you, the man who had the power to fire you at will, along with his wife, alone at the scene of the crime for more than forty minutes when the FBI showed up?"

"Yes."

"Thank you, Deputy Williams."

#

Fire: Dante's Inferno

The smoke in the stable was getting thick enough to make it impossible to breathe and see through. Hannah pulled her tee shirt over her ball cap and ponytail. She dipped it into one of the horse troughs to soak it and wrapped it around her head covering her mouth and nose to let her breathe through the wet tee shirt.

Hannah turned back to Dante and it didn't take much to entice the stallion to kick the rear door again and again. Each kick rattled the entire stable and Hannah worried it might bring the structure down around their ears. Her eyes and throat burned with smoke and she was coughing continually. The flames had climbed the sides of the building outside and the hay and straw in the loft had started to smolder. Time and again, she slapped the big horse's haunches. Several times she had to strike him multiple times in order to get him to kick. The irony of being cruel to the animal in order to save it, and all the other horses, flashed through Hannah's mind and she flicked the leather reins again, making sure Dante could not see her.

At last, the entire sliding door fell as one piece. Hannah had expected the cross boards to break, but instead, Dante had kicked the entire door down.

Even through the smoke, it was easy to see the horror outside. Beyond the fallen door and all around it, walls of flame surrounded the stable.

#

Trial: With Friends Like These

"At this time, I would like to call Mr. Merle Starcher to the stand," the Commonwealth attorney announced to the court.

Mac just closed his eyes. He knew what Carpenter had in mind and dreaded it for his friend.

Who is Merle Starcher? You could all but hear the thoughts of the assembled gallery.

An enormous biker-looking behemoth walked slowly to the witness stand, escorted by a Fayette County sheriff's deputy, and stood before the bailiff.

"Do you solemnly swear to tell the whole truth and nothing but the truth?"

"Most indubitably."

The bailiff looked at the judge.

"A simple 'I do' will suffice, Mr. Starcher," Judge Gibson clarified.

"I do."

The Commonwealth attorney stood at the central podium to begin his questioning.

"Good morning, Mr. Starcher. Do you prefer Merle or as the Mounton locals more commonly call you, Ginny?"

"I prefer not to be called at all," Ginny replied. After a look from the judge, Ginny answered, "Ginny is fine."

"Thank you for coming today," the state's D.A. continued, "I know you are busy in the mornings. I appreciate you dressing appropriately for court."

Everyone had already noticed Ginny was wearing one of his trademark classic rock band tee-shirts, Aerosmith on this occasion, which prominently displayed his bulging biceps, covered in tattoos. Ginny's long hair, short, stubbly beard, work boots, and well-worn jeans completed the biker-enforcer look.

"I attired myself with all the reverence and accord I believe these proceedings merit," Ginny answered with a straight face. He looked at the judge seated to his left, "With heartfelt apologies to Your Honor."

"No apologies necessary, Mr. Starcher."

"Mr. Star—Ginny," Carpenter corrected, "are you the proprietor of *Ginny's Diner*?"

"I am currently the owner-of-record."

"Are you one of the best friends of the defendant, Jacob MacDowell?"

"You would need to ask him," Ginny replied. "I can but attest to the fact he is *my* best friend. As to whether I remain his friend will likely depend on how this goes."

"Please just answer the questions yes or no."

Ginny just sat there. Mac smiled. *Ginny has probably never used a one-word answer for anything in the last ten years.*

"What was your involvement in the shooting of Judge Stemple last year on January 14th?"

"Uh, yes?"

"Excuse me?"

"You told me to answer all your questions yes or no," Ginny answered with a hint of a smile on his face.

"Your Honor, I ask to be allowed to treat this Mr. Starcher as a hostile witness," Carpenter stated.

The judge sat looking at the Commonwealth's attorney.

"Well?" Carpenter demanded after several moments of silence.

Now, it was Carpenter's turn to close his eyes in frustration. "Your Honor, may I treat this witness as hostile?" Treating Ginny as a hostile witness would allow him to ask more leading questions and to approach the witness stand.

"Hmmm. Let me think on it a bit." The judge looked at Ginny and then at the prosecutor. "No. You instructed him to answer yes or no to the best of his ability, and he did. Doesn't necessarily make *him* hostile. You can't hold him responsible for you not asking non-binary questions. Request denied. Please proceed with your questions."

The judge's decision wasn't necessarily a point for Mac's side, but Carpenter wasn't endearing himself to Judge Gibson.

"Okay, Mr. Starcher," Carpenter said, deliberately not using the preferred and more casual Ginny. "Let's try this. Please just keep your answers as short and succinct as possible. Were you involved with the shooting of Judge Stemple last January 14th?"

"Depends on your definition of *involved*," Ginny answered, "I speculate you could say yes, I was involved. I shot him."

"*You* shot him?" Carpenter was feigning surprise for the jury. He was extremely familiar with the events of the 14th and the days leading up to it. "Did you shoot him in defense of your life? And in case you are not aware, that is a yes-or-no question, Mr. Starcher."

"No."

"Did you shoot him in the chest?"

"No."

"I see. Was he facing you when you shot him?"

"No," Ginny said from between gritted teeth.

"So, you shot him in the back?"

"No."

"No?"

"I shot him in the head," Ginny said. "From behind. Not in the back."

It was all the judge could do not to snicker.

"To the best of your knowledge, was Judge Stemple under arrest or wanted for any crime?"

"No."

"Were you working for Jacob MacDowell at the time you shot the judge?"

"I suspect you could infer that. He deputized me the day before."

"Did you later learn Judge Stemple had concerns about Jacob MacDowell's qualifications as sheriff?"

Ginny looked at Mac, sitting at the defendant's table. Everyone knew this was coming, but to say it facing his best friend, was painful.

"When the judge started to—" Ginny began.

"No, Mr. Starcher." The prosecutor looked at his notepad. "Yes or no, you learned the judge had questions about Jacob MacDowell's qualifications as sheriff?"

"Objection, Your Honor. These are ALL leading questions," Hollister spoke up from the defense table.

"You're showing up too late to the party, Mr. Hollister," the judge admonished. "You should know better. You can object to one question at a time, but you can't wait until he asks a half dozen and then expect me to instruct the jury to forget the last ten minutes. I'll sustain the objection to the last question, but the rest are already on the books. Would the jury please disregard Mr. Carpenter's last question. Mr. Carpenter, you may continue, but play a little more Ginger Rogers and a little less Fred."

"Yes, sir. Mr. Starcher, are you and Jacob MacDowell currently named in a wrongful death suit regarding Judge Stemple?" Carpenter was purposely avoiding using Sheriff MacDowell's title in order to deprive him of any legitimacy.

"Yes."

"Here is a copy of the suit, Your Honor. I would like to enter it into evidence.

"Let me get this straight, Mr. Starcher," Carpenter teed up, "your best friend, Jacob MacDowell, deputized you the day before you shot the county judge from behind. The duly elected district judge who suspected MacDowell's qualifications to perform his duties as sheriff?"

"Yes, but—"

"Let's change directions for a moment, Mr. Starcher. Did Judge Stemple have any children?"

"Yes, he had a son, Adrian." Ginny knew what was coming from his deposition and decided adding Adrian's name to his one-word answer would just save time. Anything to get him out of the hot seat faster.

"Were you present when the murder victim, Adrian Stemple, met with Jacob MacDowell at your diner on the day of Mr. Stemple's murder?"

"Yes."

"Did you happen to hear any of their conversation?" Carpenter asked.

"It's a possibility. It was somewhat hectic if I recall accurately."

"Yes or no, Mr. Starcher." The prosecutor added for the jury, implying Ginny may lie for Mac, "I would like to remind you that you are under oath."

"Yes."

"So, you overheard their conversation?"

"No."

"You did not?" Carpenter said, genuinely confused now. This did not fit his deposition notes. "Which is it? Yes, or no?"

"Both. I was barely privy to brief excerpts of their discourse," Ginny explained. "And only out of context."

"During those portions, did you happen to overhear who was financing the lawsuit against you and Mr. MacDowell?"

"Objection," Mac's attorney plied. "This line of questioning involves hearsay. We are unable to verify this conversation due to the inability of the victim to refute the testimony."

"Overruled, Mr. Hollister," Judge Gibson said. "Mr. Starcher is testifying to what he actually heard, not what was told to him. Mr. Carpenter is not asking him to testify to the veracity of any statements but to recount what he, himself, heard. Because Mr. Stemple is unable to refute or acknowledge this statement, Mr. Starcher is the only witness to it."

Ginny sighed. He understood where the prosecutor was going with this and couldn't see any way out.

"Yes. Adrian disclosed to Mac something to the effect he had paid for his kids' attorney," Ginny said quietly.

"I see. So, the murder victim told the defendant he was the one who was paying for the attorney who was suing MacDowell for the wrongful death of his father? This was the day before the housekeeper found Adrian Stemple murdered with Jacob MacDowell's Colt?"

"Objection!" Mac's attorney raised his hand as he stood abruptly. "Mr. Carpenter is asking two questions before the witness has a chance to answer one, essentially testifying himself, AND he is referencing facts not yet in evidence."

Before the judge could agree, Carpenter said, "I withdraw the questions." But as is often the case, the jury could not *unhear* them. According to Mac's attorney, this was not an uncommon tactic in jury trials.

"Let me try it this way. Mr. Starcher, you heard the murder victim tell the defendant he was the one who was paying for the attorney who was suing MacDowell?"

Ginny waited to see if Mac's attorney could pull any of his own legal tricks out of his bag to stop this. When greeted with silence, Ginny muttered, "Yes."

"Just a few more questions Mr. Starcher," Carpenter said, essentially telling the jury this line of lengthy and damning testimony was near an end. "Did you overhear Mr. Stemple say anything else to Mr. Mac-Dowell?"

Prior to giving his deposition to the Commonwealth's attorney's office, Ginny had looked up the penalty for perjury. He would gladly face the music for any prevarication, but he knew what Mac would want.

"Yes."

"What did you hear?"

Mac could see the physical anguish his friend was in and simply nodded. Ginny looked as if he had tasted something bitter.

"I heard Adrian say Mac was responsible for the loss of jobs in Mounton, the fall of the Stemple empire, his own personal neutering, and some other stuff."

Carpenter paused for effect. He had already placed the ball on the tee, taken his practice swings, and could now envision the ball going to the hole.

"What else did Adrian Stemple say?"

"He said Mac, specifically, was responsible for the allegedly unlawful death of his father."

#

Fire: The Roof is On Far!

A bruised and battered Howdy drove Sonny Stamper to the *New Darlene's Beauty Emporium/Barbershop/Tanning Salon* for his once-a-month grooming. The beating Howdy had taken outside *The Hole* looked worse now than it had a few days ago. His bruises turned nasty shades of purple and yellow and his left eye had swollen shut. Sonny called 911 on the bar phone once he found his friend the next morning. After the ambulance had taken them both to Bardstown Hospital the doctors diagnosed Howdy with multiple contusions, a cracked occipital bone above his eye, and several broken ribs. The ribs were not threatening to puncture a lung and after two pain-filled nights, the hospital reluctantly released a well-wrapped Howdy. Mac drove the two men back to *The Digger's Hole* where Sonny lived and Howdy had parked his truck. Sonny refused to leave Howdy's bedside while he was in the hospital. No one visiting had seen Sonny's hands unclenched during the entire time Howdy spent in the hospital. The bar temporarily closed without its manager and bouncer to keep things running smoothly. With Mac in attendance, Deputy Davis took a statement from Howdy who was unable to positively identify his ski-masked attackers, but from the description of how one limped and how they spoke, both Mac and Sonny guessed it was Syrus and Spencer. This fit with their suspicions, as identical ski-masks were used in the MacDowell home break-in. Without enough evidence to prove it in court, Mac and Davis drove up to the Stamper shack to rattle their cage, but were unable to provoke either brother.

The hospital had released Howdy after two days with the promise he would stay still.

A few days later, Howdy couldn't stand staying cooped up anymore. He had taken a few days off from the bar to heal, while Sonny, Peggy, and the rest of the staff kept things alive. He announced he was driving into town for groceries. Sonny thought for a second and asked if Howdy could take him to see Miz Darlene. It was a week or two before his regularly scheduled appointment, but he wasn't about to let Howdy go into town alone. Besides, lately, he wanted to look a little more…dapper around Peggy.

Hannah had taught Sonny how to shave his neck and face to keep his beard trimmed and shaped as well as how to maintain his hair, but Howdy swore the boy grew hair faster than wild mountain grass. Every month, Howdy would bring Sonny into town to have Darlene give him a solid once-over. Sonny insisted on paying for Darlene's services, but Hannah secretly picked up the majority of the bill since she knew Darlene had to work extra hard to keep him trimmed neatly and she knew how much Sonny made.

Sonny barely fit into Howdy's little pickup, but he had never gotten his own driver's license. He needed the little leprechaun of a bartender to drive him into town. While Howdy could barely see over the hood of the small truck, Sonny had to hunch over and bend his neck to keep his head from banging on the ceiling. He didn't mind though. Truth be told, now that he had cleaned up his act and had a lawful job earning his keep, Sonny looked forward to his trips into town. People treated him nice and not like his brothers did at all.

About halfway into town, Sonny looked away from the beautiful Kentucky sunset to see a glow lighting up the clouds in the east.

"What you reckon that might be?" the big man asked.

Howdy looked at the glow in the sky. "Fire."

"Far? Must be pretty big to light up the sky," Sonny said. "Hey! Ain't that over by Sheriff Mac and Miz Hannah's house?"

"It sure is, Sonny me boy." Howdy pressed his foot hard on the accelerator.

Moments later, the small pickup skidded to a stop in front of the sheriff's station. Howdy was the first to enter since it was easier for him to extract himself from the cramped pickup. He was coming from the front door as Sonny finally wedged himself out of the truck.

"Nobody's there." Both men looked in all directions as if it would make a deputy or the sheriff appear.

"Miz Darlene's!" Sonny exclaimed as he started running for the beauty shop half a block away.

The two men burst into the shop. Darlene sat counting the last of the day's proceeds from the register and comparing them to the receipts. Mr. Darlene was sweeping up hair from the last customer of the day.

"Far! There's a big far over by Sheriff Mac 'n Miz Hannah's place!" Sonny bellowed.

"We already tried the sheriff's office and found nobody there," Howdy explained.

"Fire?" Darlene gasped.

Last year her shop burnt to the ground as part of a scheme to destroy Sheriff MacDowell's reputation and after a year of rebuilding, the shop was better than ever. All of the single tanning bed's bulbs actually lit up. They rebuilt the shop in its original location, just a few doors down from the sheriff's station on The Side Street. The sole piece of original equipment left from before the fire was the swirling barber pole out front. Ever since, Darlene had a deep fear of fire.

She hoisted her 300-plus pounds onto her five-foot three frame and waddled to the window, looking out to the east.

Mr. Darlene stopped sweeping up hair from the floor long enough to stand beside her and look out.

"Sonny's right. You can see the sky lighting up and smoke billowing," Darlene agreed. "I don't reckon I know if it's Mac and Hannah's place but someone's in trouble. Ever since that little ass-boil Douvez had our place burnt down, I jus' got a sense about fire."

Mr. Darlene studied the smoke-filled clouds reflecting the flames.

"I'm gonna finish lockin' up," she told him. "You call yore buddies on the volunteer fire department and see if'n they got any calls. You tell them to suit up and get their truck headed east. There's a fire out there and somebody needs their help. Howdy, you and Sonny head over to Mac's and if it ain't their place, let them know. What are ya'll looking at me for? Git!"

#

Trial: No Free Will of His Own

"Ms. Maynard, could you give us a bit about your background and credentials?" Washington Carpenter asked the witness.

"Why, of course. I am a board-certified forensic document examiner with over thirty years of experience in examining and testifying about disputed documents. I have worked for the private sector, the Federal Government, and law enforcement. I have a Master of Science degree in forensic science from the University of Kentucky, and received extensive specialized training in questioned document examination from the FBI and United States Secret Service."

"In other words, you're a handwriting expert?" Carpenter asked.

"Your Honor," Cummings interjected, "the defense acknowledges Ms. Maynard is an expert in the field of handwriting analysis. Can we move on?"

"Mr. Carpenter?" the judge asked.

"Ms. Maynard, I would like to direct your attention, and that of the jury, to the holographic will found at Jacob MacDowell's." Carpenter nodded to the audiovisual tech who projected the document on several large screens positioned in the front of the courtroom as well as on the screens in front of the judge, witness, and jury. To the jury, he explained: "A holographic will is one that is handwritten." To the document expert, he asked, "What can you tell us about this document, Ms. Maynard?"

Amanda Maynard was a stout woman with shortish hair and glasses. Dressed well, but not expensively, she sat straight in the witness chair.

She studied the screens for a moment before answering. She testified in court on a regular basis, especially about signatures and wills.

"Document examiners typically use a number of characteristics in analyzing handwriting: line quality, spacing, size consistency, pen lifts, pressure, slant, baseline habits, et cetera. I studied numerous documents and notes of Mr. Stemple's to establish a baseline. Based on inborn movement forms and acquired movement patterns, we can tell the same person wrote all these documents. I do this quite often. Holographic wills are notorious for legal challenges."

The assistant projected two handwritten documents on the large screen, side by side.

"Without boring us by educating us on the scientific techniques used, what did you concur?" Carpenter asked for the sake of the jury.

"Based on comparisons of past writings, without question, Adrian Stemple wrote the holographic will. What you see here is a textbook example of *Vi coactus* or *V.C.* Essentially that's Latin for 'having been forced.'" She then proceeded to use a laser pointer to show exactly how she came to those conclusions. The jury ate it up.

"Adrian Stemple wrote this will under duress," Carpenter reiterated, turning to the jury. "Quite a coincidence. The document in question leaves Jacob MacDowell in charge of a fortune, bequeaths the Stemple estate to him and the county of Mounton as beneficiaries, and names Jacob MacDowell as the sole executor with unlimited restrictions. Someone forced Adrian Stemple to write the will. This is the same will MacDowell claimed he found at the crime scene at the exact time of the murder of Stemple."

"I don't know about any of that," Maynard stated. "I just know Adrian Stemple hand wrote this will under extreme stress."

"Ms. Maynard," Dayton Hollister began his cross-examination, "do you believe handwriting analysis can tell you about someone's personality?"

"Yes and no. Firms in Europe and the UK use it heavily in recruiting and hiring as another factor in their decision processes. I personally believe a piece of writing does not magically represent someone's whole personality over his or her entire life, but rather is representative of a person at a particular life period and in a specific situation. By analysis and comparison of past documents, we know Adrian Stemple wrote this will. We can tell, as I have shown, he wrote this will under extreme tension."

"No one has scientifically verified handwriting analysis, have they?" asked Cummings. "In fact, no regulation of handwriting experts exists? Am I correct?"

"I believe those statements may be true."

"Then why should we believe your testimony?"

"I guess your beliefs are entirely up to you," Maynard said, facing the jury, "but forensics experts are statistically correct far more times than most people. It doesn't take someone with my educational and experiential background to see that these samples, while written by the same person, are clearly different. Many were written in a day-to-day casual environment and the document in question was written while he was under duress. If it helps you feel any better about it, the FBI concurs with my assessment. Maybe you would believe them?"

"No further questions."

#

"The prosecution would like to call Jebediah MacDowell," Carpenter announced.

A bailiff led Jeb into the courtroom, his holster empty. After Jeb swore an oath to tell the truth, he took his seat in the witness stand.

"You are Jebediah MacDowell, senior deputy of the Mounton County Sheriff's Department?"

"No. I am the acting sheriff of Mounton County until this all gets cleared up."

"You are the son of the defendant, Jacob MacDowell?" Carpenter asked from the podium.

"Yes."

"I'll get right to it," Carpenter said, handing Jeb a large Ziploc plastic bag containing a firearm. "Is this your father's gun?"

"It looks like it. I guess there might be a few of them around."

"Not exactly. There were about 1,200 manufactured in 1873. There are approximately 840 in existence today, but this one's unique. Of the 1,200, many were blue steel, but only a very few were like this. It's not actually chrome-plated, but polished, nickel-plated, and an engraved, certified antique. Quite an expensive one, from what I understand. Several antique firearm experts from the FBI and a representative from your father's insurance company have authenticated the serial numbers to match the weapon owned by Jacob MacDowell," Carpenter said, snatching the bag back.

Mac winced at the cavalier handling of the hardware. The potential value of the antique weapon wasn't quite the value of their house, but it was a close second.

"Then, I guess according to them, it's his," Jeb agreed.

"Are you familiar with this weapon?"

"I am a little familiar with my dad's. I'll have to take your word for it's his. I've seen his Colt a number of times, but I've never seen him fire it."

"Prior to August 14th of last year, had you ever touched this weapon before?"

"No."

"According to eyewitness statements, you've worn this Colt. On August 14th. In fact, you fired it at an unarmed man."

"Objection," Mac's attorney piped up. "Is there a question in there or is the prosecutor just testifying?"

"Sustained," the judge said. "Will the jury please disregard Mr. Carpenter's last statement. Mr. Carpenter, strike two. Let's not have a third one."

"Yes, Your Honor. Deputy MacDowell, did you fire this at an unarmed man?"

Jeb looked down. "Yes. But—"

"Who gave you this gun?" Carpenter interrupted.

"My dad, but—"

"Did your father have a grudge against the unarmed man you fired on?"

Jeb thought before answering. "Yes."

"Excellent. Let's move on." Carpenter lifted a large, foamed filled, Pelican case. "Is this the storage case in which your father keeps the Colt?"

"It certainly looks like it," Jeb answered. "You'll have to have your experts certify that as well."

Several jurors tittered at the jab. Carpenter, while inwardly fuming at the jury's amusement, smiled broadly.

"It is. For the record, the FBI's forensic specialists found one, and only one, set of fingerprints on the case handle and the weapon itself. Your father's." With a look at the defense attorney and then back at Jeb, "Were you aware of that?"

"No. The FBI doesn't share its investigative files with us."

"Especially when your father is the target of the investigation?"

"I think 'target' is an especially appropriate word, Mr. Carpenter," Jeb said without humor.

"Are you aware the ballistics from the bullet that killed Adrian Stemple matched the sample from your father's weapon, exactly?"

"Yes."

"How are you aware of that?" Carpenter asked.

Jeb knew he had painted himself into a corner. "The FBI told us."

"So, I guess they *do* share some investigative information with your department." Carpenter pulled a document from a file and handed it to Jeb. "Let's move on. Do you recognize this document, Deputy?"

"Can't say I do."

"It's a copy of an application for a business license, dated December of the year before last. Whose signature is at the bottom, approving the application?"

Jeb looked at the form. "My dad's."

Carpenter smiled warmly at the jury. "Are you aware the business there was a front for a methamphetamine lab, mere steps from the sheriff's office?"

"Objection, Your Honor. Relevance."

"Mr. Carpenter?" Judge Gibson turned his head toward the prosecutor.

"I am establishing a pattern of criminal behavior, sir."

"Objection overruled, but let's cut to the chase, Mr. Carpenter. Deputy MacDowell, please answer the question."

"Uh, what was it?" Jeb asked.

"Mina, please read back Mr. Carpenter's last question," the judge directed the court reporter.

After flipping back through her record, "'Are you aware the business listed was a front for a methamphetamine lab, half a block from the sheriff's office?'"

"I am aware now," Jeb answered.

Carpenter rubbed his chin for effect, "Deputy, who was the person physically closest to Judge Stemple at the time of his murder?"

"My dad, but I wouldn't call it—"

"Would it be safe to say, if not for your father's presence, Judge Stemple would be alive today?"

#

Fire: Great Barns of Fire

Jeb had just tucked Naomi in, already asleep as her head hit the pillow, one of the benefits of her rising at Oh-God-thirty in the mornings. The stress of testifying earlier, the weight of command, and helping his mom with the farm, had exhausted him. After shutting off Naomi's nightstand light, he turned to close the blinds of her second-story window when he saw the stable engulfed in flames.

"Naomi!" he whispered urgently, grabbing his daughter by the shoulders. "Get up, baby."

"Wha—?" the half-awake girl asked.

"Baby, I need you to come with me."

"What's going on, Daddy?"

Wrapping her blanket around her, he scooped her up and practically ran down the stairs, out the front door, and into the center of the circular drive near the flagpole.

"Baby, I need your help. When the fire trucks come, I need you to send them back to the stable. Can you do that?"

"Why? Is the house on fire?"

"No, it's the stables. I don't have time to talk now. Stay here and send them back to the back, okay?"

"Is Bob okay?" her voice sounding much younger than her seven years.

"Bob's probably fine. I gotta go."

Jeb ran back into the house, pulling his boots on as he screamed, "Mom? MOM?"

Getting no answer, he ran toward the back kitchen door, snagging his cell phone off the hallway charger. The 911 call forwarded to Deputy Davis William's radio, who in turn, informed the Mounton Volunteer Fire Department of the situation, as he ran to his SUV. After hanging up with Davis, Jeb immediately speed-dialed his dad's cell phone.

Halfway to the stables now, he could see the flames engulfing the building except for the aluminum garage door. Two hundred yards away, the old barn where they stored the tractors and equipment was also up in flames.

#

Trial & Fire: Motives, Men's Rooms, & Molestation

Mac walked into the men's room of the courthouse. He needed to splash some water on his face and clear his head after a punishing session in the courtroom. Washington Carpenter was just stepping up to a sink when he looked up to see Jacob walk in.

Mac stepped up to a sink a couple down from Carpenter. He turned on the water to let it get cool.

"What's the story, Mr. Carpenter?" Mac asked the prosecutor as he washed his hands.

"You know you are not to discuss the case outside the courtroom, right?" Carpenter replied without looking up from the sink.

"I don't want to discuss the case," Mac replied. "I just want to know what your motivation behind all this is. You seem to have a personal vendetta against me. This is much more than seeing justice done. That's your job. You seem like you're taking this a might personal."

Carpenter grabbed some brown paper towels to dry his hands and turned to Mac. The prosecutor studied the man in front of him who was wearing his fifteen-year-old sport coat, polished boots which had seen better days twenty years ago, and Mac's signature brown Stetson hat.

"You know, Mr. MacDowell," Carpenter said, his voice flat of any inflection, "hypothetically, some may take it personally about your involvement in the murder of a district judge. Some people may resent the fact you arrested my friend, Commonwealth Attorney Douvez, called into question all the convictions he ever had in his career, and a whole lot of bad people are now on the street, setting the justice system in Kentucky back decades. Some people could look at all the questionable lines you've crossed and see a man who played in the gray areas. But I don't. Hypothetically, I might see a man who made himself rich from criminal enterprises, destroyed any who opposed him, and who has taken it upon himself to raze the criminal justice system from within. A system I have dedicated my life to. So, pardon me if I am *hypothetically* taking this personally."

Carpenter slammed the wadded-up paper towels in the trash can and left the men's room. Mac stood, hands on each side of the sink, staring into the mirror.

#

Mac was still reeling from the direction the trial was heading when he received the latest onslaught.

He was returning from Lexington and pulled his truck into the *New Texaco* to fill up with gas when Mrs. Fisher pulled up on the opposite side of the pumps. He could see a few *Piggly Wiggly* shopping bags in the back of her car and guessed she had just come down The Side Street where the grocery store sat.

After his conversation with Carpenter, he needed to get home and talk with Hannah.

As he put the nozzle back in the pump, with a sniff and a *tsk*, Mrs. Fisher threw her nose up in the air and muttered under her breath, "You should be ashamed."

She spoke quietly enough to appear as if she didn't want Mac to hear her, but Mac knew she did it on purpose.

"Can I help you with something, Mrs. Fisher?"

"The way you helped the Stemple family?" Mrs. Fisher turned as she accused Mac.

"I'm not sure what you mean," Mac replied. "I didn't shoot the judge or Adrian. The trial will bring the truth out."

"I'm not talking about poor Mr. Stemple! It's all over town about you and young Mandy."

"What?" Mac asked, truly shocked.

"You know what I'm talking about," Mrs. Fisher said, now completely stopped at her car door. "While she was babysitting little Naomi several years ago, you were taking advantage of that poor girl."

"You mean not paying her enough?" Mac guessed, truly confused.

"You know what I'm talking about. You were abusing her. Sexually abusing her!"

"Mrs. Fisher, I don't know what you heard, but I never laid a hand on Mandy Stemple in my life."

"More likely, when her father found out, you had to do something about him as well," Mrs. Fisher hissed as she climbed into her car and sped off.

Where did that come from? Mac wondered.

#

"Jeb?" he heard on the phone as his father picked up.

"Dad! You've got to come quick. The stable and the barn are on fire! I can hear the horses screaming."

"Call 911. Get Naomi out of the house and tell your mother. I was already on my way home and will be there in five minutes."

"I already called 911 and have Naomi out front," Jeb said. "Dad. I can't find Mom. I think she might be in the stable."

After a second of silence, Jeb looked down at his phone, to find his father already gone.

#

Hannah fell to her knees, the smoke and coughing burning her throat raw. She looked around and through the diminished visibility, but could barely see the few stalls closest to her. Horses were rearing up and pawing at their walls. Froth flicked from their mouths as they coughed and panicked. The tears ran down her face and into the shirt wrapped around her mouth and nose and not just from the smoke. The wet shirt—

Wait! The wet tee shirt!

Hannah clambered to her feet toward one of the horse troughs. Feeling her way through the smoke, she found the hose and spigot to feed the troughs. She burnt her hand on the spigot, already too hot to touch. Pulling the damp shirt from her face, she wrapped it around the metal knob and twisted it as fast as she could.

Water sprayed from the hose. Hannah held it above her head and soaked herself. Grasping the running hose between her knees, she re-tied the newly soaked shirt back around her face. Pulling the hose with both hands she dragged it toward the now broken back door of the stable. She sprayed the flames sprouting up around the fallen door, dousing them as much as she could, soaking the rear wooden door. She aimed the hose at the door and dropped it to turn back toward the horses. Untying Dante's reins from the stall post, she turned him and slapped his haunches to propel him out the back door. The flames while not entirely out, had diminished enough to let the horses escape.

Stall upon stall, Hannah released horse after horse. As soon as each stall door opened, the panic-stricken equine bolted for the back door, the flames now rising higher again. Halfway through the stable, Hannah stumbled and fell. She had inhaled too much smoke. She couldn't get up.

Just as Hannah passed out from the smoke, an explosion erupted from the front end of the building. The sound of rending metal, the roar of the flames, and the sound of screaming horses were the last thing Hannah heard as she succumbed to the smoke.

#

Fire: Bronco Bust In

Mac was less than a mile away from the house when he first saw the flames. The clouds and smoke above lit up the sky with reflected firelight. It was hard to tear his eyes away, but he had to. While paved, the road to his house curved like a snake. He swore as he all but ran off the road more than once. He had turned on the light bar and siren on the top of his Bronco and was doing close to 100 miles per hour on roads marked for 45.

Power braking and sliding sideways, he turned up the gravel road beside their drive, spraying rock and dirt as he turned. He glimpsed Naomi holding on to the flagpole in the front, blanket wrapped around her and thumb securely in her mouth, a habit she hadn't reverted to in years. As he sped past the house, Mac saw Jeb using a garden hose from the house to make a path through the flames to get into the stable. Flames roared all around in the front of the building, with the exception of the rolling metal door. The garage door would heat and buckle, but it was unlikely it would burn. In his peripheral vision, Mac saw the big, red barn used to store equipment off to the side, burning uncontrolled.

Mac pressed his foot to the floor as he roared down the gravel lane leading to the stable.

At 50 miles per hour, he flew through the fire burning the grass around the stable, and rammed the aluminum door with an explosion of metal on metal. The garage door frame ripped off both side mirrors when he crashed through. Ford had manufactured the Eddie Bauer

Edition of the Bronco with airbags, one of the first to have them, but unfortunately for Mac, Ford installed them thirty years ago and they failed to deploy. His head smacked the steering wheel.

As soon as he hit the metal door, he jammed both feet on the brake pedal.

God, don't let her be behind the door!

Mac jumped out of the Bronco, its engine killed by the impact. The big Bronco filled the entire doorway, leaving just inches of space to either side. Luckily, he was able to get out since the Bronco's doors were just past the garage door frame.

The smoke was thick. He couldn't see more than a few feet.

On the floor, halfway through the stable, Hannah lay on the ground. Not moving.

NO!

Mac raced to her and turned her over. He couldn't see any burns, but was well aware smoke inhalation was the greatest danger. She lay in the straw, her lacy white bra, blackened with soot and smoke, her John Deere cap pulled back halfway down her ponytail. Cradled in his arms, he couldn't tell if she was breathing because of the tee shirt wrapped around her face. Rather than spend time with that, he scooped her up and turned to the sliding back door she had managed to break down.

Just as he started to walk toward the opening, straining with his precious cargo, a half-ton of burning hay fell from the second story loft, finally loosened by the crash of the Bronco into the garage door.

Blocking the exit.

#

Jeb stepped back as he watched his father ram the two-and-a-half-ton SUV into the aluminum garage door of the stable without touching the brakes. As the door ripped down, Jeb couldn't see his father get out of the cab with the front doors of the truck on the other side of the doorway.

He did start hosing down the truck. Regardless of how his parents were doing inside the building, the last thing they needed was the 32-

gallon fuel tank in the Bronco exploding.

Mac stared at the opening at the back of the building. The broken bales of hay burned high in front of the exit. What's worse, the burning hay was generating an incredible amount of smoke, much more than the fire outside. He had mere moments to get Hannah out before he too succumbed. Still holding his wife in his arms, he turned back toward his Bronco, which wasn't wedged into the doorframe, but filled up the space enough he knew he nor Hannah would fit in around it. One look at the front of the truck told him it would never start again. He considered trying to push it back out of the way, but the metal from the door had jammed around the axle and tires too much. By the time he might be able to free it from the metal, he would still have to push it back out of the stable enough for them to pass. Long before that, either the fire or the smoke would kill them.

If there was just an escape tunnel or hidden passageway. Just before panic could set in, Mac spotted a spray of water from over the roof of the Bronco. Jeb. He had seen Jeb out there with a garden hose. Spraying the Bronco down might buy them a few moments. *Hey! There was his tunnel!*

Mac carried Hannah toward the Ford. While still holding her, he used one hand to open the front truck door. He was afraid to put her down, because he might not be able to get her up again. He backed up, still holding the door, and eased her, still in his arms, around it. He placed her in the driver's seat and once he had her in position, he reached down and pulled the seat back release. Hannah flopped backward as the seat reclined. Reaching under the tilt steering wheel, Mac raised the wheel as high as it would go. *God bless Eddie Bauer.* Climbing in on top of his half-dressed wife, he crawled over and past her to drag her through to the backseat of the SUV, very aware of the thirty gallons of flammable fuel he had just filled up with. Once they were half in the backseat, he reached around until he found the release to lower the folding bench seat in the back into the storage area behind.

Mac could see Jeb spraying with the hose through the smoke, but the roar of the flames and the screams of the horses made it impossible for his son to hear him. After banging on the rear window to no avail, Mac scooted back down the length of his wife, back toward the front seat, and kicked the steering wheel numerous times. *The steering wheel housing the horn.*

Hearing the horn, Jeb now saw his father clambering back to the rear window of the SUV and directed the hose at the ground behind the vehicle, the window, and the rear of the truck. Once he had extinguished the flames enough to allow him to, he dashed to the back door and yanked on it, but it wouldn't open. Either the crash or fire had warped it in its frame. The stable and the Bronco trapped his dad and the smoke and flames were closing in on the Bronco.

A giant fist smashed through the SUV's rear window...spraying Mac and Hannah with broken glass.

Jeb looked up and watched Sonny grab the rear door through the broken rear window, rip it off its hinges, and toss it into the backyard.

It was then Jeb saw his mother lying beneath his dad.

"Help me get her out," Mac croaked, his throat raw from smoke.

Mac climbed out as Howdy, Sonny, and Jeb pulled Hannah free of the SUV. Once clear, Sonny gently picked her up and carried her a safe distance from the fire toward their house, as Mac fell to all fours coughing smoke and soot from his lungs. He staggered to his feet to rush toward Hannah. He pulled the shirt from her face and leaned down to see if he could feel or hear her breath.

"Is she—?" Jeb asked, his voice trembling.

"She's alive and breathing, but barely."

Mac heard sirens in the distance, approaching rapidly. Just then, the upper storage loft of the stable completely collapsed into the ground floor completely enveloping the building. The Bronco's gas tank finally exploded. The screams from the horses went silent.

Fire: Smokin' Hot Wife

Davis arrived seconds ahead of the volunteer fire department. He squealed into the circular drive to allow the trucks access to the gravel road leading to the stable and barn. For some reason, they were already en route in the general direction when he called. After Davis checked on Naomi still holding the flagpole, he ran around to the rear of the house. The ambulance arrived seconds later and the EMTs began working on Hannah immediately. The driver tried to tend to Mac, but the sheriff waved him off, refusing to leave Hannah's side.

One EMT took her blood pressure and pulse while the other inspected the inside of her throat with a flashlight for tracheal burns. After a quick inspection, the medic replaced the oxygen mask over her mouth and nose. Mac was thankful for the blanket they wrapped around her. They did it to prevent shock and while Hannah was not overly modest, Mac knew she would not cotton to rolling around in her bra and jeans. Her eyes fluttered open as she coughed violently and tried to rise from the stretcher they had placed her on. Mac gently pressed her down without much resistance.

The EMTs lifted her gurney into the back of the ambulance and began to secure their gear. One came over to Mac.

"I think she's okay. Inhaled lots of smoke, but there doesn't appear to be any esophageal or tracheal burns. We're taking her to Bardstown Hospital. It's closest and I think she is past the worst of it. You want to come?"

"Son, I don't think you have enough men to stop me," Mac remarked without a smile.

"No doubt," the EMT said. "While we're at it, we need to get someone to take a look at you. The soot around your nose and mouth alone tells me you got a lungful or two yourself. Hop in, we leave as soon as we can clear a path."

The EMT pointed a thumb toward Sonny.

"We treated the big guy for some cuts and abrasions on his knuckles. I'll never know how he didn't break his hand into a hundred pieces when he hit the window. He doesn't have to, but I suggest we take him in for some X-rays."

"So, what's the problem?" Mac asked.

"Frankly, we can't get him to step away from your wife."

Mac turned to Jeb.

"Take care of that," pointing to the fire with his thumb. "I'm going with your mamma. I'm gonna take Sonny with me. They think she's fine, but are taking her to Bardstown to make sure. The fire has totally destroyed the stable and barn, but make sure the boys save the house. No one wants to be around if your mamma gets out of Bardstown and her family home has burned down. Make sure Naomi stays safe and I'll call you as soon as I can."

"Will do, Dad."

Despite all the noise of the fire, water hoses, and men yelling, both Mac and Jeb heard the low moaning sound coming from the fence at the edge of the training arena between the burning barn and stables.

Standing in the light of the flames and strobing red lights from the fire trucks, Naomi scanned the rescued horses in the training area again.

She turned toward her dad and Pappaw with tears in her eyes, her blanket had fallen to the ground.

Bob wasn't in the training arena.

#

Trial: One Day Earlier

"OBJECTION!" Mac's attorney interrupted. "Calls for speculation. Mr. Carpenter is asking Jeb MacDowell to speculate whether Judge Stemple would be alive if it were not for his father. Clearly trying to influence the jury to link Judge Stemple's death with proximity to Jacob MacDowell."

Which you just unnecessarily did again, Mac thought.

"Sustained," the judge said. "The jury will please disregard the prosecutor's last question. Mr. Carpenter, officially your last swing at bat. Next one involves the word 'contempt.'"

"Okay, let's move on to more recent events," the prosecutor started. "On the date of Adrian Stemple's murder, did your father receive a phone call from the victim?" Carpenter made sure to emphasize the words *murder* and *victim* for the sake of the jury.

"Yes."

"What was gist of the conversation?"

"Objection. Hearsay."

"Sustained. Mr. Carpenter, would you like to rephrase or move on?" the judge asked. "I'm going to let that one slide by as an honest mistake. As usual, I would like to instruct the jury to disregard Mr. Carpenter's question."

"Acting Sheriff MacDowell, you answered the phone and it was Adrian Stemple, correct?"

"Yes."

"And he asked to speak with your father?"

"Yes."

"What happened then?" Carpenter asked.

"Dad agreed Adrian sounded strange and he had asked Dad to come out and see him. Right then."

"Did you, or any deputy, accompany Jacob MacDowell out to the Stemple home?"

"No, he went alone. He was getting off duty and was going to stop there on his way home."

"Do you know a Mandy Stemple?" Carpenter asked. One of his tactics was to suddenly change directions to throw witnesses off track and get them to say something they shouldn't.

"Yes. She used to babysit my daughter a few years ago," Jeb replied.

Carpenter looked at his notes. "Are you aware of the rumors circulating of your father molesting her while she babysat Naomi and shutting down those accusations became a part of the reason for killing Adrian?"

"OBJECTION!"

"Yes, I agree," Judge Gibson said. "Mr. Carpenter, even *you* know hearsay is inadmissible. Sustained. I am instructing the jury to once again please disregard Mr. Carpenter's last question."

Mac winced. The jury absolutely could not *unhear* it.

"Yes, sir. Mr. MacDowell, do you recognize this?" Carpenter asked while holding up a plastic grocery bag sealed inside a large Ziplock bag.

"Looks like a Piggly Wiggly grocery bag," Jeb said. "Anyone for a thousand miles, or smart enough to read the logo, could tell you that. I guess I could see where you needed my help."

"Do you know what was found in this bag?"

"Uh…groceries?"

"No. This bag was found at the scene of the murder," Carpenter went on. "Inside this bag were microscopic traces of liquid molybdenum and liquid PTFE, a synthetic polymer. These are additives in Hoppe's Elite T3 Gun Oil. Would it surprise you if it is the same one your father uses to clean his Colt?"

"Actually, it would."

"What? Why?"

"Because Mom is the only one who cleans his Peacemaker," Jeb said. "Dad would, but Mom typically cleans his when she cleans hers. He rarely ever uses his or has it out. It gets cleaned way more than it gets used. If it gets cleaned, she does it. So no, he doesn't use Hoppes."

"Regardless of who cleans it, traces of Hoppes Elite T3 Gun Oil were found inside this bag at the crime scene," Carpenter continued. "Is it true Hoppes Elite is the gun oil used on your father's Colt?"

Jeb had done a little research since his deposition. He knew this would come up.

"His and several million other weapons since Hoppes is one of the best-selling gun oil companies in America. Hoppes discontinued the Elite T3 gun in 2019, but Mom and Dad like it, and since she cleans his Colt two or three times a year, their supply has lasted a while."

"I see. Hoppes hasn't manufactured the oil your father used since 2019," Carpenter mused. He was planning all along to lead Jeb down this path, but the young man had found his own way. "Is Hoppe's Elite T3 Gun Oil fairly rare in its use today?"

Damn. This snake somehow knew where I was going and let me get there, Jeb thought.

"I reckon I'm not really sure."

"All right, Acting Sheriff MacDowell," Carpenter took a deep breath. "I have a question for you requiring strictly a yes-or-no answer.

"I want to make sure I have my facts straight. Here's what I remember from your testimony. Your father, in his capacity as county sheriff, authorized a business license for a meth lab a block from the sheriff's office, less than a month before he watched Judge Stemple's murder by your father's best friend and employee. The Colt I showed you is your father's. You used this weapon to try and kill an unarmed man last year, after your father gave it to you to wear, specifically for the meeting. He handed you a weapon he had never allowed you to touch before the day you fired at the unarmed man your father had a grudge against. A bag with microscopic traces of the rare gun oil your family uses was found at the scene. You identified the case your father stores this handgun and its accompanying holster and belt. His case had one set of prints on it, your father's. Your father receives a phone call from the victim on the day of Adrian Stemple's murder and goes to his house to meet him. Alone. We've heard from the state's medical examiner, the FBI, and the Kentucky State Highway Patrol's ballistic experts state without question the bullet which killed Adrian Stemple came from Jacob MacDowell's unique handgun. Please, Acting Sheriff MacDowell, remember, we are looking for a yes-or-no answer and you are under oath. Does this summarize the testimony given here today?"

"Objection. The prosecutor is testifying again."

"Overruled. I'm interested in what Mr. MacDowell has to say."

Jeb thought long and hard. Carpenter had engineered everything all the witnesses testified about, but out of context. He couldn't see a way to escape.

"Yes."

"So, to be clear, did I just summarize your testimony?"

"Objection. Asked and answered."

"Never mind, Your Honor, I withdraw the question," Carpenter allowed.

As Carpenter sat down, Dayton Hollister rose and stood at the podium and addressed Jeb.

"Mr. MacDowell, or do you prefer Acting Sheriff MacDowell?"

"Jeb's fine."

"Jeb, would you say you know your father better than anyone?"

"I reckon my mother knows him a tad bit better than I do," Jacob testified. "But I reckon I know him better than most."

"In fact, I've heard it said you know your father so well you finish most of his sentences," Hollister asked. "Would you say this to be true?"

"We work well as a team and I know him well enough to be able to do a bit of his talking. He tends to be on the quiet side."

"So, knowing the sheriff as well as you do, would you say he shot Adrian Stemple?"

"Objection. Calls for conjecture and speculation."

"Sustained. Mr. Hollister, try again," the judge said.

"Thank you, Your Honor. Jeb, knowing your father as well as you do, do you think he shot Adrian Stemple?"

"No—"

"Objection!" Washington Carpenter barked. "Same question, same objection."

"Sustained. Ladies and gentlemen, please disregard the last two questions and Mr. MacDowell's answer." *Despite being unable to unhear that, how much weight will the jury give to the words of a son trying to save his father?* Mac wondered.

"No further questions."

Gibson looked at his watch. "Mr. Carpenter, would you like to redirect?"

"Yes, Your Honor. I will keep it brief."

"Thank you," the judge said.

"Jeb—"

"*You* can call me Acting Sheriff MacDowell," Jeb interrupted. The gallery and jury smiled at that.

"Fine. Acting Sheriff MacDowell, you stated you know Jacob MacDowell about as well as anyone?"

"As I said, probably not as well as Mom," Jeb mused. "But, yes. I guess. You could say he's known me my whole life."

The gallery tittered. Even the judge smirked.

"Last year, this man, who knows you better than anyone, handed you a revolver before you went to shoot the man who you both thought was responsible for murdering your wife and unborn baby and whom Jacob MacDowell held a grudge against?"

"It wasn't—"

"Yes or no, Acting Sheriff MacDowell?"

"Yes."

Judge Gibson cocked an eyebrow and glanced at the defense table. Dayton Hollister sat silently looking at his notes.

"Did you believe your father handed you a loaded gun?"

"Yes."

"So, you know him better than anyone else and you thought he handed you a loaded gun on the way to confront the man you thought murdered your wife?"

"Yes."

"No further questions, at this time, Your Honor."

#

Fire: Childhood's End

Joseph Dawe went home after his night shift, changed into some jeans and an old tee shirt, grabbed some leather gloves and a tool kit and drove over to the MacDowell farm. Jeb had called in sick and Jesse and Davis were covering his patrols. Dawe was helping the MacDowells by sifting through the ashes of the stable to see if anything was recoverable. Mac called Hollister to let him know about the fire and that he would be absent from court today. Hollister went ballistic. He insisted Mac appear in court. A murder defendant not at his own trial would look horrible to a jury. Mac just hung up on him mid-sentence. He needed to see how much of his life with Hannah the fire destroyed. Picking up his wife from the hospital was more important than sitting in a room acting like a statue.

Besides Dawe, Sonny, Howdy, Darlene, Mr. Darlene, and Duncan came by to help. Half the town wanted to, but Mac waved them off. He would protect them from seeing the burnt carcasses of the horses if he could. Darlene stayed with Naomi in the house to keep her away from her beloved Bob.

By the time Jeb got home, changed into some work clothes, and kissed Naomi on the forehead, Dawe and company had just started to search the old barn that housed the equipment. If forced to tell the truth, Jeb was glad he missed going through the burnt stable. The shame pushed him to work twice as hard on the barn. The fire razed the structure nearly to the ground. One and a half of the walls remained, but the inferno completely destroyed the roof and the rest of the building.

Jeb stood in the partial doorway and looked at what remained. The barn's loft was completely gone. The heat melted the tires of the big tractor, bailer, and plow to the ground. He imagined the stench of burnt rubber smelled better than the seared horseflesh in the stable. The fire blackened and charred their metal frames. One wheelbarrow sat in the corner, its wooden handles burnt off. The thick beams that supported the structure were still standing but scorched through with surfaces like blackened alligators. Soot-covered metal hooks held the crisp remains of the 125cc motorcycle Jeb had cherished when he was eleven and twelve. He had raced across the farm like it was his own private motocross track. Now, the bike, with its plastic parts and fenders melted and the tires exploded, hung like a metal skeleton on the wall. Just below the remains of the little trail bike was the corpse of a John Deere Gator. Jeb could see a splash of green here and there through the soot-covered frame. The robotic arms of a front-end loader for the tractor sat torched and immobile next to the Gator. The hardened steel bucket of the loader may still be usable, but more than likely all of the equipment was totaled.

Jeb moved toward the interior of the barn and past his father and friends, unaware a tear was crawling down his soot-dusted face.

#

Hannah informed the Bardstown Hospital staff she was leaving. Dressed in a fresh set of clothes Mac had brought her, they signed everything they needed to as a nurse wheeled her to the door. During her stay in the hospital, Hannah had been coughing up, in a most unladylike way, spitting black soot and ash into a cup. The staff did not want her to leave until her lungs were clear.

"This is just silly," Hannah complained to the nurse pushing her chair to the exit. "Don't you and this chair have sick people to attend to?"

"Ma'am, it's regulations—"

"Nurse...uh, Turner?" Mac offered quietly. "My advice is to push her the remaining fifty feet to the door and Do. Not. Engage. Everyone's day will go smoother and I still have to drive her home."

"Jacob Andrew MacDowell, are you implying I am hard to deal with?" Hannah asked.

"No, ma'am. And look here! We're at the truck already!" Mac was eager to change the subject with obvious relief and a smile.

Hannah refused any help into the passenger seat of Jeb's truck. Mac had borrowed it to pick up Hannah because it had more leg room than Hannah's Jeep. The fire totaled his Bronco and the insurance company was making noises about him purposely driving it into the conflagration.

"But I crashed it into the fire to save my wife," fell on deaf ears.

"Okay. We're out of there and I am fine, tell me everything," Hannah said.

"You know Naomi and Jeb are fine," Mac started. "The stable and barn are completely lost, but the house remained untouched. The fire investigator from Lexington says his initial thoughts point to arson. They think they found accelerants all around the outside of both buildings. They're still investigating. I'm putting a call into the chief soon."

Hannah sat for a few moments, the Kentucky countryside flying past her window.

"What about the horses?"

Mac hesitated. "You got about half of them out before you collapsed. From what you told me, Dante kicked down the back door and you got the fire under control enough with the water hose to get some out."

"Just half?" Hannah asked quietly, but a tear trickled down her face.

"Yepper. Most of the horses you saved belonged to customers. A good portion of the ones that...didn't make it......were ours. The insurance company is balking, but they may not have a choice but to pay off the claim as soon as the adjuster can figure out all the damages. But Hannah, I am truly sorry. I know what those animals meant to you."

"What about Bob?"

Mac didn't trust himself to speak. He shook his head slightly and stared ahead as he drove. Naomi had taken to the gelding, making it practically a part of the family. More than her grief over the loss of the horses and the suffering they endured, Hannah now worried more about her granddaughter.

#

Hannah raced from the truck to the door and was met by Naomi, whom she hugged and kissed until neither of them could breathe. Afterward, the two MacDowell girls took a long stroll through one of the pastures, carefully avoiding the stable and the barn.

"Mammaw, were you scared when you was in the fire?" Naomi asked.

"Yes, I was, SweetPea," Hannah answered honestly. "I was scared. I was frightened to death I would never get to hug you again in this world. I was petrified I wouldn't be here to watch you grow up. I was afraid the horses might suffer. And if you promise not to tell, I was a little bit afraid of what trouble Pappaw might get into without me around. If you're asking if I was scared of dying, then I would guess I would have to say no. I know what's coming afterward and no matter what happens here, I will always be watching you."

The two walked through the pasture for a bit silently.

"Mammaw," Naomi began, " do you think Bob is with Jesus?"

"I sure do, SweetPea," Hannah replied immediately.

"Do you think he misses me?"

"I can't imagine he doesn't," Hannah said. "I was barely in the hospital for a few days and I missed you like crazy."

"Do you think he's lonely?" Naomi's voice didn't quiver as she held her Mammaw's hand as they walked.

"He sure isn't. Most of his friends are there. Some of them from the same fire," Hannah said. "Don't you worry one little bit about Bob, honey. Someday, a long, long, long, loooonnnggg time from now, you'll get to ride him again and feed him angel carrots."

"Do you think Mommy's met him?"

"Who do you think is feeding him angel carrots right now?"

After their walk, Hannah took Naomi back to the house for her nap. Knowing Hannah needed some time and space, Mac had driven back to Lexington for afternoon court. Hollister had given him a hard time about taking the morning off, but Mac replied if the jury wanted to give him the needle for picking his wife up from the hospital, they were welcome to.

After kissing Naomi on the forehead, Hannah walked back out to the barn to survey the damage. Standing in the burnt rubble of the door frame, she looked at what remained of the once-solid structure. Her great-great-grandfather had built this barn with the help of his neighbors. The thick, solid beams had stood firm for over a hundred years, withstanding blizzards, thunderstorms, more than a century of the hot Kentucky sun, and in spite of a brush or two with tornadoes. She had helped her grandpap and her daddy work on a tractor right over there. Well, if she was honest with herself, she just handed them tools. On the left, at fourteen, she earned some nasty blisters mucking out stalls, long before her grandparents built the stables. She looked at where the now missing hayloft resided and remembered her first kiss with Tommy Whitaker when she was twelve years old. She didn't know whatever happened to Tommy, but she would remember that kiss forever. She wondered if Grandma kissed Grandpap for the first time there decades ago. Unbeknownst to her, a tear rolled down her face. She was not sad about Tommy, or the memories and secrets this barn held all these years. She was heartbroken over the fact it wouldn't hold any for Naomi.

With a final sniff, she turned toward the house, determined to rebuild her farm. She wanted a place for Naomi to build her own set of memories. And kiss her own Tommy Whitaker. She was not turning toward the house. She was turning toward the future.

#

Mac and Hannah were sitting at the bank manager's desk. It was a lunch break from the trial and Hannah had called the day before to make an appointment.

"I don't understand, Henry," Hannah demanded. "How can you withdraw our line of credit?" Mac had tried to pay the jury consultants yesterday, simply to have the payment declined. He decided early on to pay Hollister when the trial was over.

"I'm afraid, Mrs. MacDowell," the bank manager explained, "your collateral has reduced greatly in value and exceeds the amount we discussed."

And...here we go, Mac thought.

Mac sat quietly but believed he understood what was coming. He felt sorry for Henry Potter. He was a miserable, frustrated, pennypincher who had spent his whole life in the banking business, but despite all that, Mac didn't believe he deserved what was coming.

"What is all this *Mrs. MacDowell* crap, Henry F. Potter? We've known each other our whole lives. My grandparents were customers of this bank back when your grand-daddy ran it." Hannah implored. "How can we be overextended? We put up the farm as collateral and you know as well as I do it is worth at least triple what we asked for."

"Before the fires, Mrs. MacDow—Hannah. The loss of those two buildings reduced the value of the property significantly. Add the major loss of equipment, livestock, and several streams of revenue, the bank has decided you may not be as creditworthy as you were a month ago. I'm sorry, but this is a business."

Hannah fumed.

"The bank decided, huh? Well, *Mr. Potter*," she said through gritted teeth, "this may be just business for you, but I can assure you from now on, the MacDowells will no longer be banking at *this* business. We will be closing our accounts today. I imagine Jeb will be in to close his in the next day or so. When we leave here, Jacob and I will be having lunch at *Ginny's Diner*. If you have lunch there as well, you may be able to hear me discussing, quite loudly, how this bank does not care about loyalty, decades of patronage, or the character of its depositors. I know you are not a part of the ladies' bible study, but I may choose to discuss it there as well. Good day, sir."

Potter flinched visibly at the mention of *Ginny's*. *Ginny's Diner*, aside from the best food for miles around, was the wellspring of gossip for Mounton. Anything overheard in *Ginny's* at lunch would be all over Mounton County by dinner. One of the largest sources of information in Mounton was Hannah's Church Ladies, a multi-denominational bible study group, that met Wednesday nights. Tonight was Wednesday night.

Hannah stuffed the cashier's checks into her purse as she and Mac left the bank, cutting over one block to The Side Street. Mac chuckled at his wife's recent actions.

"Where to now, 'Mrs. DeSade'?"

"Where else? *Ginny's* for lunch."

"I can't imagine we'll see Henry Potter there."

#

Flip The Script

Felicia Williams told her son, Gabriel, to ring the doorbell. At six years of age, Gabriel thrilled at doing such a grown-up thing as *ring the doorbell*. With equal excitement, he awaited the answer, because behind the door his best friend, Naomi, lived with her grandparents. Wife of Deputy Davis Williams, Felicia heard of the fire and wanted to be one of the first to see if she could help. When the Williams had moved to Mounton and Davis accepted the position of deputy, Hannah, Beth, and Naomi had been the first to welcome them. With the Williams being the sole family of color in Mounton, that meant something.

"Gabe!" Naomi hollered through the screen door, stretching to reach the latch to let the mother and son in.

"Is your Mammaw home, sweetheart?" Felicia asked.

"Back here, honey," Hannah called out. She was just wiping some flour off her hands. A small bandage still decorated her forehead but her bangs covered it.

Felicia set a casserole dish on the counter.

"With all the fire craziness, I didn't know if you would have time to cook. We brought you a little something," Felicia said.

"We're gonna make a Southerner out of you yet," Hannah smiled.

"Well, don't get too excited, it's vegetarian and gluten-free. I'm not done trying to get you and Mac to eat healthier."

"That's okay, we're not done trying to turn you into a Baptist," Hannah laughed.

Mac walked in as the two women visited. Naomi and Gabe sat at the table a few feet away trying to piece together a picture puzzle. When one of them would find a piece to fit, they would let out a squeal of delight. It quickly turned into a friendly competition between the two best friends.

"Felicia, Gabe," Mac acknowledged as he leaned over and kissed Naomi on the forehead, before turning to Hannah and Felicia. "What are you two fine ladies discussing this afternoon?"

"Vegetarians and Baptists," Hannah laughed as Mac stepped behind her at the counter and planted a kiss on her cheek.

"That's gonna make the fried chicken, pot-luck dinners after church more interesting."

"Davis told me you can't really talk about the trial," Felicia started, "but if there is anything we can do…"

"Just keep us in your prayers…er…thoughts," Hannah said.

"Some people down at the community center," Felicia reported, "heard the lawyers were objecting to everything and the jury ordered to disregard just about anything except what makes you look guilty."

"*People* at the community center, huh?" Mac said and looked at Hannah.

"Ezekiel," they both said at the same time. Felicia didn't deny it.

"It's a shame they won't let the real story be told. What happened to 'the whole truth and nothing but the truth'?" Felicia asked.

"Takes a third seat to 'win at any cost' and 'whatever makes us the most money,'" Mac said.

"Back when I was working advertising in D.C., if a competitor would make a bunch of negative claims against one of our clients, we would just ignore it or admit to it, and then focus our efforts on changing what we could make the consumers *see*, *hear*, and *feel*. If they feel something strongly enough, they will buy it. Their impression was more important than snippets of evidence out of context. If you get them to *feel* a certain way about something, they will buy it, regardless of the facts. We usually used our competitors' tactics against them."

"Pappaw?" Naomi asked while still studying the puzzle intently.

"Yeah, SweetPea?"

"Why don't you just arrest the bad men?"

"Because we need to have enough evidence to make sure they are found guilty in court," Mac told his granddaughter.

"Why? It sounds like the men what arrested you don't want anybody to hear about half the ebidence."

Felicia, Hannah, and Mac just looked at each other, unable to answer Naomi's question.

#

Trial: Resting Guilt Face

"I just spoke with Carpenter out in the hall," Hollister whispered to Mac. The two men were sitting at the defense table several minutes before the gallery would start filling up following the afternoon break. It was late in the day on Friday and Gibson had a tendency to push new testimony to the next court day. "Based on how well his case is going, Carpenter was letting me know he has decided to pursue the death penalty."

"WHAT?" Mac barked

"Quiet down," Hollister said. "We half expected this."

"We haven't even presented our case yet."

Hollister looked at his client, "What case?"

"Your Honor, the Commonwealth of Kentucky rests its case," Carpenter said smugly as he looked at the jury. "We have proven beyond a shadow of a doubt Jacob MacDowell shot and killed Adrian Stemple with planning and forethought."

"Well, you won't mind if we bother to let the defense take a whack at it, will you?" the judge replied. "I mean, they did take the time and trouble to show up. Mr. Hollister, are you ready to make your case, if it's all right with Mr. Carpenter?"

"Uh…yes, Your Honor," Hollister answered somewhat shakily.

"And there we have it. First thing Monday morning we will begin the defense portion of our show." The judge instructed the jury, "Ladies and gentlemen of the jury, normally we only sequester a jury during deliberation, but unfortunately, due to the media frenzy involved in this case, we will require you to be guests of the Commonwealth for the weekend. We could send you home and advise you not to look at any news, TV, or social media, but in today's world, that's a virtual impossibility. Even if you could avoid viewing any media, the hounds are out there and will shove a microphone in your face the moment you step away from the courthouse. That being the case, the bailiffs will discreetly escort you to one of our finer motels, where they have removed the TVs and radios from your rooms. We won't take your phones, but if we catch you watching anything related to this case or discussing it with anyone, we will totally dismiss you and I will personally make it my life's mission to provide you with free accommodations in one of our not-so-fine county jail cells for an unspecified amount of time. Do not discuss this case in any way, shape, or form, even amongst yourselves, nor watch or listen to anything related to this case. Thank you and see you first thing Monday. Bailiff?"

Mac stood as Hollister packed up his briefcase. Carpenter left his assistant to pack up their cases while he made a beeline toward the throng of reporters and cameras awaiting outside the courtroom.

As Mac and Hollister made their way to the back door of the courtroom to exit quietly, Mac looked at the courtroom and wondered if this was his last weekend as a free man. When the defense portion of the case concluded in a few days, he may be facing life in prison or worse. He could feel the clock ticking, despite the fact it may be digital. Based on what he had seen from Hollister, he didn't think it would be prudent to start any long-term projects around the farm. Then again, Hannah probably wouldn't let him anyway.

Follow The Money

On Saturday, the Mercer County Sheriff's Department finally supplied the list of customers from the tire store robbery. Jeb was reviewing the list in his email when he stumbled over a couple of local names and addresses. He scribbled the noteworthy names onto a notepad and used a law enforcement database to retrieve their work and home phone numbers. He picked up the phone and called the first name.

"Mr. Dalton, this is Acting Sheriff MacDowell with the Mounton County Sheriff's Department." Jeb thought the temporary title would garner more cooperation than saying merely deputy. "I am looking into the robbery at the Michelin tire shop from a week or three ago. We're assisting the Mercer County Sheriff's investigation." *Technically, true. Not officially, but still…*

"I heard about the break-in," Dalton said, checking out the caller ID. "I was just there a few weeks ago."

"Yes, sir. I can see from some records here you purchased four top-of-the-line performance tires for a BMW M4 convertible about two and a half weeks ago."

"Hey! I'm not a suspect or anything, am I?"

"No, sir," Jeb said. "We're just following up with some recent customers, based on interviews with the Mercer County Sheriff's Department. I promise we are not looking at you in any way. Could you tell me about your experience at the tire center?"

"Sure. I didn't buy them there. I ordered the tires on the internet weeks earlier. I just had them installed there. It was sort of a gift to myself. Paid with my credit card. I have the receipt here somewhere. The family and I drove down there and made a day of it. I guess you already know we have a spread up here, closer to Mounton."

"You stated you were with your family?" Jeb asked.

"Yeah, my wife and fourteen-year-old son. We had the tires installed, went to an early dinner, and came home."

"Nothing unusual? No stops?" Jeb was starting to think this was a dead end.

"Not really. We stopped on the way home at a shop we go to when we're down in Harrodsburg and picked up a couple of bottles of Pinot Grigio to celebrate."

And just like that, another piece fell into place.

"Do NOT jump to conclusions," he could almost hear his dad say.

"Mr. Dalton, is there a time when I could come down and speak with your family?" Jeb asked over the phone. "It won't take long."

"I guess so. Is this afternoon too soon? I have to be in Lexington all day Sunday and I would kind of like to be here when you talk to them," Dalton said.

"How about four o'clock? Shouldn't take more than twenty, thirty minutes and then I will get out of your folks' hair."

"Four will be fine. See you then."

#

It didn't take Jeb long to drive down to the address he had for Dalton and was running ahead of schedule. His ex-Marine dad had programmed him well. The Dalton residence was just inside the border between Mounton County and Mercer County, but much closer to the village of Mounton than the larger town of Harrodsburg.

Dalton called this a SPREAD, but he was being modest. Calling this an estate would be an understatement, Jeb thought. *Not a mansion, but mansion-adjacent.*

His GPS had led him to the sprawling grounds surrounded by a split-rail fence around the entire acreage. The house, one Jeb tried to not think of as a *manor*, was bigger than "The School in Mounton" and that was saying something since The School in Mounton educated grades pre-K through middle school. After the gate buzzed to let him enter, Jeb drove up the winding driveway to the paved loop at the front door and was met at the entryway by Reginald Dalton. Dalton was in his late thirties and trim in a way that regular visits to a gym alone can accomplish. *Scratch that, the house probably has a fitness center.*

After Jeb entered through a palatial marble foyer, Dalton introduced his wife. Stepping into the house, Jeb could detect the aroma of roses and lavender. Probably artificially infused into the air conditioning system. Jeb preferred the front yard which was strong with the smell of freshly mowed grass.

"Nice comfy little place you have here," Jeb noted.

"Thanks. We like it. I'm sorry my son, Denton, isn't here," Dalton began. "He left just a bit ago to go motocross racing with his friend, Chaz. Chaz had a cycle, and of course, Denton had to get one. You know how it was to be fourteen. And before you get the idea a motocross bike is a bit extravagant for a fourteen-year-old, I garnished Denton's allowance until he pays it off. It should be free and clear about the time he needs a car. I don't think he would be able to add anything about the robberies we couldn't."

Jeb was actually pondering the fact they named their son *Denton Dalton.*

"Sheriff, before we begin, I need to tell you I am a civil attorney and I am recording everything we say. It's nothing personal, but you know how it is today."

"Actually, for the time being, it's acting sheriff, not sheriff." Jeb asked, "You're an attorney?"

"Yes, I'm a partner at a practice in Lexington. Mostly, corporate and personal injury suits. Some occasional defamation cases, but you know how it is."

Evidently, I know how a lot of things are.

"Have you ever heard of an attorney by the name of Dayton Hollister?" Jeb asked.

"I—" Dalton began.

"Oh, honey, that's the firm you talked about so much," Mrs. Dalton spoke up for the first time. Until then, Jeb might have assumed she was just a gorgeous mannequin placed on the loveseat for decoration. "They're the ones you said were shady."

Dalton closed his eyes in exasperation as he faced his wife.

"Yes, I have heard *of* him. I don't know him personally, but word gets around."

You know how it is, Jeb thought.

"I don't like to spread rumors, especially about other law firms, but word around Lexington is the firm doesn't color strictly within the lines," Dalton shared.

"Good to know," Jeb said. "I guess we can get started and I can let you get back to your lives." Jeb amicably questioned the couple for about fifteen minutes and then stood to leave. "Thank you for your time."

"I don't know how we helped," Dalton said sincerely, "but if there is anything we can do to help catch the guys who broke into the tire store, please let us know."

"Will do," Jeb replied. "Tell Denton I'm sorry I missed him, but maybe I'll catch him some other time."

#

Yard Work of the Heart

"Miz Peggy? I wuz wonderin' if'n you didn't mind, mebbe me and the younguns might spruce up the yard a bit," Sonny asked. "We could make a game of it."

"Sonny, I told you to call me Peggy. You don't have to do that." but as she spotted the disappointment in his face, she quickly added, "I mean, it would be neat if you would, but that wasn't why I asked you to come to lunch today. I just thought you might like a change of pace from your hot plate."

"I shore do appreciate it. 'Ceptin' for Miz Hannah's, yours is 'bout the best cookin' I ever et," Sonny smiled. *Sonny, you idjit! You made it sound like Miz Hannah's cookin' was better'n hers. Why don't you just keep yore stupid trap shut!*

"Why thank you, Sonny, that's about the nicest thing you've ever said to me." Truth was: other than some drunks at the bar trying to get into her pants, it was the first compliment ANYONE had given her in a long time. "Why don't you go play with the boys, and I'll fix lunch. Mama's down to the *Piggly Wiggly* and 'll be back soon."

Peggy turned to the kitchen to busy herself with lunch. She had decided to make something a little special for Sonny. She had splurged with a bit of her tip money and bought chicken breasts to fry, some Idaho potatoes to bake, corn, pop-n-fresh biscuits, and her mother was coming home with the makings of a salad. From her earlier lunches with Sonny, she knew she had to make a lot of extra as the big man had a giant appetite. While working on lunch, she would look out the back kitchen window and see Sonny working with her boys cleaning up the yard. Her boys loved Sonny. His childlike nature seemed to be able to turn any job into a fun game. And he genuinely liked them. Peggy thought it might have been from years of abuse and siblings who were as selfish as they were wild. As her boys picked up the broken toys and an old Big Wheel from the yard, Sonny hoisted to the street a rusted-out old sink Wilbur had left there years ago for the weeds to grow around. Peggy hardly ever thought about her late husband anymore. There was a time when she thought her whole life, and the life of her boys, would be nothing but pain and fear and dread, but now light and hope had crowded her past out of the way. And she knew it was mostly because of Sonny.

"I swear, the prices go up week after week," her mama announced as she bustled her way into the front door of the mobile home with several plastic bags of groceries. She paused at the door and used her heel to keep the door open. Behind her, Sonny carried the rest of the dozen plastic bags entwined in his large fingers. "Just put them on the table, Sonny. We'll put them away."

"Yes, ma'am," he said as he went back outside to be with the Clay boys.

"Mom, I thought you just went to get a few things!" Peggy blurted as she looked at all the bags.

"You know how it is. You go for one thing and see ten you didn't know you needed. Never go shopping when you're hungry."

"Mama, if you put the refrigerated stuff away, I will get the salad fixin's you bought ready for lunch," Peggy said.

"Salad for lunch? Any special occasion?"

"No. Not really. Sonny's just workin' extra hard in the yard and I thought it would be nice to fix a big meal," Peggy explained.

"Seems like Sonny's not the *only* person working extra hard."

"I have no idea what you are talking about," Peggy lied.

"I'm just happy you found someone to spend time with who's completely different from Wilbur," her mother said. "It does worry me his job is to scare people and his family…"

Peggy looked back out the kitchen window as Sonny lifted both her two boys up and all three laughed hysterically.

"Mama, I think I can safely say Sonny wouldn't hurt a fly."

#

F.N.G.

"So, *that's* the new rookie?" Patricks asked Jeb as Heaven walked toward the sheriff's station. Patricks sucked in his already tiny waist and puffed out his V-shaped chest as the comely new recruit walked toward them.

"Yepper."

"Definitely a step up from the kid," Patricks commented. "I'm not saying Jesse isn't a good deputy, but he's nothing to look at."

"It would be awkward if you thought he was."

"Deputy Carlysle reporting for duty, SIR!" Heaven announced upon reaching the duo at the front door of the station. Despite her new deputy's uniform, she was hot.

"Sarcasm, Deputy?" Jeb asked sharply.

"No, SIR!"

"Damned shame because your gonna need alla the sense of humor you can muster to make this job fun," Jeb smiled.

"You got *that* right," Patricks muttered.

"Did you say something Deputy Patricks?" Jeb asked.

"Just agreeing with you, Acting Sheriff MacDowell."

"Heaven, this is Deputy Lawrence Patricks, but you can call him GQ or Dickhead. depending on how he acts. Mostly, we just call him Patricks. Joseph Dawe comes on at eleven and usually has the night shift to let him be with his boys during the afternoons. Jesse Hendricks and I do the morning patrols for now. When my dad comes back on duty, he is the *real* sheriff and the schedule will change around. I'm just acting sheriff in his place temporarily. Right now, we have worked it out to let you work at *The Hole* four nights a week, sleep-in the next morning, and have a few days to work up at the community center. You ready to start your first day of probationary training?"

Jeb turned to head into the station and Patricks waved his arm with a low bow to allow Heaven to go first. As Jeb held the door for her, he gave Patricks 'The Look' to warn him to put it back in his pants.

Patricks amped up his 10,000-watt smile and followed the beautiful new recruit into the office.

Jeb shook his head and wondered if his dad ever had days like this.

Following an afternoon of procedural training, Jeb sat his new deputy down in the chair opposite the deputy's desk. Patricks reluctantly left earlier to patrol the county.

"Here's the thing, Heaven. Yes, I want you to study the criminal statutes book, but more importantly, I want you to get a feel for this town and how we do things. Meet the townsfolk. When Patricks first started, he was by-the-book, but we're a little more lax here. Our job is to protect and serve, not arrest and ticket. Be early, be careful, and be friendly. Do all that and you'll do just fine. We're gonna have you work with Patricks, Davis, and Dawe on enough shifts you'll be able to handle just about anything. All the shifts except Dawe's overlap. You'll never be on duty by yourself. You'll be on part-time swing shift to cover various day shifts. When I'm not available, Dawe is next in command by seniority, but Davis has the most experience. If anyone gives you a hard time or you feel uncomfortable for any reason, I want you to come to me immediately. Change doesn't come easily to Mounton."

"I think I can handle a few drunk coal miners."

"I was thinking more along the lines of Patricks," Jeb said. "He's a handsome guy, and he knows it. To make matters worse, there are not a lot of eligible single women in Mounton. An attractive female deputy might draw some unwanted attention. But come to think of it, there might be more than a few housewives who might get their noses out of joint."

The two sat in silence for a moment pondering the situation.

"Are you saying you think I'm attractive, Jeb?" Heaven asked coyly.

"Of course you're attractive, but don't take it the wrong way, I'm married," Jeb said as he looked down at his wedding ring.

"Oh. I'd heard your wife passed a year ago," Heaven said seriously.

"She did. But in my heart, I'm still married to her. Maybe someday I'll feel differently, but for right now, she's still my wife."

"I'm just busting your balls, Jeb. Can I speak candidly for a moment? The Looks Fairy didn't just come overnight. I know I'm a good-looking woman. I was a good-looking girl. I have been dealing with guys hitting on me since forever. You either learn how to use it against them or how to deal with it and get on with your life. I occasionally *test* a guy's character. You passed. Had you not, this would have probably been my last day here."

Jeb looked at her for a moment in astonishment.

"Good to know," Jeb smiled. "How did Patricks fare?"

"Jury's still out," Heaven said. "Deep down, he's probably a good guy, but he's going to have to get over himself. Until I know more, I can handle him. Until then, as far as he is concerned, I am just another F.N.G. Plus, he's not my boss. It makes a difference."

"You are definitely different, Deputy Carlysle. Any other questions?"

"Hundreds. But let's go with an easy one. Where's your father if he's the *real* sheriff?"

"Might require a longer, more complicated answer than you might think. Have you heard about Adrian Stemple?"

"Yeah. He was my landlord until someone killed him. Word has it, they arrested your father for it."

"I guess it wasn't *all that* complicated."

"Did he do it?"

"What! No! Of course not. Adrian and my dad were good friends."

"That's what I thought. Then where is he? Why isn't he chasing down any lead he can? If he's as innocent as you say, then why isn't everybody in this town doing everything they can to prove his innocence or find the real killer?"

Jeb looked out the window for a moment.

"You know Heaven, you're going to do just fine here."

#

No News is No News

It was late Friday night and Jeb had put Naomi to sleep a couple of hours after dinner and was just sitting down at the desk in his parents' den with a laptop they recently purchased. They had retired for the night an hour ago, but Jeb was wide awake. He was reviewing the notes and reports from Adrian's murder, trying desperately to find something they missed. He knew his dad had until the trial finished to find anything to prove his innocence. With all the false alarms, Jeb had not been able to give his father's case his full attention. Court wouldn't resume until Monday morning, but they had days, at best, until his dad may lose his freedom forever, or possibly his life. They had to find some evidence *now*. All of the testimony had gone poorly according to what Ginny, Davis, and he had shared privately. The landline phone rang and startled him enough to jump.

"MacDowell residence."

"Jeb? This...Howdy...*Digger's Hole Saloon*...Figured ye want to...a white, county SUV abandoned...by the lake on 44. Tried calling 911, but figured...you...check it out."

Jeb could barely understand the man. The garbled static on the phone was terrible. Cell service in Mounton County, especially out by the lake, was known to be spotty at best. Jeb looked at the phone and then shut down the computer. He dialed the sheriff's office direct.

"Mounton County Sheriff's Office. How can I help you?"

"Carlysle? It's Jeb. I just got a call here at home, sounded like Howdy out at *The Hole*. I could barely make out his voice. The call broke up quite a bit. I thought he mentioned there was one of our SUVs abandoned out by the lake. Anyone out right now?"

"Jesse's out cruising around town on patrol," Carlysle said. "I think he is intent on finding that Grogan guy, you know, the one that got away. Patricks will be in to relieve us any minute."

"Howdy told me he called 911, but no one answered. You been there all night?"

"All night. I grabbed a soda from the fridge, but other than that, been sitting here holding down the desk. You want me to go take a look?" She seemed eager to get away from the office.

"Nah. I'll drive on out there. Give me a good excuse to get some air and get away from this Stemple case." *I need to be doing something. This sitting around and waiting is killing me.*

"Any luck?"

"Lots of it and none of it good," Jeb said. "I'll give you a call once I get out there. I will have my radio on in my truck in case there's no cell coverage. Maybe it's Jesse and he just stepped out to take a piss or check on something."

"Let me know, I'm here if you need backup."

#

Marcus Grogan wadded up the tin foil he had wrapped around the burner phone to distort his voice. There was a possibility he would have reached Mac, but Jeb was actually the intended recipient. His boss had other plans for the old man. Tossing the ball of aluminum foil out the open window and into the weeds, he backed the stolen van farther off the road and waited.

Jeb slowed his truck down as he approached Lake Mounton on Highway 44. The road paralleled the lake's edge for miles until it ran into County Road 248. He slowed to a stop. He had to release his seatbelt to get his mobile phone from his pocket.

"Mounton County Sheriff's Office. How can I help you?"

"Patricks, it's Jeb." *Weird. The call I got from Howdy was all broken up, but I'm getting a decent signal.*

"I got you, Chief."

"First of all, knock off that chief shit. Dad will be back to work in no time and I, for one, am ready for him to come back. This being-in-charge is not all it's cracked up to be. I had no idea it involved this much paperwork. Or this much waiting around."

"That's why they pay you the big bucks," Patricks snorted.

"You idjit. I am making the exact same amount I made two weeks ago. Listen, there's nothing out here. I'm going to head over to *The Hole* and talk to Howdy and find out what I can. I can't understand it though. The cell reception on this call seems pretty—"

CCCRHUMP!

Nothing makes the sound like metal hitting metal in a car accident. The silver van hit Jeb's old truck broadside at the driver's side door at full speed, picking the Ford up on its two passenger wheels. The impact exploded the windows and propelled Jeb from the left side of the cab into the passenger door. The truck rolled onto the passenger side, then slowly onto the hood as it flopped into the ditch next to the road, upside down.

As the van still idled, despite the smashed front-end, Markus put the vehicle in park, jumped out, and ran toward the overturned pickup truck. Anyone watching would have seen a concerned driver coming to the aid of the truck he just hit. Anyone looking closely would have seen the half-gallon plastic container of gas he was carrying. Reaching the truck, he sloshed the gas all over the bottom of the truck, now at about eye level. Waiting until he saw Jeb crawl part way out of the wreck, he sat the plastic container down for a second, struck a match, and tossed it on the fuel-soaked truck. When the WHUMP of the fuel ignited, Grogan snatched up the plastic gas can and ran for the van. As the bottom of the truck blazed just a few feet above him, Jeb lay unconscious, scalp bleeding, on the ceiling of the overturned cab.

#

"Honey? Have you seen Jeb this morning?" Hannah asked Mac as she fixed breakfast. It was just after 6:00 a.m., but the MacDowell family were notoriously early risers.

"He probably slipped out to work," Mac suggested as he set the table for him and Hannah.

Naomi was sitting at the table eating a bowl of cereal with gusto. Hannah had tried to get the girl to eat a substantial breakfast, but bacon and eggs lost out to 'magically delicious.' Naomi said the box reminded her of Mr. Howdy.

"Noper," Naomi mumbled between mouthfuls of dehydrated marshmallows. "Daddy always comes in and kisses me before he goes to work. I'm up before he is most days, but today, no kiss."

Mac and Hannah exchanged concerned glances just as the landline rang.

Hannah snatched the phone off the cradle. "Jeb?"

"No, ma'am, this is Patricks down at Bardstown. Can I speak to the sheriff?"

"Patricks, if this is about Jeb, you talk to me right now or so help me, I'll come down there and pray the truth right out of you. Multiple times."

"Uh…yes, ma'am. Seems there was an accident last night and Jeb's truck got hit—" Patricks began.

"WHAT? Is he okay?" Hannah barked at the phone. Mac was now standing next to her and Naomi stopped eating cereal. Mac reached over and pushed the speakerphone button.

"Patricks, this is Mac, I'm on the line too. As is Naomi." Mac told the deputy to prevent him from saying anything traumatic.

"Jeb got a call last night about an abandoned county vehicle and went to check on it. He called it in and Carlysle spoke with him. Once he got out there and didn't see anything, he called in and got me. His truck got T-boned and then caught fire. Jeb tried to crawl out of the smashed cab, but collapsed not too far away. I actually heard the accident while he was on the phone with me. I was able to hear everything until the truck blew up. Dawe came on duty right about then and Jesse and I took one of the SUVs out to Jeb's general location. We called the fire department and ran Jeb to the hospital. He's there now."

"Why didn't the fire department call me?" Mac asked. "Just because I'm not sheriff doesn't mean I can't help with fires." Mac had been on the Mounton Volunteer Fire Department since he and Hannah moved there.

"I'm guessing because it was Jeb's truck, they didn't want to worry you. They have him here at Bardstown. They've got him in for testing and he hasn't woke up yet all the way. I called as soon as I knew you would be up. There was nothing you could do here. Jesse dropped us off. He ran back to the scene to see if he could help or find any evidence. At the very least, it was a hit and run."

"Lawrence Patricks, you and I are going to have a serious talk about when it's appropriate to call a boy's parents about him being in an accident," Hannah pointed out quietly.

"Uh…yes, ma'am. But Jeb's not exactly a boy. He's the acting sheriff and he was awake just long enough to tell me not to call you till now. And, ma'am, he's my boss."

Patricks, let it go, son, Mac thought.

"All right, I'll…" Mac caught a glare from Hannah. "—er, *WE'LL* come right down to the hospital. We'll bring Naomi with us since it's too early to drop her off to school. She'll want to see her daddy anyway. Call Dawe to come get you and take you home. You and he are now at least fourteen hours into your shifts and you'll need to get some rest before your shift again this evening. Call Jesse and tell him to hang tight until I can get out there. See if Carlysle can cover some hours this morning. And this is important Patricks…TELL NO ONE. You brought Jeb to the hospital and that's it."

"Uh, sure, Sheriff. But as for you going to the scene, you know you're not on active duty now, right?" Patricks hated to remind a man he respected of his suspension.

"Yepper, but I am in the volunteer fire department and am headed to the scene of a truck fire. Hang tight, son, we'll be there shortly."

Hannah was already getting Naomi ready to travel. Mac looked at the single set of keys left on the wooden key hooks next to the door and thought of his treasured Bronco burnt in the fire at the stable. "I guess we're taking your Jeep."

#

Reading & Revelations

Sonny sat in the hospital waiting room with Naomi while Hannah and Mac looked in on Jeb. Howdy closed the bar early and drove Sonny into town after Jesse came by with news of Jeb's accident.

Hannah came out to the waiting room with tears in her eyes. Mac kissed her on the cheek and then stomped out of the hospital without another word. He was so angry he couldn't trust himself to speak.

As Hannah dabbed her eyes, Sonny asked, "Is Jeb gonna be okay, Miz Hannah?"

Hannah looked down at Naomi and smiled weakly. "I can't talk about it right now, Sonny." Hannah turned away from them to blow her nose. "How are you two doing?"

Both Sonny and Naomi instinctively felt it was not a good time to press Hannah for more.

"We're doing good, Mammaw. I'm teaching Sonny how to read!"

Sonny blushed, from under his well-trimmed beard down to his clean-shaven neck.

"Pa didn't cotton much to school learnin'. Syrus went for a few years afore they had me, but I never spent much time gettin' schoolin'."

Hannah looked at the giant of a man who seemed larger sitting next to her seven-year-old granddaughter, "Well, let's just do something about that," as she picked up the *Highlights* book. "Why the sudden interest in reading, Sonny?"

Sonny blushed again.

"No reason, I reckon. Just don't want to be a stupid-head no more."

"Sonny, you're not stupid. You are one of the best men I know. I think it's great you want to improve yourself."

"Thank ya, Miz Hannah. I reckon lately I jes' wanna be a better man."

#

The day after the accident, Mac parked Hannah's Jeep at the sheriff's station and walked slowly the hundred yards to the newly rebuilt *Darlene's Beauty Emporium/Barbershop/Tanning Salon*. The shop burned down the previous year when the storefront next door, a disguised meth lab, caught fire. *Darlene's* being the closest building was the other casualty. The outer facade was now more in line with the town's new historical tourist style.

Mac sat in one of the chairs in the small waiting area, staring straight ahead, his face a blank, ignoring the outdated magazines on the little coffee table, while Darlene seated Doris Burnett. Both born and raised in Mounton, the Burnetts had long passed their seventieth birthdays, and would probably end up in Mound Hill Cemetery up the road.

"Doris, why don't you let one of my girls give you something a bit more up-to-date?" Darlene asked Mrs. Burnett as she sat in her in one of the three cutting chairs.

"Honey, I have had this same style for forty years and Mr. Burnett still lives at home. I think it's just fine."

Mac grunted to himself. *Change was NOT something the residents of Mounton embraced. That should be our town motto.*

Darlene signaled Mac to take the third chair.

"How 'bout you, Mac? Got a little silver peppering your crewcut. Let's darken your color some," Darlene asked. "Or maybe shave it off. It's the style now. You'd look like a new man."

Mac jerked his thumb toward Mrs. Burnett and said quietly, "I'm with her. I come home with a shaved head and Hannah may not recognize me and just shoot me for trespassing. I'm just going to need to look a little nicer in the upcoming days. Just a trim."

"Gotta special event?" Darlene asked.

"'Special' is NOT the word I would use," Mac replied.

"What's the latest about the trial?" Darlene asked Mac as she wrapped a plastic cape around his shoulders. "How's it going?"

"Sorry, Darlene. My attorney and Judge Gibson told me I shouldn't talk about it to anyone."

"Well, I can." Ezekiel Thompson sat in the third chair. He was in for his twice-a-month haircut, the same as he had been for the last thirty years, long before Darlene had graduated from stylist to owner. Darlene charged him the same amount the owner had back then. Since he had little hair left, it would have been robbery to charge more. Now, nearly one hundred and five years old, Ezekiel lost a lower leg in one of the three wars he served in. The jerky-tough strip of leather had lived in Mounton his whole life except for his tours overseas. He was one of the few residents the prosecutor had not listed as a witness, and as a result, Ezekiel could sit in the gallery and watch the trial progress. At his age, trial gossip was about as close to entertainment as you could get.

"No offense, Sheriff, and I don't really care if you get offended, but it don't look none too good," Ezekiel said while Sally finished trimming his hair. "Them damned lawyers is objectifying to everything and interrupting to the point I cain't make heads or tails of what's going on."

"Yepper," Mac agreed as Darlene trimmed his already immaculate hair.

"Meh, it don't matter no how, I cain't hear but about half of what they say anywho," Ezekiel disclosed.

Mac thought as he watched the old man get his hair cut in the mirror, *I don't think anyone is supposed to hear about half of what they have to say.*

"How's Jeb doing?" Darlene asked. "We heard about the accident. Word has it he crawled out of the truck before it blew up. Whatta the doctors say?"

Mac sat for a long moment before answering. He had been dreading this part of the conversation but knew something had to be said.

"Don't believe everything you hear, Darlene," he whispered barely loud enough so Mrs. Burnett and Ezekiel could overhear. "I need you to keep this to yourself. Hannah and I haven't explained everything to Naomi yet. After the thing with her mom last year, and lately Bob, we just don't know how to tell her about Jeb."

Darlene stepped back from his chair, her mouth wide open.

"Oh, Mac!"

"Yepper. You can't imagine what the house feels like without him around. The boys are feeling his absence something awful at the office. Naomi misses him terribly and she doesn't even know all the details yet. There's this giant piece missing out of her life and she doesn't know why. Seems in a wreck like that, it's pretty common to suffer internal injuries that don't show right away. And if you add in a head injury and smoke inhalation…well, Jeb's always been a good, God-fearing boy and Hannah swears he's going to be sitting with Jesus."

"Mac. Why didn't you say something? You let me prattle on about hair color when Jeb…" Darlene sobbed in her perpetually gravelly voice. "Oh my Lord, Hannah! That poor woman."

"She's been through a lot lately," Mac agreed. "Please don't say anything. We don't want the word to get out till we've had a chance to talk to Naomi. We'd appreciate it if you wouldn't come by until then. Just act like everything is normal…for now. We're gonna pretend he's still with us until we have to tell her otherwise."

"Of course. I won't tell a soul. You just give my love to Hannah and Naomi."

Right after Mac left, Ezekiel got up out of his chair and left his dollar bill on the counter without a word.

#

Mac drove straight home. Word of the conversation at Darlene's had gotten around town before he reached the farm.

"How's Naomi?"

"She's taking a nap in her room," Hannah said.

"Did you talk to her?" Mac looked up the stairs where his little angel would be sleeping.

"Not yet. I hope she understands. It'll be a tough concept for a seven-year-old. Sonny is sitting on guard outside her door. I guess in case she wakes up and needs anything. I can't get him to come down."

"He'll be fine. Does he know about Jeb?" Mac asked.

"Yes. I don't know if he understands or not. He seemed...confused. Where did you go?"

"I needed to get a haircut. Felt like I needed to look my best for the next few days coming up. I wanted to speak with Darlene. I told her what I could since Ezekiel and Mrs. Burnett were sitting right there."

"With those two, I think it's safe to say everyone in town knows what you talked about by now," Hannah said as she shook her head. "By nightfall, everyone from here to Lexington will know."

"I'm glad we decided to keep Naomi out of school for a few days. We can save her from having to answer a bunch of questions. Keep her here where you can be with her. I'll take Sonny back out to *The Hole* later today and talk with him again about Jeb."

"Mac...when can we go get our boy? I hate the idea of him just laying up there."

"I'll make the arrangements after I drop off Sonny. You have the hard part. You need to make sure Naomi understands everything."

#

When It Rains

"Mr. MacDowell?"

Mac stepped out his kitchen door, to-go cup of coffee in hand, and headed toward his rental truck parked in their drive and saw a man he didn't know walking up the drive toward him.

"Yepper."

"Mr. MacDowell, my name is Stotts. George Stotts. I am an insurance investigator for Midwestern Fidelity, your insurance company," the man said as he held out his hand to shake the other's. He was in his mid-fifties and clean-shaven. A slight bulge around the waist declared he was an athlete in his youth,. His slacks and polo shirt matched his dress shoes which were just one shade too nice for northern Kentucky. His blue rental car was relatively new, but clearly a fleet model, and on the-least-expensive side. "I apologize for calling on you this early and unannounced."

"Mr. Stotts, it's 7:30 a.m. This is not early for farmers. But I am on my way to court and in a bit of a hurry. What can I help you with?" Mac asked.

"I just wanted to introduce myself and meet you."

"Is this to cancel our policy?"

"No, sir. Midwestern Fidelity would cancel your policy in a form letter from one of our home office representatives." Stotts explained. "No, I am here to look into the claims you have filed in the last year or so."

He now had Mac's full attention. This man wasn't here to socialize.

He was here to find out who was responsible for all the claims Midwestern needed to pay, or had paid out, over the last year. If he couldn't find the person responsible, he would focus his attention on who he could find.

"Which is why I want to talk to you. If now is not a good time, can we set an appointment when we can talk? I would like to speak with your wife and son."

"We can do it in the evenings. You may not have heard," unsure if he should say this to an insurance investigator looking into their claims, "but I am on trial for murder right now. In fact, I am running late to court as it is. You can come by any evening after seven and speak with my wife and me. Talking with our son may be a little…difficult, at this time. He was involved in a hit-and-run a few days ago."

"Oh, yes, I heard about his accident and your legal issues," Stotts said, sounding genuinely concerned. "My understanding is since he was acting in an official capacity, the county's insurance, and not Midwestern, will handle those claims."

Mac's tone chilled, "Your concern touches me deeply."

"Don't take anything I say personally, Mr. MacDowell," Stotts appealed. "Midwestern flew me down here to find out the truth about what really happened here over the past year. In what little research I have had time to do, you have an exemplary arrest record as a county sheriff. In fact, it looks as if you have solved every case and crime, *except* for what has happened to your own property and family. But between the totaled tractor, the fires at this lovely farm, the break-in here recently, the car accident with your son, and the murder of your daughter-in-law, a great number of questions remain unanswered. It strikes me odd your personal insurance claims continue as mysteries."

At the mention of Beth's murder, Mac unconsciously tightened his grip on his metal coffee mug. "What are trying to say, Mr. Stotts?"

"Not much. Except I look forward to speaking with you and your wife. And I want you to rest assured I won't stop looking until I find whoever is responsible for all the tragedies to have befallen your family. Like you, I feel like I have a mission in life. I will personally see to it whoever's responsible goes to prison for a long, long time, if for no other reason, than insurance fraud. No matter who they are."

"Give us a call and we'll see when we can fit you in," Mac said icily.

"Oh, I will definitely be in touch, Mr. MacDowell. You can count on it."

#

Shock & Aw

The news of Jeb's accident traumatized the town of Mounton. The murder of Beth and her unborn child the year before hit the town like a bomb. Everyone loved Beth. She was the nurse at the walk-in medical center and her upcoming baby was like a symbol of hope to a town that had seen better times. The true depth of the town's sorrow was because of the impact it had on the MacDowell family. They couldn't imagine how her passing ripped through them.

And now "this thing with Jeb." No one could bring themselves to say it out loud. Born and raised in Mounton, and except for some time in Lexington to do a partial stint at the police academy, Jeb had never spent any serious amount of time away from his hometown. Locals now qualified conversations all over town as "Before *The Accident*" and "After *The Accident*."

He played baseball, first in Pop Warner as a boy, and then when he attended high school in Louisville. He delivered papers to darn near most houses in town. His absence tore a scar on the town's heart.

Hannah and Naomi hadn't left the ranch since the accident. The few times Mac appeared in town, he hadn't uttered a word and had been wearing a black shirt with his jeans. There was no telling how the family would go on from here, but nothing but those closest to them knew their true feelings.

#

"Salutations," Ginny answered his phone.

"Ginny. This is Hannah."

"Ah, the fair Lady MacDowell. How may I be of assistance?"

"With everything going on, I thought I might go to a meeting. Are you up for it?"

"I concur. I, too, would savor some positive reinforcement. These are indeed trying times."

"Great. I will swing by and get you in a few."

Due to only her second use of alcohol, Hannah had been the victim of a date rape decades ago. It was just before she started dating Mac and she has attended AA meetings ever since. She didn't truly believe she was an alcoholic but felt a calling to attend meetings to retell her story as a cautionary tale to other women. She felt it was her way of acting in God's service and reciprocally, she gained strength from the stories of survival she heard there.

The Mounton Alcoholics Anonymous meeting met in the basement of the Baptist Church twice a week. Mac had secretly learned of her attendance and incident years ago but respected her right to privacy. Had it not come up in the Douvez case last year, he might never had told her he was aware of it.

"How does Mac feel about you attending meetings?" Ginny asked as they climbed out of Hannah's Jeep.

"He's fine with it," Hannah replied. "He knows me better than anyone and believes I really don't have a problem, but he understands my wanting to help others. It's a lot easier on me having to not make excuses to go out. More than the meetings, I was really keeping my experience with Douvez from him. I sort of suspected you would know how he felt about it."

"I do," Ginny admitted as he held the door open for Hannah.

She and Ginny sat in the back of the meeting and listened to the various stories. Hannah didn't see any new female attendees. She saw no need to reiterate her story. She shared it about twice a year when there were new women at the meeting who might benefit from the story. It was a challenge in a town the size of Mounton to keep attendance anonymous, but since Hannah's story came to light, she began sponsoring several women to help them in their journey.

Toward the end of the meeting and much to Hannah's surprise, Ginny stood up and walked to the podium.

"Hello, everyone. Most of you probably know me. My name is Ginny and I am an alcoholic." This was something he had never done in Mounton before.

"Hi Ginny!"

"I won't bore you with the details of my lackluster origin story," Ginny began. "I can summarize it by conveying the stress of obtaining an education while working, the passing of my mother, and the administration of a business contributed to my adopting alcohol as a crutch. Years ago, I finally acknowledged my helplessness in conquering my own inner demons and physical addictions and was able to find the help I needed to stay sober since then.

"I'm up here today because my stress indicator is registering higher than usual and I have no desire to backslide into any old habits. Not long ago, a deliberate conflagration ravaged my best friend's farm. He is on trial for murdering one of our mutual friends." Ginny looked back at Hannah. "You may have heard about it." A small titter of laughter emanated from the room. A few faces glanced back at Hannah. "You might not have heard that I recently testified at his trial and I fear, despite his innocence, may have irreparably damaged his case. WHEN he stands exonerated, a wrongful death suit names both us regarding the late Judge Stemple. The suit is for millions. Losing will cost us everything: our homes, my diner, his farm, and possibly our futures. More recently, his son, another one of my best friends, was the victim of a hit-and-run vehicular homicide attack.

"I recognize that as much as I want to help my friend, I must also take care of myself. I can't revert to my previously destructive patterns. I know this is not a struggle I can prevail by myself thus I ask you to please pray for me and my friends. We do our best to look after our friends, family, town, and each other, but ultimately, we usually need help to look after ourselves. Thank you."

Ginny sat back down next to Hannah.

"Nice share," she whispered. "I think it was the first time I ever heard you speak here, Ginny."

"Well, sometimes you just have to ask for some outside help. With all this, if not now, when?"

"I would say right now is as about as good a time as any."

#

Necessity is the Mother Of Intervention

"Mac, we require a little intercourse," Ginny said as he and Duncan pulled Mac into *Duncan's Mercantile & General Store*. He had finished another day in court and was walking around Mounton and then would head home. Ginny and Duncan stopped him on the street just as he was hustling to get to the truck he had rented while the insurance company balked about paying for his Bronco.

"I'm going to assume you mean 'talk.' What's up?"

"We got a wee problem," Duncan explained. The store was empty this early in the evening, but Duncan uncharacteristically turned the OPEN sign on the door to say closed. Something Mac had never seen him do in the daylight. "Appears some dunderheid in this county has gotten his self in a spot of trouble and is too blind or too daft to get his self out of it."

"I'm not the sheriff right now, but it doesn't mean we can't help," Mac said. "What's the problem?"

"Therein lies the conundrum," Ginny explained. "It appears this fellow supposes if he ignores these quandaries, the universe will simply handle everything justly."

"Sounds like he has his head buried in the sand," Mac said, turning from one friend to the other. "He needs to take on these problems head-on. Let's go have a talk with him. Who is this guy?"

"You, ya bloody dunderheid! We're talking aboot you!" Duncan smiled.

"What?" Mac asked his friends.

"Mac, even for a tourist, you're one of the best men I know, but surely you can see which way the toilet's swirling."

"Duncan, if you're talking about the trial, it will be fine. I didn't kill Adrian and everyone knows it. I have nothing to worry about," Mac denied.

"Buddy, were you in the same courtroom I was?" Ginny asked. "If you don't step up, Carpenter will be filling your prescription for a potassium chloride vaccination."

"Aye, and it's nay just that," Duncan continued. "In the last few weeks, someone murdered one of your best friends, some dobbers framed ye well and good for the same; then some other eidjits burned your stable, barn, and farm equipment to the ground, not to mention killing some beautiful animals and damned near frying your lovely hen. Just this week, some dotty dobber smashed into Jeb, wrecked, and set his truck to explode. Someone is out to kill you and your whole family. It's time to take this shite seriously."

"I am loathed to concur with our resident Scotsman, but those are just the physical threats," Ginny began. "Besides the corporeal damage, there's the psychological mayhem. Vandals broken into and desecrated your domicile. Imagine how this impacts Hannah and young Naomi, knowing someone violated their most protected sanctum. Then there's the stress for them knowing their husband and grandfather may be executed for a crime he didn't commit. Some reprobate arsonist killed Naomi's pony among other animals. None of which begins to account for the attacks on Hannah and Jeb. Add in the helplessness your loved ones have to be feeling over your trial and there is no way your family will not end up scarred by all this."

"You—" Mac started.

"An' then there's the financial pressure," Duncan jumped in about an issue near and dear to his heart. "Hannah mortgaged her family home for the first time in two hundred years. Ye lost your income while this boggin excuse for a mistrial goes on. Yer family income has been cut by the fire ruining Hannah's boarding and training business. Ye're stuck for the loss of yer barn, stable, horses, and vehicles. The insurance company is dragging their feet aboot paying ye. Rumor has it the damned fool bank cut off yer line of credit and ye can't pay your eijit lawyer, who is robbing ye blind anyway. With the farm half burnt and the bank agin ye, ye can't afford to replace yer trucks. Ye've lost your Bronco to one fire and now this thing with Jeb. Boyo, ye've got to admit it. You're under attack."

Mac looked at both men.

"Once again, circumstances force me to accept Duncan's analysis," Ginny cautioned. "You're under physical, financial, and psychological siege, and the query du jour begs, what do you intend to do about it?"

The store was unnaturally quiet except for the compressor on the red, antique soda refrigerator sitting on the floor.

"I don't know. I watched my father focus on his own needs till he died lonely and unloved. I've dedicated my life to doing just the opposite. I don't know if I can change my ways after all these years," Mac stood up straight. "But you are right about one thing. If this was happening to anyone else in this town, I would be tracking their attackers down and making them pay for this. I guess I just thought because I was innocent it would all work out. But Jeb's attack was the last straw.

"Good," Duncan said. "Now, can I be opening me bleedin' store back up? This stuff isn't going to sell itself ye know."

#

Mac pulled over on his way home from *Duncan's*. There was a scenic overlook on Highway 248 with a view of the lake and he needed a moment to think. The rental truck crunched in the gravel as he killed the engine. His day in court and his conversation with Ginny and Duncan exhausted him both physically, mentally, and emotionally.

He stared out at the calm lake vista and wondered how his life had gotten this jacked up this quickly. Was it just a few months ago he had thought he and Hannah had the perfect life? Now, he was on trial for murder and in a few days was facing life in prison. He wasn't afraid of prison or dying, but he wasn't ready to end his life with Hannah. And Naomi. His little angel deserved a Pappaw to play with and watch over her as she grew to be the beautiful woman he knew she would be. Hannah was as strong a person as he had ever met, but he wasn't sure how she would take it if the trial followed its current direction and he ended up convicted for a crime he didn't commit. She loved Naomi as much as he did, but would she be able to disguise her anger and loss from Naomi?

The horrors kept piling on as he thought of the frustration of not being around to solve Jeb's accident, Adrian's murder, the break-in and desecration of Naomi's room, and the fires that had close to killed Hannah and devastated their farm. If by some miracle, he beat the murder trial, the remaining problems seemed insurmountable. Hannah's family farm mortgaged for the first time ever, the cancellation of their insurance, their credit ruined, their income ravaged, no equipment or vehicles to run the farm, plus the insurance investigator, Stotts, nosing around and implying Mac is his main suspect.

Now this rumor of him molesting Mandy. Someone beat Howdy within an inch of his life. The timing of everything was bad enough Mac thought there was no way it could be coincidental. At what point is it just too much for a man to stay strong?

Mac became acutely aware of the knot in his throat and his eyes welling up as his knuckles turned white gripping the wheel. *NO! We haven't done anything wrong. Hannah and I are good people and we take care of our family. If we just play by the rules, God will fix all this. Won't he?*

Whoever this may be is coming after me and they are trying to go through my family to do it. Big mistake. I may not be sheriff right now, but maybe it's time I started acting like one.

Somewhere in the back of his mind, he could hear a voice suspiciously like Hannah's:

"So do not fear, for I am with you; do not be dismayed, for I am your God. I will strengthen you and help you; I will uphold you with my righteous right hand."

He also remembered her saying *"You put your big girl panties on, get your bony ass out of my rocking chair, and get out there and 'protect and serve'."*

With a sniff and a wipe of his eyes on his shirt sleeve, he started the engine. He wouldn't let Hannah see him like this. Real men don't let Life get them down. Then again, real men don't usually have these many burdens laid at their feet. As he drove and the more he thought about it, the more he realized this was an *unusually* large stack of hardships. Much more than could occur in nature. The question is: what to do about it?

#

Heaven Help Us

"Sheriff MacDowell?" a female voice called out.

Mac turned on the sidewalk. Despite his suspension, he still walked and patrolled the streets of Mounton in the evening and before court. Acting as the county's protector wasn't a job to Mac, it was a calling.

A beautiful young woman in a Mounton County deputy's shirt, dark brown deputies' uniform pants, a white cowboy hat, and boots strode quickly to catch up to him. *How did she get her deputy's uniform shirt so tight?*

It was just shy of 6:30 p.m. Mac had just driven from court in Lexington and wanted to get in a quick walk about town before heading home.

"Sheriff, I'm—"

"Heaven Carlysle. My son told me all about you." Mac didn't mention he had read the background check Jeb had done on the young woman. "Nice uniform."

Looking down, Heaven smirked, "Yeah, I know we're allowed to wear jeans on duty, but the only ones I have are skinny jeans and I think I am going to have a hard enough time getting the women around here, let alone the men, to accept me as a deputy. So, polyester it is."

"I would agree that embracing change is NOT Mounton's motto," Mac replied. "Patricks wears the uniform pants because he lives By The Book. Jesse wears them for a very similar reason to yours. I will say you are prettier than I heard."

"Jeb told you *that?*"

"Nope. As a matter of fact, he surprisingly didn't mention what you looked like at all. Word gets around town is all."

"Boy, I'll say. Just go to the diner for lunch and it's like you have X-ray eyes into everybody's home."

"It does keep the BS factor low in a small town if everyone knows the truth. What can I do for you, Deputy Carlysle?"

"Just Heaven, sir."

"Heaven, huh? How'd you get a moniker like that?" Mac asked the young woman.

"B.B. King sang, 'Everybody wants to get to Heaven, but nobody wants to die to get there.'"

She noticed he looked her in the eyes instead of at her chest when he talked to her. Looks like the apple fell right at the foot of *that* tree. "I just wanted to say it's an honor to work for your department and I look forward to you coming back. Jeb was a great boss, but he swore you were better. I'm truly sorry about his accident."

"Well, his daughter lives with us, which made him obligated to say those things."

"I know you don't know me, but I've been thinking about my conversation with Jeb." Heaven asked, "Would it be okay if I share something with you my dad once told to me?"

"Sure. Dads give great advice. I know. I am one."

"I was about sixteen and I was riding my motorcycle around when a car ran through a red light and hit my bike at an angle. I had a broken leg and some road rash, pretty much laid up for a few weeks." Heaven's eyes focused on the past as she recalled the story. "That night I was laying in the hospital bed, expecting my loving dad to be sympathetic to his injured baby. He sat down next to my bed, held my hand, looked me in the eye, and said, 'Why'd you let him hit you?'

"I laid flabbergasted. The man I treasured most in the world was blaming me for some maroon running a red light and hitting my bike.

"I said, 'Dad, I had the right of way.' And he asked, 'Yeah, but why'd you let him hit you?' 'No, Dad, you don't get it, I didn't do anything wrong.' 'But why'd you let him hit you?'"

Heaven paused as she looked at the suspended sheriff.

"I heard all about Adrian's murder and your trial," she said. "The word in this small town is your trial isn't going too well."

"Yepper. I would be lying if I swore it couldn't go better," Mac replied. "Just to let you know, it was a frame-up. I'm innocent."

"Sheriff, I'm going to say this once, since you're not my boss right now, and then I gotta get to work down at *The Hole*.

"*Why'd you let him hit you?*"

Heaven turned and walked quickly toward her rented house to change for work.

Mac stared after the young woman and thought about what she asked him.

#

Losing at Legalized Gambling

"What do you mean they aren't paying?" Mac asked his wife.

"They didn't say they *weren't* paying, they just said they weren't paying *right now*," Hannah explained.

The two were sitting in their living room after Mac got home. They had determined Hannah shouldn't attend the trial most days. Someone had to stay on top of the day-to-day chores at the ranch. For the long, drawn-out expert witnesses and non-critical testimonies, she would stay home and keep the home fires burning. Almost literally.

Three Days Earlier:

Hannah surprised Mac with how she had taken the news earlier of Carpenter's intended pursuit of the death penalty. He had expected fireworks or at least a silent fury. What he got was:

"Doesn't matter."

"What do you mean it doesn't matter? They could kill me," Mac asked.

"That's if they find you guilty, and they're not, because I won't let them," Hannah declared. "If I have to, I will say I did it."

"You will not! First of all, the prosecution will see it as an obvious attempt to protect me and will just get you a perjury charge. Second of all, phone and cell tower records will show you at home during the murder, giving you an alibi, whether you want one or not. And finally, I am not letting my wife take the rap for something neither of us did."

"Fine," Hannah hissed. Mac hated when she said 'fine'. It meant she was mad and would just find some other method to get her way. "Then you need to go speak with Pastor Allen. No husband of mine is getting the death penalty unless he is going to heaven. Just because you're a good man doesn't mean God's going to give you a pass. You need to believe and accept. Are you ready to do that, Jacob Andrew MacDowell?"

Mac needed to change the subject. "Have you heard we have a new deputy? Heaven Carlysle."

"Yes. The Church Ladies say she is quite a looker. And young. And stacked."

"Hey, I have an idea. Let's go talk to Pastor Allen," Mac said as he headed toward the door.

Present:

"What's the point of having insurance if it doesn't cover you when you need it?" This was not the first time they had this conversation. Mac looked at property insurance as legalized gambling with minimal risk to the insurance companies and Hannah saw it as a necessary evil. We stored the new tractor, hay baler, tiller, Gator, and most of their farming equipment in the barn. The structures themselves were worth as much as the farm equipment. A forty-horse stable is not cheap.

If the financial losses weren't enough, Naomi was having nightmares on a regular basis about the suffering of the horses and her beloved Bob. Try as she might, Hannah was unable to comfort her as she, too, was agonizing over the horrific event.

"They are saying the investigation into the fires is ongoing and they are investigating the cause of the arson. Until their investigation is complete, they are withholding payment of the claims," Hannah relayed her conversation with the insurance company. "It gets worse. This is the last straw for them. Between the tractor's destruction last year, the break-in, and now the fires, we needed to start looking for new insurance about two months ago. It doesn't help all those claims sit marked 'deliberate' and 'unsolved'."

Mac stood up from the loveseat sitting in front of the large living room window. Pacing across the floor, while Hannah sat patiently, he looked on the verge of exploding.

"I hate to admit it, but they're right," he stated.

"What?" Of the million things he could have said, Hannah would have never guessed that.

"I should have cleared all of these cases," Mac admitted. "I'm so busy taking care of everybody else's problems I haven't taken care of our own. Now add all this to this stupid trial and the lawsuit and Jeb's accident. There's just no excuse. I just always assume because we're innocent of any wrongdoing, it would all work out. I haven't taken any of this seriously enough. I've been a fool."

Hannah sat quietly in her rocker. Mac glared in her direction.

"What? You expect me to argue?" Hannah said with a smile. "If all these things happened to one of our neighbors, what would you do?"

"I would make things right," Mac told her. "I'm going to find out who's behind all these incidents and get strong, hard evidence. But you already knew that. This is exactly where you were leading me, isn't it?"

"I know it's not from the Bible, but it applies in this case: God helps those who help themselves."

"No, God help whoever's behind all this. And I hope *their* insurance is paid up."

#

Affordable Advice

"Your Honor?" Mac called down the street. After a day of sitting in court, he was happy to be walking down the Main Street of Mounton when he spotted Judge Brown.

"Mac!" the judge smiled, waved, and waited for Mac to catch up. "I'm sorry to hear about Jeb. If there's anything I can do, just let me know."

"I appreciate it Judge."

"You know you can call me Josiah. We're not in court now."

"I know, but I have a legal question and I need a lawyer's take, not a fishing buddy's."

"We can't discuss your case. It's out of my jurisdiction now but some yahoo might interpret it as ex partè."

"No, it's nothing like that. I want to hire you as a consultant for some generic legal advice about rules of evidence," Mac told the judge. "And inadmissibility."

"Well, if that's the case, we can step into my office annex," the judge said, pointing to *Ginny's Diner*. "I'm gonna have to charge you my standard fee…say…the cigar in your shirt pocket."

"I think you're overcharging me," Mac smiled as he handed the judge the cigar.

"Sue me."

Mac laughed as he held the door open for his friend and the bell inside jangled their entry. "After this cigar, I don't think I can afford a lawyer to do that."

#

"Let me make sure I have this right," Mac started. "There's a specific date both sides have to present each other with all the evidence they have collected? And then neither side can admit any other evidence into the trial, because both sides have to review it, vet it, and possibly call in expert testimony to dispute it? Hollister called this the discovery process."

"Yes, the discovery deadline is usually about thirty days before the trial."

"So, if a defendant found evidence to exonerate him during the trial, it would likely be deemed inadmissible because it showed up after the deadline?"

"Most likely. At least until both sides have had a chance to review it," the judge explained. "But for the most part, there are almost never any surprises in court. Both sides know what the other has in terms of evidence long before it goes to trial. The lawyers already know what the witnesses will say BEFORE they ask the questions.

"Per these Rules of Discovery, the same goes for witnesses," Judge Brown continued as he sipped from his coffee cup. "Both sides have to tell each other beforehand who they are calling as witnesses to let the opposing side can call their own rebuttal experts."

"Speaking of witnesses, I've recently heard the phrase 'leading the witness.' Can you tell me what that means?" Mac asked his friend as he took another bite of Ginny's apple pie.

"When an attorney attempts to prejudice the testimony by asking a question worded in a way to put words in the witness's mouth, the opposing counsel objects on the basis of leading the witness. The judge usually sustains the objection and instructs the jury to disregard the leading question, but in reality, they can't unhear something and it usually sticks with them."

"I could see where a bunch of leading questions could lead a guy to a lethal injection."

"Mac, let me tell you something I have learned in forty years of the legal profession," Judge Brown explained. "There are three kinds of lawyers: good, bad, or both. A bad one either doesn't know his ass from a hole in the ground, may or may not be corrupt, or probably got a D in law school. A good one knows every trick in the book, knows the law inside and out, and knows how to play the game. He colors just barely inside the lines. A lawyer that's *both* is most of the above. They're the ones you have to watch out for. On both sides of the table."

"So, when you were a DA, you were a good one?"

"Now *that's* a leading question."

#

Toys in the Attic

"Jacob MacDowell, what're you doing up there in that dusty attic?" Hannah asked her husband.

Mac struggled to climb down the hinged ladder leading up into the attic while he carried a large box.

"Seeing as how I've got some time on my hands, when you were telling Davis about the junk up there after the break-in, I thought there were a few things I either need to fix, use, or get rid of. Figured if I did it one box at a time, it might be easier to sort through. Some of this old stuff is Jeb's that…well, we just won't need anymore."

Hannah nodded sadly and peeked down inside the box.

"I'm not all that sure the Polaroid camera works or if the film is even good anymore after all this time. The toaster may just need a new cord. That old blender hadn't worked for years, just get rid of it, don't bother to try to fix it. Oh, Mac. Not the baby monitor!" Hannah moaned.

"Honey, I don't think with what happened to Jeb he will need it anytime soon and unless you're thinking about getting pregnant again at your age…"

"And what's *that* supposed to mean? Like you got another one in you!" Hannah feigned outrage. "No. I know we won't need the baby monitor now, but I don't think I'm ready just yet to let it go. Can we put it back?"

"Sure, babe. Let me put this box down in the den and I'll take the monitor back up today."

"Thank you. I know it's silly, but it reminds me of Beth and the baby."

"Consider it done," Mac said.

Using a tissue from her pocket, Hannah dabbed at her eyes, eyeing the box of Jeb's old stuff. "What are you going to do with the rest of that old junk?"

"I'll tinker around with it. Or just donate it or trash it. Some things I think I can find some use for."

#

Mac walked into the Mounton County Sheriff's office and Deputies Jesse Hendricks, Heaven Carlysle, and Davis Williams stopped and stared. Mac wore his usual Wranglers, old cowboy boots with pointy toes, his worn brown Stetson, and a black Polo instead of his usual tan sheriff's shirt.

"Boys."

"Uh…hey, Sheriff," Jesse Hendricks stammered. He wasn't sure how to avoid the topic of Jeb.

"Nice shirt," Davis commented, opting for humor to defuse the tension.

"What? You don't think this is *me*?" Mac asked with a smirk.

"Oh, yeah, it brings out the color of your eyes," Davis smiled. "Sheriff, I don't mean to be *that* guy, but didn't the council say you couldn't be sheriff until your trial was over." Davis Williams was the singular black deputy and one of the few men of color in Mounton county. He hated the phrase African-American. He had never been to Africa. Technically, he was a Baltimoreon-American. Mac and all the officers in Mounton treated him like a *man*, and that's just how he liked it. He had moved his family from D.C. to get them away from the crime and drugs of the capitol, as well as take a law enforcement job in the much slower-paced Mouton County.

"Relax, boys," Mac said. "I'm not here to work. The council was right to take me off the job until all the dust settles. I'm just here to take my mind off things. And you can call me Mac."

Jesse looked at Davis and back at Mac. "I don't think I can do that, sir. You were sheriff here before I was born and probably will be after I'm gone. I'll just stick with Sheriff."

"I got no problem with Mac," Davis smiled. "In fact, can I call you Big M?"

"Not twice," Mac said with a grin. "What's happening in Mounton County?"

"The usual. Couple of fender benders. A twelve-point buck ran afoul of a vehicle and has now changed its Facebook status to roadkill. A slight disagreement out at *Digger's Hole*, but Sonny handled it and Howdy called us in to haul away the unconscious offenders. Been a few more of those lately. Word out around there's no new sheriff in town."

"Sounds like you boys have it in hand," Mac said.

"Sheriff, I'd like to apologize about my testimony in court the other day..." Davis began.

"Water under the bridge. The prosecutor was doing his job of painting the worst possible picture and you just happen to be the brush du jour. I was there. He painted you into a corner no one could have gotten out of."

"I know. But I think I did more harm than good," Davis said.

"Well, it ain't over yet," Mac stated. "Speaking of which, you got any more on the break-in or homicide?"

Jesse shuffled some papers nervously. "I don't know if he's supposed to talk to you about it or not, sir."

"Davis, did anyone tell you not to?"

"Well, no."

"Is it against any law you are aware of?" Mac asked Jesse.

"No, sir."

"Then no worries," Mac smiled. "The town council told me I couldn't be sheriff until this gets straightened out. They never said a word about not hearing about your progress. Judge Gibson told me I can't discuss my case with the jury, the prosecutor, or himself during the trial, but never said a word about you boys talking to me. You've already testified, but no matter what, I'm not influencing your testimony in any way, I'm just listening. Besides, we're not talking about the Stemple murder case, we're talking about the break-in, robbery, and fire at my place. All that aside, if you're uncomfortable talking about it, I understand."

"Oh, hell no," Davis laughed. "I wouldn't give two craps what some pencil-necked prosecutor thought. The truth of the matter is, not much new has popped. You probably know more than I do since the FBI took over and you're hearing most of it in court. In fact, the FBI has taken us off the cases completely."

"Taken off or not in charge?" Mac asked. "And Jesse, you keep right on speaking up. It's okay to be respectful of your elders, but it don't mean they're always right. Question everything."

"Sheriff, we're real sorry about Jeb's accident. Is there anything we can do?" Jesse asked.

"Glad you asked. What're you fellas doing tomorrow night after Dawe comes on at 11:00?"

#

Supply the Pie

Mac left his rented truck at the station and walked down what everyone referred to as The Side Street to *Ginny's Diner*. There were really two streets in the town of Mounton. The town blocked off Main Street from vehicular traffic to allow for its reinvention as a tourist destination. The Side Street paralleled Main Street one block over and housed a few of the town's more "charismatic" businesses. The whole town stretched approximately four blocks long and was home to a biscuit over six hundred people. The walk down to *Ginny's* took only a few minutes and Mac strolled grimly through *his* town.

"Ginny. Shirley." Mac acknowledged both with a tip of his hat.

"Mac," Ginny replied.

Mac stopped halfway to his booth.

"For twenty-plus years, you've always called me *Sheriff* or occasionally *Constable* when I walked in. What's up?" Mac asked his friend.

"Heard you got fired."

Mac sat in his booth and took off his hat, setting the crown down on the table.

"Temporarily relieved of duty pending the outcome of the trial."

"You say potato, I say bowling shoes. How's the trial faring?" Ginny asked in a quiet, more serious voice as he sat at Mac's table, handing his friend a cup of coffee.

"Not as well as I would like it to."

"That's the word around town," Ginny said.

"The word?"

"I regret my usual sources have resorted to speculation and idle gossip in lieu of any real news or fact. However, it appears Ezekiel Thompson was not on the witness list, permitted into the courtroom, and has been providing regular updates on events," Ginny explained.

"Ah. Makes sense. Carpenter would not see Ezekiel as a credible witness since he wasn't at any of the main events. Both Hannah and I have seen him in court, plus he gave me his impressions the other day at *Darlene's*." Carpenter wasn't alone in underestimating Ezekiel. He wasn't as fast as he used to be, but he was still sharp as a tack and just as feisty. "Plus, we suspect he is a primary source of gossip with the community center women."

"Mac, I would sincerely like to apologize for my less-than-sterling performance on the witness stand," Ginny confessed. "And I am truly mournful regarding Jeb's mishap."

"Don't worry about it. There's a lot of all of it going around." Mac sipped from his mug.

As Ginny returned with his pie, Mac asked, "What are you doing tomorrow night after the diner closes?"

"To the best of my recollection, I have a scintillating rendezvous scheduled with Netflix."

"Good. I'm getting a few of the boys together about 11:00 p.m.," Mac said. "And oh yeah, and by the way, it's here."

"Nice of you to invite me," Ginny snarked.

"Hey, figure'd it be an easy commute for you. Plus, it will make it easy for you to supply the coffee and the pie."

#

At 10:15 p.m. Mac stepped quietly to the kitchen door of their house.

"Where do you think you are sneaking off to at this time of night?" Hannah asked from the kitchen entrance to the living room. Dressed in her robe, holding her Bible, and reading glasses perched on her head, it was clear she was reading when she heard him try to sneak out.

"I thought I would go out and get a piece of pie down at *Ginny's*," Mac confessed.

"Jacob MacDowell, you know good and well there is a fresh, uncut pie right there in the refrigerator."

"Did you bake it?" Mac asked his wife.

"You know I did."

"I'll tell Ginny you said *hey*," as he pushed his way quickly out the back door through the mud room.

It was 10:31 p.m. when Mac arrived at the diner. A leftover from his days as a Marine, Mac thought of fourteen minutes early as running late. When Mac relayed the story of his narrow escape from home to Ginny said, "You know you will pay for that tomorrow, right?"

"I'm not too worried. They stole her thirty-ought six."

Ginny was just finishing up cleaning the kitchen, his last customers had left twenty minutes earlier. Davis Williams and Heaven Carlysle were just sitting down when the other deputies arrived.

Jesse, Dawe, and Patricks showed up at five minutes after the hour and Jesse quickly took off his Mounton County Sheriff's cap as they sat at a nearby booth. Dawe had the night shift, but forwarded the 911 calls to his radio and cell.

"Any problems?" Mac asked Jesse.

"No, sir. I called my dad and told him I needed to work a little late to keep him from worrying. I hated lyin' to him, but I guess you're right. The fewer people who know about this, the better," Jesse said.

"Good man." Mac smiled at the boy.

"No Duncan?" Dawe asked.

"He volunteered to help keep an eye on some of bad actors," Mac replied.

Ginny pulled off his perpetually stained white apron, revealing a once black tee shirt with a flaming guitar designed like a flying saucer on it. He poured Davis and Mac coffee and Dawe and Jesse sweet iced teas.

"Before we get started, I have a question," Davis turned to the big diner owner. "Ginny, do you have any tee shirts made *after* the 1980s?"

Ginny looked down at his shirt and grinned. "Boston will live forever as one of the greatest debut bands of all time."

Jesse looked perplexed. "Who's Boston?"

Ginny snatched the sweet iced tea out of Jesse's hand. "No tea for you."

"I guess you're all wondering why I called you here tonight," Ginny said turning to the rest of the group. "Oh. Wait. I didn't."

"Fellas, you know about Jeb and why he isn't with us tonight," Mac started. "But that's not why we're here. I can't talk about that right now. However, I'll be straight with you, the trial isn't looking promising. The prosecution is just doing its job of trying to put what they think is a bad man in jail, but I know I didn't kill Adrian and it looks as if I am going to have to find out who did. And I need to do it quickly. If I don't find out who did it before this trial ends, we can color my goose cooked. I have a couple of days at most and the clock is ticking. I'd like your help. I've decided it's time to be a little more proactive. Instead of just sitting around hoping for the best and letting someone trash my life, I think maybe I should find out who is behind all this and return the favor."

"I'm in."

"You can count on me, sir."

"Me too."

"Forget it, I hope you hang."

Everyone stared at Ginny in raw shock.

"Just kiddin'. I wanted to see if you gentlemen were paying attention. More coffee, anyone?"

Mac shook his head at his friend's attempt at levity. He fully expected everyone assembled to want to help and had come to realize in the last year he wasn't the *sole* guardian of justice in Mounton.

"Now that *everyone's* on board," Mc said with a glance at Ginny's big toothy grin, "I have a few thoughts about some things we can look into."

For thirty minutes Mac relayed his thoughts about the various crimes to their friends.

In the end, he summarized, "Here's what we've got: Adrian's murder, the fire that dang near destroyed our farm and killed Hannah, the break-in there, Jeb's hit and run, and Howdy's beatdown."

"We can circumstantially tie the Stampers to some of that," Patricks said.

"I get the impression the Stampers don't have the brains to put together something this devious. There's a lot of questions left unanswered," Davis added, "And a lot of supposition. We need solid evidence of all this. There was one other person involved in the break-in, and from what you tell me, I can't see Mandy or Jasper with the skills to pull it off. Still looks like a professional from out of town."

"Yepper," Mac said. "I don't want to put any pressure on you boys, but if we don't lock down some hard evidence before the trial ends, I may be doing my investigating from down at Big Sandy. Or from somewhere much warmer. And then you would be left behind with an extremely pissed-off Hannah.

"Davis, since Jeb's...not here, you're in charge. I've talked it over with Dawe and though he has more seniority, we both agree you have more experience in the field. Get Bernie from *The New Texaco* to help cover some shifts. Also, you've got Heaven now. Besides your regular duties, could you follow up on the break-in? I think Jesse will be more than willing to help if I am not mistaken."

"I can follow up with the Lexington, Louisville, and Frankfort police departments Davis called. Maybe their detectives know which pawn shops are most likely to be fences," Dawe said. "I can then call those shops after I get off work in the mornings. The kids are at school and Patty-Jane will be at work. It's a lot of boring phone work, which may be exactly why the prosecution didn't do it. It might not lead to much, but we need to make sure it gets done."

"Speaking of which, I have a few things Patty-Jane could check on if she doesn't mind," Mac said. "Davis and I will take a drive out to the Stamper holler to have a look-see."

"We'll never get a warrant," Davis maintained. "We don't have enough, or actually any, evidence to get a judge to issue us a warrant to check out their place. How do we get in and see if they have your stuff?"

"I don't think we'll need one," Mac asserted.

"How do you plan to manage that?" Davis asked.

"One of the Stampers is going to invite us in," Mac said with a grin.

#

Relatively Family

"Sonny."

"Sheriff Mac," Sonny greeted the man. "Is Miz Hannah with you?"

"Not this time, Sonny," Mac replied. He shook the big man's hand just outside *The Digger's Hole*. Mac's hand looked like a child's in Sonny's grip.

"How's her and Naomi doin', after the far and Jeb and all?" Sonny asked.

"She's as good as she can be. I wanted to thank you for all your help," Mac said. "You probably saved both our lives the night of the fire. How're things going with you?"

"Uh, good, I guess."

"Sonny, what's the matter?" Mac asked. "Let's go inside and get some of Howdy's coffee and talk."

"That'd be okay, I guess. The bar won't be busy for a few hours and I gotta be at the door at 7:00 sharp. Mr. Howdy don't mind if I just hang around, but I tol' him I'd be at the door every night at 7:00."

"We'll make sure you're back out here."

After Howdy left a cup of coffee and sweet tea at their table, he went back to cleaning the bar in preparation for the night's business. The bar was open, but empty at the moment. Since Sonny had started and tamed the rougher trade by his mere presence, the local watering hole had become quite the night spot in the county. It didn't hurt the next two closest counties were dry.

"What's the matter, son?" Mac asked the big man. Sonny rivaled

Ginny in size and strength, but the colossus had crapped out in the genetic dice game of life, born both mildly retarded and a Stamper. Not that there's much of a difference.

"Sheriff Mac, you ever torn between the right thing to do and keeping your family happy?" Sonny asked.

Mac thought about Sonny's family and then his own. He tried to think back to any time he had done the right thing versus what Hannah wanted. Her ideas on falsely taking the blame for Adrian's murder came to mind.

"Well, I'll tell you, Sonny," Mac started, "doing the right thing might not always make your family happy, but it is usually the best for them in the long run."

"Not shore I unnerstant, Sheriff Mac."

"Yeah, me neither," Mac smiled. "Let's try this. A good man should always do the right thing. The right thing might not always make his family *happy*, but it is probably the best thing for them. Family and friends are some of the most important things in the world. Hannah and I kind of think of you as a little like family."

"You do?"

"Yeah, Sonny. You're kind of like the nephew we never had."

"Dang, Sheriff Mac. I ain't never been anyone's nephew before."

"Well, I've met your family," Mac smiled again. "You're better off."

Sonny sat and stared at the banged-up wooden table for a few moments. Then his eyes moved up to the red knobby, oval candle jar in the middle, and finally to Mac's face.

"Sheriff Mac, there's sumpin I have to tell ya," Sonny said in a deep, yet child-like, voice.

Sonny proceeded to relay to Mac the highlights of his argument with his brothers at this actual table. He told Mac of someone hiring the brothers to break into Mac's house. Mac asked a few questions for clarification. Howdy edged up to the table.

"Tis all true, Sheriff," the leprechaun-esque bartender confirmed. The swelling from his eye had gone down and the remaining evidence of his mugging was some purplish bruises on his face. "I overheard the tail end of it. Them brothers of his were trying pretty hard to get him to come back and help them with some mischief. I din't know the whole story or I'd called you to warn you. When they raised their voices and threatened me, Sonny here, suggested they leave. I heard later what happened to your house and farm. I've got no proof, but I wouldn't be a bit surprised if it were those two hooligans that way-laid me the other night."

Mac considered the words of both men.

"Sonny, you know how we talked about doing the right thing?" Mac asked. "How would you like to show me your house?"

"Will I be back at the front door by 7:00?"

#

We Don't Need No Steenken Warrants

Mac, Davis, and Sonny got out of the newer of the two county's white patrol SUVs. When Sonny climbed out of the vehicle, Mac heard the shocks and springs groan lightly with relief. As the three men walked toward the Stamper shack, Spencer came bounding out to intercept them. Right behind him, Syrus put his hand on his younger brother's shoulder to restrain him.

"Howdy, Sheriff, good to see ya agin—wait, you ain't sheriff now, are ya?" Syrus asked with a smile. "Hey, by the way, where's your boy, De-pew-tee Jeb?" Syrus jabbed at Mac, deliberately ignoring Sonny's presence. Mac gritted his teeth and did not respond to Syrus's remark. Davis's hand edged toward his sidearm.

"Syrus," Davis started, "we're here to take a look around. Please step aside."

"Hold on there, Marshall Dillon," Spencer drawled. "I ain't no Perry Mason, but I reckon you need a warrant to search a person's house."

"You're right." Mac looked at the middle Stamper. "You *ain't no* Perry Mason. According to the county records, your Pa, God rest his larcenous soul, left all his property and estate to all of his sons, in equal shares. Sonny invited us in to look around. With the owner's permission, we don't need a warrant."

"Sonny—he cain't do that! He ain't a Stamper no more," Syrus sputtered. "We disowned him."

"Well, this deed lists his name as one of the owners of this…*domicile*," Mac said, holding several photocopies. "I'm looking right at a copy of his state issued ID and his last name is Stamper. I guess when you disowned him, you must have neglected to take his name off the deed. Doesn't matter anyway. As you said, I am not a sheriff today. I don't need a warrant. By the way, you owe Sonny for his share of the profits from the last three quarters of Stamper's Paint Thinner."

"Yeah, that's right. You ain't no sheriff," Spencer twanged, pointing at Mac. "We don't gotta let you in."

"Again, you're right, you don't," Davis said. "But he will," pointing his thumb to Sonny. "As part owner, the law entitles him to have anyone he wants in his house, no matter how nasty it may be."

Davis started to walk past Syrus when Spencer stepped in front of them.

"Well, listen here, Deputy Spook, Sonny is purely a third owner," Spencer said. "Didja think of that? Means you get to see only a third of the house!"

Davis shook his head. "Yeah Spence, *that's* how it works. Tell you what, we won't look at anything hidden under your law degree."

As Mac and Davis moved toward the screen door of the shack, Sonny stayed behind.

"Sheriff Mac, if'n you don't mind, I'd prefer to stay with the car." Sonny seemed to shrink away from Syrus's stare, despite the size differential.

"Sonny," Mac told his friend, "It would probably be better if you came with us." As he looked hard at Syrus and Spencer, he said, "There won't be any problem."

"If you say so."

The five men crowded into the shack. The inside overflowed with garbage and looked decidedly more disastrous than the outside, if such a thing could be possible. Davis opened a few doors to reveal closets piled high with dirty clothes and more trash. Syrus and Spence didn't seem to notice the stench. Mac strolled around the small rooms, his hands in his pockets. Sonny stood in the corner while Syrus and Spence glared viciously at him. When Davis found two double-barreled shotguns, and after breaching them and unloading them, replaced them back in the closet. "Not Hannah's."

"Where is it?" Mac asked Syrus.

"Uh...where is what?" Syrus said.

"The still."

"Sheriff—Mister, you knowed damned well, making 'shine ain't legal," Syrus said.

"Okay," Mac smiled. "I'd like to see the manufacturing devices used to produce Stamper's Paint Thinner."

"Oh. That. I guess it'd be okay."

"You sure you don't want to check with your attorney?" Davis asked tilting his head toward Spencer.

Syrus led them out the back door to a wooden shed which barely qualified as a lean-to. Inside the shed were four large copper kettle boilers, a couple of old folding lawn chairs, and crates of empty Mason jars. An extension cord led from the roof of the shack to the roof of the shed. A single lightbulb with a pull cord hung from the ceiling of the shed. Incongruous with the rest of the hovel, a large, flat-screen TV hung on the wall.

"Still shipping in Mason jars?" Mac asked.

"Them's what's left over from the good ole days," Syrus said.

Syrus and Spencer stood at the door of the shed as the three others started back toward the SUV.

"Hey, Sonny," Syrus called out. "Be sure to say hey to that barkeep!"

After looking over the property, Mac, Davis, and Sonny climbed back into the SUV and headed back toward *The Digger's Hole* to get Sonny back in time for work.

"All those Mason jars and with Adrian no longer overseeing them, it wouldn't take much of a leap to guess your brothers were about to go back into the 'shine business," Davis said.

Sonny sat quietly.

"I didn't expect to see the laptop," Mac said, mostly to himself. "That'd require one of those fools to know how to use it. Thought maybe we find Hannah's guns. Seems about their speed. I guess the third man probably insisted they give them up. I know I wouldn't trust them with them. Sonny, when you lived there, did your brothers have a TV in the shed?"

Sonny shook his head.

Mac worried about how quiet Sonny had become. For Mac, this could be considered babbling. He was talking, mostly to entice some conversation out of the big man.

"Did you notice the cut coaxial cable hanging down from behind the set? I would bet if we checked, it would match the cut cable at your house," Davis said.

Sonny stared at the passing landscape.

Mac looked out the windshield. "Not really a surprise, as far as I know, there's no cable service out in the holler. Did you see a satellite dish?"

Sonny didn't speak all the back to *Digger's Hole*.

#

Burying The Lede Under Lard

Mac and Davis ate dinner at *Ginny's* and discussed their progress looking into some of the details of the case. Ginny walked up to refill Mac's coffee and Davis's sweet tea.

"How was supper, boys?" Ginny asked.

"Would it matter if we said horrible?" Davis replied.

"Do you really want to piss off the guy preparing your food?"

"Good point. It was *awesome*!" Davis said, his dark brown face splitting with a grin.

"Guaranteed or your money back," Ginny grinned.

"I didn't think the MacDowells paid for meals here," Davis smiled.

"Really? I hadn't noticed. By the way, when did you change your last name to MacDowell? You don't look like family."

"I'm just happy to finish a whole plate without it being jerked out from under me," Mac said, thinking of how many partial meals Hannah had aborted.

"You inevitably have room for pie," Ginny noted.

"Just *your* pie, Ginny," Mac laughed.

"Now, you're just flattering me. No matter how much you cajole, you cannot get into my pants."

"As tight as those jeans look," Davis smirked, "I don't know how *you* got into them."

"Lard is just not for cooking, Deputy." Ginny asked, "By the way, are you two still interested in any non-locals in the area?"

"Yeah, you seen any?" Davis stopped eating to look at the big diner owner.

"There's this one guy, blows through here on occasion. Doesn't investigate any of the new tourist traps, and partakes of some breakfast, lunch, and occasionally dinner. Keeps to himself, no visible means of income, gray van out of Cincinnati, and has a certain *look*."

"Sounds promising," Mac said as he pushed his empty plate away. "You got a description to go with said *look*?"

"Long, brownish-blond curly mane, late twenties, quite tan, six-four or so, relatively athletic build, designer beard stubble, slightly above average looking."

"Could be a thousand guys," Davis complained.

"Or…you could look right over there. He's sitting in booth two."

"WHAT? Why didn't you lead with that? Instead of fishing for compliments and talking about money-back guarantees and lard in your jeans, you could have pointed to the guy we are looking for all this time?" Davis complained as he tried to stand just enough in the booth seat to see over the divider.

"Relax, Elliot Ness," Ginny said as he pushed Davis back down into his seat. "He's not even close to finishing his dinner."

Mac wiped his mouth with the paper napkin that was wrapped around his silverware. "Let's let him finish his meal and speak with him outside. We don't know if he had anything to do with the shooting of Adrian or Jeb's accident, but better to not endanger Ginny's customers if we can help it. They're taking a big enough risk just eating here."

"Sir, can we speak with you for a minute?" Davis asked as they followed the man leaving the diner.

"Eh…what about?" the man said opening the driver's door of his van.

"We'd like to speak with you for a moment if it's okay," Davis spoke up. He was wearing a Mounton County standard deputy shirt, jeans, and a Mounton County Sheriff's cap. He had a John Brown belt on with his nine-millimeter holstered there. And his badge.

Mac was wearing his trademark Wrangler jeans, his old cowboy boots, his brown Stetson, and a black polo shirt as he walked next to Davis. The closest thing he had to a badge was his rodeo-style buckle which gleamed in the midday sun.

The man at the car turned toward them and partially closed the door. His pressed, black slacks, black long-sleeved dress shirt, buttoned at the neck, and dazzling white tennis shoes screamed out non-local.

"How can I help you, gentlemen?"

"First, if you don't mind, if you have a minute, we would like to ask you for some ID," Davis asked with his hand out.

"Right after you tell me what this is all about."

"We're looking into a recent break-in and some other events and would like to talk to you about them."

"And you think I had something to do with all that?"

"Not until we see your ID," Davis said, with his hand still out. Mac stood behind the deputy to one side, letting him take the lead. The longer the man took to produce the ID and the more resistant he was to the idea, the more Mac edged to the side and closer. Since he wasn't wearing a sidearm, if things went bad, he would need to physically tackle the man.

"I don't think so, Barney. Unless this turned into 1940s Germany and you have probable cause, you can't just go around demanding someone's papers," the man stared at Mac. "You're not a cop, are you?"

"Not at the moment," Mac said.

"Right. I know you. I read about you in the paper. You're the sheriff who got suspended while he's on trial for murder." Looking at Davis's name tag on his uniform shirt. "Based on your pigmentation and because your name tag says Williams, I'm guessing you're not his son. Where *IS* your son, Mr. MacDowell?"

"He's not here Mr...?"

"Nice try. Well, when you see him, say hi for me," Grogan smirked. "By the way, your minute is up."

"Jeb's not here right now, but I am. Say cheese!" Davis said as he quickly snapped a picture of the man with his iPhone when Grogan turned toward him. "Can we ask what you are doing in Mounton?"

"Do you question all the tourists who comes into town? I could see where it would impact tourism. And…I didn't give you permission to take my photo."

"I didn't ask for it. No, sir. We do not question every tourist in town. We just have some evidence indicating someone unknown to us was at the scene of a crime and we are checking out strangers," Davis replied.

"So, this is just a random questioning, huh? Should I call my lawyer, or maybe a civil rights attorney? *You* probably know a good one."

"No, sir. We apologize for any inconvenience. Please have a nice day," Mac uncharacteristically jumped in with a tip of his hat as he motioned Davis toward the county SUV.

"No problems, Sheriff. Oh, wait. I forgot. You're not a sheriff anymore, are you?"

"Noper."

Both Mac and Davis watched as the man drove off.

"Nothing shady about *that* guy," Davis said staring after the car. "What a douche."

"Mommy van with Cincinnati plates. Record this number on your phone before I forget it. You're gonna want to look up the registration. Compare your photo to the FBI bolo. I have a feeling we just spoke to Mr. Grogan."

"You think there's something fishy about him, too?" Davis asked.

"No crime in wearing black on black, a deliberately stubbled beard, and a ponytail if you're in New York. If you're in Mounton, that's practically probable cause.

#

Dishes & Deities

The next night, Hannah was putting away the dinner dishes as Mac finished drying the last of the plates. Naomi had gone up to her room to read. She was missing her father and was not as talkative as she usually was.

"How was court today?" Hannah asked.

"About the same," Mac replied as he dried his hands with a dish towel.

"That bad, huh?"

"Well, let's just say unless Hollister steps up his game, you will either be visiting me down at Big Sandy or buying me flowers each week," Mac said with a wry smile.

"Don't be ridiculous. Do you know how much flowers cost these days? Besides, they'd just rot and die on a grave site. A plastic bouquet is much more sensible. Plus, it would be more like a every couple of months or three. With the money from your will, I could probably swing some silk flowers occasionally. Just the cheap ones though."

"I'm glad you find this funny, Mrs. Dillinger," Mac said. The two were carrying cups of coffee into the living room. Before speaking again, Hannah glanced up the stairs to make sure Naomi wasn't listening.

"Heard something interesting today. Seems you were molesting Mandy Stemple when she babysat Naomi back in the day."

"I heard that, too. Seems like her brother wasn't man enough to handle the job," Mac said, sipping his coffee. "Where did you hear it?

Mrs. Fisher?"

"Not just her. It was the topic of conversation before and after bible study. The room got unusually silent when I came in, but three different women couldn't wait to let me know privately after the meeting. I got to act surprised two times."

"I wouldn't worry about it," Mac assured. "Idle gossip has a tendency to fade away."

"Jacob, you might want to think about taking this a little more seriously," Hannah cautioned. "If it was at the Church Ladies' Meeting, it is all over town by now. With what happened to poor Adrian, people may start believing it."

"Baby, with what happened to Adrian, the trial, you in the fire, the insurance, the mortgage, and…Jeb's accident, God wouldn't dump one more thing on me."

"Don't presume to know God's will, Jacob Andrew MacDowell. 'He will not let you be tempted beyond your ability, but with the temptation, He will provide the way of escape, that you may be able to endure it.' Corinthians 10:13, if you want to look it up."

"He may provide a way of escape, but I sure don't see it right now," Mac said. "Duncan and Ginny have given me a stern talking to, but it may take more than encouragement to find our way out of all this."

"'We were under great pressure, far beyond our ability to endure, so that we despaired of life itself. Indeed, we felt we had received the sentence of death. But this happened that we might not rely on ourselves but on God.' 2nd Corinthians 1. Don't you worry honey, God may give you more than you can bear, but that's to make you rely on Him to get you out of it."

"Well, I hope He hurries up. My trial is going to end in a day or two and if something doesn't change, I am looking at a short stay and a long sleep. I do have a question, though. How come the times we talk about things looking bad, everything with you always seems to begin and end with God?"

"Because it really does, silly."

#

Two Bits & A Shave

Mark Grogan looked at himself in the rearview mirror of the van he was driving. As always, he liked what he saw, but living out here in the sticks had thrown him off his grooming game. Time to do something about that.

Mark had asked his waitress, Peggy, at the diner what the hair styling options were here in Mounton. After giggling a bit, Peggy had said, "Mister, I hate to break it to ya, but there's just one option, *Darlene's Beauty Emporium/Barbershop/Tanning Salon*. It's right down on The Side Street about a quarter of a mile from here. You can't miss it. It has a barber pole spinning outside."

Tanning salon too? This could be my lucky day.

"Right down the road toward town, huh?" Grogan asked as he left a big tip.

"Yessir. About a hundred yards from the sheriff's office. If you go past the station, you went too far."

"Got it. I won't go past the sheriff's office."

#

Once he finished his little chat with the former sheriff and his deputy outside the diner, Grogan smiled to himself. *They got nothing. Let's have a little fun with this.*

He drove straight down to *Darlene's* and parked in front. He could see the sheriff's station from where he parked and if they looked, they could certainly see his van parked outside the shop. *Might as well rub their noses in it some.*

The door jangled as Mark walked in. Several customers sat in chairs in the larger middle room in front of mirrors. All eyes turned toward the tall tan man as he stepped into the shop.

"Welcome to *Darlene's*," An enormously fat woman who couldn't possibly stand more than five-three waddled up to him. Mark towered over her. "I'm Darlene. I own this fine establishment. What can I do you for?"

"I'm hoping you can help me," Mark said. "I'd like my hair trimmed a tad just a little and my beard cleaned up. I like it to keep it stubbly, but not a full, thick beard. I feel like it's getting a little shaggier than I like. Can you help me out?"

"Sure can," Darlene smiled. She looked at his beard and couldn't discern any shagginess, but if he wanted to be persnickety about his face, who was she to not charge him for it? "Just let me get this station cleaned up and we can get you going."

"I'm see from the sign outside you have tanning booths. I moved from Florida not long ago and my tan is fading just a bit. Possible I could use one of your booths while you clean up?"

"Actually, you can use ALL our booths since we have just the one," Darlene laughed in her gravelly voice. The man already had the most tanned face in Mounton. *Persnickety and vain.* "Come on back and I'll show you where it is. It's a relatively brand-new machine and all the bulbs work. It would surprise you how little call we get for a tanning booth in Mounton."

As Darlene led the stranger back to the tanning room, she tried to remember where her book on beard grooming was. She had trimmed a lot of beards, most recently Sonny's, but no one ever asked her to do a stubble cut on one.

Mark emerged from the tanning room fifteen minutes later with a deeper tan. A half-hour later, he left the salon with his beard trimmed perfectly and just the minimum of his curly blondish-brown hair cut. The ponytail remained untouched.

#

The next evening, the MacDowell family sat at their dining table for their traditional Thursday night dinner. When Beth was alive, it was mandatory Jeb and his family come to have dinner at his parents on Thursday night. It was the one school night of the week the MacDowells allowed Naomi to stay up a little later. After Jeb and Naomi moved in, Hannah thought it was important to keep the weekly tradition. After all, it was her rule to begin with. With Jeb and Beth's seats empty, it didn't feel the same.

"I'm telling you, Hannah, we know who this guy is, but we sure as heck can't find him," Mac said between forkfuls of food. "If we could locate him, we could pick him up."

"Who are you looking for?" Hannah asked as she put some potatoes on Naomi's plate.

"This guy Grogan," her husband replied. "We don't know much about him other than his rap sheet, but he's going by the name Calhoun."

"Tall? Tan? Blondish-brown hair? Ponytail?" Hannah asked.

"Yeah. How did you know?" Mac stopped eating to stare at his wife.

"He came into *Darlene's* yesterday. He wanted to get his beard groomed and use the tanning booth. Darlene had never seen him before and he never asked about the prices of anything. She figured he was from some big city. He said he hailed from Florida. Paid in cash and didn't blink an eye when she innocently charged him the out-of-town rates."

"Darlene has out-of-town rates?" Mac asked.

"That's your takeaway? Oh yeah. You don't think she charges the tourists the same price she charges us, do you? Anyway, from what I gathered in bible study group last night, he's not married. At least he wasn't wearing a ring and Gladys Stearns practically swooned talking about him. Mable Barnes, you know, the tenor in the choir, she knows a bit about him. He's driving a silver van and staying at the B&B Mable manages over off of Highway 55. The old Barbour place, out by the woods."

"God bless those Church Ladies," Mac said as he started to rise from the table. "It's like the Internet but with coffee cake."

#

Sibling Rivalry

It was just past nightfall in Stamper's holler. Spencer was shutting down the stills. They wouldn't have to watch the stills overnight. Syrus carried a case of filled Mason jars to their rusted-out pickup truck. The moonlight filtered through the leaves and gave everything a leopard-like dappling. Syrus turned to see his youngest brother as Sonny stepped from the shadows.

"Sonny! I knew you wouldn't desert yore kin..." Syrus began, but the look on Sonny's face was like storm clouds about to give birth to a tornado. Syrus edged back toward the truck bed and reached back with one arm while never taking his eyes away from his youngest brother. "Spence, get over here. Sonny's come back home."

As Sonny closed on his oldest brother, Syrus pulled a wooden bat from the bed of the truck and swung it full force at Sonny's head.

Sonny caught the bat mid-swing in the palm of his hand.

Jerking the bat away from Syrus's grip, he rammed the wooden club like a piston, catching Syrus in the face, knocking him several feet back and off his feet near the front tire of the truck.

Spencer was heading in their direction and seeing the commotion, screamed as he charged his younger brother. Without missing a beat, Sonny backhanded his middle brother with the bat hard enough to send him flying.

The two brothers lay underneath the pickup as images flashed through Sonny's mind: the robbery of Sheriff Mac and Miz Hannah's house; the horrible things done to Little Miz Naomi's room; a far dang-near killt Miz Hannah and did kill a bunch of innocent horseys, including Little Miz Naomi's Bob; the way Mr. Howdy looked all purple and broken after they beat him; what they said about Peggy. HIS Peggy.

With a roar, the giant of a man screamed out:

"You. Will. Never. Go. Near. Sheriff. Mac. Or. His. Family. Agin."

Punctuating each word with a devastating slam of the bat, alternating between the two brothers.

"Never. Talk. About. Her. Agin."

Over and over the bat swung down and struck the two brothers. Syrus tried to shield his head as much as possible by shimmying under the truck, all the while pushing his brother Spencer closer to Sonny with his feet. His vision was fading to black around the edges, but he could still see…there was no mercy in Sonny's face. Hell, there was barely anything human. For the first time in his life, including when their Pa beat them senseless as young'uns, Syrus Stamper feared for his life.

"If'n I see you in Mounton agin…" Sonny panted as he loomed above his two beaten and broken brothers, grabbing the bloody bat with a hand at each end. "Ahhhh!" he roared as he snapped the bat in his hands like a twig in winter. Sonny threw the two bat shards to the ground, disgusted with himself and his brothers.

As he turned away, he mumbled, "Oh, yeah, Mr. Howdy says 'hey' back."

#

Photos & Phone Calls

"What the hell?" Grogan snapped to no one.

He was holding an envelope with the name Mark Calhoun printed on the front. The envelope had been slid under his door at the B&B. No return address. No postmark. Just a plain white number 10 envelope with one of his aliases typed on the front. Someone must have slipped it under there quite early in the morning. Grogan would have seen it if it had been there.

Without hesitation, he ripped open the flap. Inside were two Polaroid pictures. One photo depicted an antinque Colt Peacemaker laying on a gray plastic shopping bag and the other of his van parked out in front of the motel out on Route 44.

Those damned kids! The sheriff couldn't do it, his gun's been locked in evidence since his arrest. The girl must have taken the picture of the van when I delivered the gun back to her brother. They were the two who knew about my involvement in any of this. This is some kind of half-ass blackmail attempt.

#

At the same time, someone taped a sealed envelope to the door frame of a room at *The Motel 44*. The outside of the envelope displayed no names, but inside two Polaroid snapshots awaited discovery. One snapshot was of a Colt revolver resting on a *Piggly Wiggly* plastic shopping bag and the other was a photo of the bright yellow Dodge Challenger parked outside the motel room. The occupants of the room wouldn't awaken or find the envelope for several hours.

#

A third envelope arrived in the mail at Big Sandy Correctional Institute a day prior and addressed to a specific inmate. The envelope suffered through the usual inspections of X-rays, a drug-sniffing dog, and after all the precautions, opened for a gloved personal inspection. After documenting the contents, deeming it non-contraband, the corrections officers resealed the envelope and delivered to the inmate on the address. The envelope contained Polaroid snapshots of a Colt Peacemaker revolver placed on what looked to be a gray plastic shopping bag and a photo of a bright yellow Dodge Challenger.

The inmate immediately demanded to call his attorney and after several hours they allowed him access to a phone. The attorney's receptionist told him of his unavailability and she did not expect him until late in the day. Slamming the phone into its cradle earned him a warning glance from one of the guards. There was no way they would allow him to use a phone again today.

His thoughts bounced between blackmail, betrayal, warnings, and murder, all the way back to his cell and for the rest of the day.

#

Far From Evidence

Mac sat through the testimony of the ballistics reports the prosecution's office put on the stand, but his mind was on other things. His attorney had provided him with a legal pad to write notes on, but Mac was using it to make a to-do list and a list of questions. There was nothing he could do to impact Carpenter's attack on him, but his attorney convinced him he should attend his own murder trial. Mac was glad Hollister hadn't asked if he had better things to do.

On the first break, Mac called the fire chief in Lexington.

"Jerry, it's Jacob MacDowell."

"Mac! I was just going over some of the paperwork about your fires. What can I do ya for?" Jerry Siegel had been the Lexington fire chief for the last ten years, having worked his way up the ranks. He and Mac knew each other for decades as Mac served on the volunteer fire department and was usually the first on the scene for anything in Mounton County. Mounton didn't have a fire investigation team. Jerry and his group investigated any suspicious fires.

"Actually, I was calling about the fires at the house. Any news?"

"Well, no suspects if that's what you're asking," Jerry explained. "The insurance company guy, Stotts, has been blowing up my phone for some results. I can tell you what I told him. It's actually what the initial investigator suspected. It's a weird one. Obviously, persons unknown started the fires and they were not a natural event like lightning. However, they used two different types of accelerants. Most arsonists have a signature and always start the fires the exact same way. One of the same guys who torched your place may have started Jeb's truck fire, but I doubt it. The truck fire was also started by gasoline but splashed hurriedly and hastily. The height of the truck upside down means the arsonist was tall in order to spread the gas as far as he did, whereas the barn and stable were all low to the ground. Different heights, different splash patterns. I would say it's different guys, but none of it is admissible in court. Just my impressions."

"You said *they* and *persons*," Mac stated.

"Yeah, this is definitely two different guys at least, maybe three. The building fires started simultaneously, which would have been tough for one person with the buildings so far apart. The arsonists started the stable fire with gasoline and sloshed it all over the sides of the buildings, including the aluminum door. They ignited the barn fire with an alcohol-based accelerant. Moonshine to be specific."

"Moonshine?" Mac asked. "How can you tell?"

"Well, it fit all the chemical profiles, but the alcohol content was too high. Then there were the containers," Jerry explained. "We found broken Mason jars outside the barn."

#

Picking Up the Trash

With the Mason jars and moonshine used as an accelerant at the MacDowell fire, Mac and Davis seeing the MacDowell's stolen TV, and Sonny's statement the brothers tried to recruit him to break into the MacDowells' house, it didn't take much urging to get Judge Brown to issue search and arrest warrants for the two elder Stamper brothers. The enforcement team decided they would roll on it about midnight to possibly catch the Stampers sleeping.

Deputies Dawe, Carlysle, and Patricks silently cruised up behind two KSP patrol units to the Stamper shack.

"Looks like their truck parked there," Dawe commented. "Carlysle, get out your cell phone and video everything. The KSP boys all have body cams, but we don't, and you never know how one of these things will go down when it comes to the Stampers. Without Sonny in their corner, they may come in as meek as lambs, or fight like cornered rats."

The two men got out, with Carlysle videoing from her phone, but they never got past the rusted-out pickup, where the four KSP troopers stood. One look at the scene told why.

"I guess we can rule out the trapped-like-rats scenario," Patricks said.

Lying in a pool of blood and all but beaten beyond recognition were Syrus and Spencer Stamper.

As one of the KSP troopers called for ambulances, the lead trooper walked over to Dawe. "How do you want to handle this?"

"Tape it off. This is a crime scene. You guys collect the blood, DNA, and trace evidence. We'll take the bat and see if there are any latents on it. Hopefully, these two will live to tell us who did this," Dawe said.

After the KSP troopers set about working the scene, Patricks turned toward Dawe.

"Okay, I'll bite. Why take the bat? Why not let them do *all* the evidentiary work?"

"Two reasons," Dawe replied. "One, I think I might know who did this…and two, that's Jeb's bat. It was on the break-in report. You can see his initials carved into it, under the blood. He carved them there when he was twelve."

"But Jeb—" Patricks started.

"I know. Let's get the bat and get those prints," Dawe said. "And call Mac."

Thirty-one hours later, the lead KSP trooper met Dawe and Patricks at Syrus Stamper's hospital room to take a statement. A junior KSP trooper stood guard outside the room. The doctor in charge of his case knew the situation and had been weaning him off painkillers for the last six hours. Dawe and Patricks entered with the senior trooper and a file folder. Patricks started videotaping as they entered the room.

"Syrus?"

"He can't speak. We had to wire his jaw shut," his attending physician announced. "His brother hasn't regained consciousness yet." Patricks had never seen so many casts on one person.

"What's the extent of their injuries?" Dawe asked the doctor as he pulled him to the side.

"It would be easier to tell you what wasn't broken," the doctor said. "The internal bleeding stopped, but there are indications of some organ damage. Broken jaw, multiple fractures, contusions, nerve damage, the list goes on and on."

"You took him off the pain meds, right? Is he competent enough to give straight answers to any questions?"

"I guess, but I don't know how, if he can't talk?" the doctor said.

"Syrus? It's Deputy Joseph Dawe. We need to ask you some questions. Do you feel like the pain or drugs are affecting your ability to answer them?"

He gently shook his head no. Syrus's eye opened and focused on Dawe. One eye was filled with blood from the beating; the other swollen shut.

"I need you to sign this waiver saying you understand you are waiving the right to an attorney and you are not currently medicated."

Syrus was frantic to sign the paper. Once signed, Dawe handed him a piece of paper and a pencil.

"Here's some paper. Just point to yes or no.

Syrus scribbled on the paper with his one good hand.

"HURRY PAIN NEED DRUGS."

"Do you know who did this to you?"

A long hesitation. **"NO."**

Patricks kept the phone aimed at Syrus and his paper, but he and Dawe shared a look.

"Maybe this is a mistake," Patricks said. He knew the clock was running out on Mac. If they didn't find some evidence in the next day or so, the sheriff's next mailing address would be Big Sandy.

"NO! CONFESHUN."

"To what?"

"EVERTHING! STARTIN FAR BARTINDER ROBBERY TRACTER OXY."

"Oh, man," Patricks whispered.

"Okay, Doc. Give me a half hour to get in here with a court reporter, some real video equipment, and then you can give him whatever drugs he needs to ease the pain."

Patricks and Dawe walked back to their cruiser an hour and a half later.

"Okay. This month is shaping up to be in the Guinness Book of

Weird-Ass Shit," Patricks said. "Syrus seemed beyond eager to confess to everything he did since he was ten. He was actually frantic."

"Being free terrified him more than spending a lot of time in prison hospitals," Dawe pointed out as he thought it over.

"Any reason you didn't mention to Trooper America back there we found Sonny Stamper's latents all over Jeb's bat?"

"If Syrus didn't want to give Sonny up for the beating, who am I to argue?" Dawe asked softly. "My guess is, Syrus tried to teach Sonny one of their daddy's lessons with Jeb's stolen baseball bat and Sonny objected. Sonny's had enough bad breaks without taking a hit for giving his two idiot brothers a small taste of what they deserve. This dumbass just confessed to starting the MacDowell fire, almost killing Hannah. And when it gets right down to it, with all the blood at the scene, and here at the hospital, I'm willing to bet the DNA results will show it was Syrus and Spencer who pissed and defecated all over Naomi's room. They're just lucky Sonny got to them before Mac did. Or worse, Hannah."

"What if Spencer doesn't wake up?" Patricks asked.

"It'll save us the energy of not having to chase him down," Dawe said. "And Patricks? Keep this quiet. At least for the time being."

"Even from the sheriff?"

"Yes, but I was actually thinking of Hannah. A prison, a hospital, or a coma won't help those boys if she finds out they did Naomi's room."

#

Ghost, Busters & Break Downs

Markus was driving out to *Motel 44* to have a few choice words with his partners. *Nobody blackmails Markus Grogan.* He had swapped out the silver van he had used to ram Jeb's truck with an identical one with no signs of impact. He went as far as to swap the plates. Unless someone got a chance to check out the VIN number, there was no way to connect him to the wreck.

Just as Grogan was passing the spot near the lake where he had set fire to the MacDowell kid's truck, he glanced out the passenger window and saw a man standing at the edge of the woods just beyond the ditch. He had driven past in a hurry but now brought the van to stop a hundred yards past where he had seen him. It was a man in a tan uniform shirt and blue jeans, wearing a baseball cap. *Is he wearing a badge?* The man was looking directly at Grogan's van. Maybe it was an investigator looking into the wreck. Curiosity tore at Grogan. Between the snapshots under his door and his orders to stay in town, the stress was eating him alive. With a quick decision, he pulled the gearshift into reverse and with his backup lights glaring white in the daylight, he roared the van back to where the man was standing. Except there was no one there now. Markus could merely see blackened grass. This was the exact spot where he had torched the kids truck.

Markus looked around nervously. It had been too dark under the cap in the noonday sun to see the face clearly, but he could swear it had been Jeb MacDowell standing there.

The problem was: according to the word around town, Jeb didn't survive his injuries from the wreck.

#

This ghost thing rattled Grogan. He decided a confrontation at the motel would not be such a good idea considering he had just seen a dead man at the side of the road. This job was starting to get more than a little weird. He would head back to the B&B and hole up for a while until he could figure all this out. His natural instinct was to pack up his gear and hit the road. It was one thing to do a little breaking and entering and he had no problem with hitting the MacDowell kid. The boss paid him well for both and the man ordered him to stay close by in case the need arose. Getting the word to do the son and make it look like an accident was unexpected and outside his comfort zone, but Grogan had no problem setting it up and executing it. He wasn't supposed to kill him, just put him out of action. *Well, he's out of the action now.* On the other hand, he hadn't counted on catching the eye of the sheriff quite this quickly. The way they rolled up on him at the diner was a sure sign he was a person of interest.

The Polaroid photos under the door were definitely not something he had counted on. And now Grogan wasn't sure they came from the kids. No blackmail demands. No note. Why would they try to blackmail him? If half of what he heard in town was true, the kids would be rolling in dough as soon as the sheriff got convicted. According to town gossip, them getting their old man's money looked like a slam dunk. In a day or two, the sheriff was either headed for a permanent orange jumpsuit or one last puncture mark.

But damned if the guy on the side of the road didn't look like MacDowell's kid. His DEAD kid. Instead of heading straight to the B&B, Grogan stopped at the sole working phone booth in Mounton. *Hell, probably the lone remaining payphone in Kentucky.* The phone was on The Side Street as it would have clashed with the retro-makeover of Main Street. After digging out some change, he called the Lexington number.

"Why are you calling here?" the voice on the other end of the line asked.

"Dude, something weird is happening," Grogan said into the receiver as he looked around. "Someone sent me some snapshots. One of the sheriff's gun and one of my van parked outside the motel. Except you can tell it was in the early morning from the angle of the sun in the picture and I was never there in the morning."

"It wasn't the sheriff. He was in court all morning. Hmmm."

"Yeah, no shit 'Hmmm'. If the pictures weren't bad enough, I just saw the sheriff's kid, standing by the side of the road. Right where his truck burnt up."

"But—"

"Yeah, I know. He's supposed to be dead. But I swear it was him. Had his stupid Cardinal's cap and everything."

"You're sure?"

"Hell yes, I'm sure. The others are too skinny or too muscular. One is Black for God's sake!"

After a moment of silence on the phone, "You still there?" Grogan asked.

"Yes. Okay. Stick with the plan. Go back to the rooming house and sit tight. Park the van out of sight and I will contact you. Whatever you do, don't call this number again."

"But what about…you know…the kid?" Grogan asked.

"If it's really his ghost, then he's dead and the effect on the sheriff is as intended and his son can't get in the way. More than likely, you just need to get some really good meds. Either way, stay the course. Stay out of sight and wait for more instructions."

CLICK.

Grogan looked up and down The Side Street, expecting an apparition to appear at any moment. He looked at the phone handset he hadn't hung up yet.

Who ya gonna call?

#

"It's still there!" Jasper looked out the curtains of the room at *The*

Motel 44.

A silver van sat parked outside on the edge of the road, too far away to see who was in it, but they knew just one person who drove a van. Between some road signage and untrimmed bushes, it was hard to see.

"Why would he just sit there and watch us?" Mandy asked as she changed the TV to a pay-for-porn channel.

"I think he's watching to see what we do. He probably planted those photos at the door and he's planning on blackmailing us once we get the money," Jasper said, staring out the window.

"But don't we think he's the one who hit Jeb's truck?" Mandy asked. "He has as much to lose as we do. I mean if they get us, they're going to get him for killing Jeb."

"I don't know what to think," Jasper whined. "I knew it was a mistake bringing a guy like him on, but our vote didn't count."

Mandy looked at her brother.

"Let's call Lexington and see if they know anything about this. Best case scenario, he's there for our protection. Worst case scenario, if he tries to blackmail us, well, they can only hang us once."

Just as the silver van pulled away from *The Motel 44*, fifteen miles down the road in Mounton, Markus Grogan was hanging up the phone from his own call to Lexington at the phone booth in Mounton.

#

"Sir, glad I caught up to you," Jesse wheezed as Mac, Patricks, and Dawe prepared to enter the courthouse.

"What's up?"

"Not too much. I wanted to give you the latest," Jesse told him. "Heaven just called from Bardstown Hospital and because it may have been related to the fire at your place and technically you're responsible for Sonny, I thought you should know. Howdy brought him in to get his hand X-rayed and thought he may have hurt it when he punched the window out of your Bronco."

"Sounds reasonable."

"Yeah, no. Here's the thing. The doc has some questions. Sonny used his knuckles on the window," Jesse said. "Doesn't explain why the bruise is in the palm of his hand."

"Is Sonny going to be okay?" Mac asked.

"Oh, yeah. They put a small cast on his hand and gave Howdy some instructions and the doc says in a few weeks, it will be good as new. As long as he stops high-fiving sledgehammers."

"Well, it IS Sonny," Mac said. "He probably quit slapping ball-peen hammers when he was ten."

Patricks squinted at Dawe, but the night deputy looked neither left nor right as he strode up the steps to justice.

#

Jasper Stemple could not stop checking the window. Mandy came out of the bathroom, wrapped in a towel which barely covered her, and found her brother perched on a chair, peering out the curtains. He had been at it for hours.

"Get away from there, Jas," Mandy said. "Do you *want* to attract attention?"

"I'm telling you, Grogan is trying to mess with us. I keep seeing a silver van parked down the road, just watching us." Jasper's nerves were shot. "I'm going to confront the son of a bitch." Unused to the conditions of the motel, the stress of their recent activities, and now haunted by the silver van, Jasper was near his breaking point.

"Do you really want to confront the guy who just ran the sheriff's son off the road and supposedly killed him? You don't have the gun anymore. Is it really such a good idea?"

After a moment's thought, Jasper mumbled, "No, I guess you're right."

Mandy looked at him and not for the first time wondered why she fell in love with him all those years ago. He was a gutless coward. She practically had to scream at him to get him to shoot their worthless father. But it was the key to inheriting the family fortune and implicating Sheriff MacDowell.

She just needed to keep him under control for a little while more. She peeled off her towel and climbed on to the king bed.

"Come here, silly boy. I know just how to steady those nerves."

Jasper turned from the window, looked at her on the bed, glanced back at the window, then shut the curtain and headed toward his sister.

#

Grogan was near panic. The man had sold this operation to him as an easy gig. *"Come down to Podunk Kentucky,"* he said. *"A couple of easy B&E's, run the sheriff's kid off the road, and collect a big payday,"* he said. Now, someone is sending him blackmail pictures without any demands, the law is sniffing around him, and on top of all that, he's seeing the dead deputy he ran off the road and killed, watching him and disappearing. He called his contact in Lexington and spoke once, but had received no new instructions yet. There was no sign of the big payday and he thought either the kids were blackmailing him or the dead guy was. Either way, this is where the suck wagon unloaded.

The best part of this whole town was the praline pecan ice cream, but those minor conveniences didn't warrant hanging around when he was seeing spooks. Grogan tried to call his contact's burner phone in Lexington again and when it went to voicemail, he made his decision.

Time to blow this pop stand!

He had just started throwing things in a bag when the knock came at the door.

Probably housekeeping. He left the Do Not Disturb sign on the door of B&B, but he questioned whether dear old Mable could read and write.

A quick peek out the side window showed him several uniformed police officers, with guns drawn.

Damn! Five minutes too late!

Grogan left his bag on the bed and quietly ran to the window on the side of his room. After sliding it open, he climbed out and as he hit the ground, he heard, "FREEZE!"

A black cop was standing twenty feet away in a Weaver stance with both hands holding his automatic, aimed straight at Grogan.

Oh, no. I am NOT going to jail in Deliverance after torching Deputy Dog's truck. I would be lucky to see morning.

Grogan turned the corner of the bed and breakfast, away from the black cop with the gun. At the other corner of the bed and breakfast stood what must be the ghost of MacDowell kid. Just standing there. Arms folded. Cap pulled down. Watching him.

Grogan skidded to a halt in the wet grass, his feet sliding out from under him. He could hear the black cop running to catch him from around the corner, but never took his eyes off the ... specter in front of him.

In sheer horror, Grogan turned and ran away from the B&B and towards the forest. If he could make it to the woods, he could possibly escape.

Right then, his leg shot forward with agonizing pain and the impact lifted his feet up from under him toward the front, dumping him on his back.

The black cop was on his shoulder mic, already notifying the cops in front of the B&B of the situation and calling for an ambulance.

The cop leaned over him and quickly frisked Grogan for weapons, "You may want to make a note for the next time you run: the average human being runs eight to twelve miles per hour and the slug from a nine-millimeter travels 818 miles per hour. I would bet on the Glock if I were you."

#

"And you shot him?" Mac asked incredulously.

"In the leg. You should have seen him land," Davis Williams smiled. "It was a classic ass-plant. The ambulance showed up in plenty of time to keep him from bleeding all over the grass. And we found some interesting stuff in his room."

"But you shot him," Mac said. "I've told you boys—"

"I know. You've told all of us, 'It's more important to respect the man than the badge…' blah-blah-blah. But once in a while, it's okay for them to respect the gun."

#

Darlene for the Defense

"Get out!" Darlene pointed toward the door. Her five-foot-three-tall frame stiff with anger.

"What?" Mrs. Fisher stammered.

"You heard me," Darlene barked. "I won't have that kind of talk in my salon."

"But I've had my hair done here for going on fifty years," Mrs. Fisher complained. She couldn't believe Darlene would throw her out. "I got my hair done here before you were born!"

"Then it's time you explore other shops!"

"There are no other shops. At least in Mounton. Where am I going to get my hair done?"

"I hear Louisville has some nice salons. Go there. And stay there!" Darlene growled in her tobacco-raspy voice.

"What did I do to make you act this way?" Mrs. Fisher whined.

"The fact you don't even know tells me what a complete and utter fool you are. I would hate for people to say, 'Hey, look at that fool. Doesn't she get her hair done at *Darlene's*?' No. This is my business and I have the right to serve who I like. And I don't like you!"

"Well! I never!" Mrs. Fisher stormed out.

"I bet you haven't either!" Darlene snapped as the older woman left.

Darlene looked at Mr. Darlene, who just kept sweeping the hair on the floor, shaking his head. The proprietress wondered if this was the last customer she would lose because of the rumor of Jacob and

Mandy. She hoped so. But she didn't know how Jacob could win a rumor battle. Some folks loved to believe the worst of others. Mandy was nowhere to be found to refute the rumor. It was years ago and there was no evidence to vindicate him. Jacob and Hannah were the best friends Darlene had and there was no way he could have done the terrible things Mrs. Fisher had chattered on about. It was simply his word against the town rumor mill. And the truth of the matter is: *Darlene's Beauty Emporium/Barbershop/Tanning Salon* was one of the wellsprings of most of the gossip. Word will be all over town by this evening of how Darlene had treated old Mrs. Fisher.

She looked at the other customers, who sat in their chairs getting permed or colored or cut.

"Anyone else wanting to spread malicious gossip about Jacob MacDowell is welcome to follow her to Louisville!"

Three faces quickly buried themselves in out-of-date fashion magazines.

#

Trial: A New Sheriff in Town

"I'll be honest, Mac. It's our turn to present our case and call our witnesses and we don't have a lot to work with," Hollister told Mac. "They've got your gun, your prints, motive, opportunity, a questionable history, and all your friends and family's testimony made you look like Al Capone."

The two men were standing in a small conference room used for witnesses at the courthouse. Jacob's defense was scheduled to begin in fifteen minutes. It was approaching the time to walk down the hall back to the courtroom.

"Then you won't mind if I jump in," Mac said.

"What do you mean 'jump in'?"

"Mr. Hollister, I need you to call my deputies back to the stand," Mac told his attorney.

"Because they *helped* your case *so much* during their initial testimony?" Mac's attorney said sarcastically. "Besides, isn't your son—"

"I'd rather not talk about him. Some new information has come to light and I think the jury should hear it. The guys are in a witness room right down the hall."

"What information?" Hollister demanded.

"It would probably be best if it came out in court," Mac said.

"Are you kidding me? You want me to put guys up on the stand who practically inserted the lethal injection into your arm, one of them your own son, and you want me to call them to the stand *without* knowing what they are going to say in advance? No first-year law student would do that."

"I think your initial reaction will play well with the jury," Mac explained as he handed Hollister a list of questions. "Just follow these instructions and it will all come out fine in the end."

"Who's trying this case? You or me?"

"Whose life is it?"

"This is the craziest b.s. I have ever heard," Hollister said.

"And you need to call Deputy Dawe," Mac continued.

"What? You want me to put up a witness I haven't deposed and have no idea what is going to come out of his mouth? If you're shooting for a mistrial, you're certainly on your way."

"There won't be a mistrial. Dawe is on the witness list. Carpenter put him there himself. He just has a few pieces of the puzzle."

"No lawyer in the history of American jurisprudence would ever do any of these things," Hollister protested.

"Then you are really going to hate this next part," Mac smiled. "I want you to put me on the stand too."

"Jacob—Mac, I don't think this is a good idea at all. I advise against it in the strongest possible terms."

"I don't think it could get any worse, do you?" Mac asked. "The jury needs to hear my side of the story."

"I agree the testimonies could have gone better, but if you get up there and go down the wrong path, it could easily go from life imprisonment to the death penalty. We haven't prepped you for testimony and I thought you didn't like talking in public."

"It may be the last chance I get to. Mr. Hollister, trust me when I tell you what I have to say to the jury won't hurt my case one bit."

"I wish I had a dime for every time a client said that," Hollister relented. "Okay, Mac. I work for you and if you insist on taking the stand, I can't stop you, but I am going to make sure the record reflects my opposition to all of this. Any appeal won't center around my *lackadaisical* representation."

"Don't worry. I won't tarnish your sterling reputation," Mac said as he opened the conference room door for his attorney. Let me tell you a quick story…

"Back when Jeb was just a baby, Hannah and I had some friends over to play Euchre. Hannah had spoiled him a bit, so I insisted that we put him in his crib in the other room so the adults could play cards. After a while, we hear 'Mom!' I told her to just ignore him and he'll go to sleep. Soon, 'Mommy!' 'Just ignore him.' A few minutes later, "MOTHER!" I shook my head. After a bit he screams out 'HANNAH!' I told her, 'Ya better go get him, no tellin' what's comin' out next.' I said all that to say this: ya never know what'll come out of someone's mouth next."

"I don't get it Sheriff, but hey! if you want to go to the gallows, it doesn't mean I want to hang with you."

"No worries, Mr. Hollister, I have no intention of hanging," Mac smiled. "You, however, are on your own."

#

During a sidebar with both attorneys at the judge's desk, Judge Gibson and the prosecutor looked with concerned confusion at Mac at different times, still sitting at the defense table. With a shake of his head, the judge shooed both attorneys away.

"Mr. Hollister, do you have any witnesses to call?" the judge asked.

"Yes, Your Honor. I actually have several," Hollister said with a glance at Mac. "I would like to recall Deputy Davis Williams."

A Fayette County sheriff's deputy escorted Deputy Davis who carried a file folder casually under his arm, into the courtroom and up to the witness stand.

The judge looked at Davis, "Sir, I want to remind you, you are still under oath."

"Yes, sir."

"Deputy Williams," Hollister began, "I understand despite having the FBI taking you off the case, you have continued to look into the break-in at the MacDowell's house. Could you tell us what you found?" After looking back at Carpenter sitting at the prosecution table, he added, "You do not have to constrain your testimony to one-word answers."

The jury snickered at the shot at Carpenter.

"Yes, sir," Davis began. "The FBI officially took over the case in coordination with KSP because it was a crime against a law enforcement officer, but technically, they didn't forbid our department from looking into it further. We just weren't officially in charge."

"Sounds like they didn't want you on the case," Hollister hypothesized.

"They didn't actually *say* we couldn't investigate," Williams continued. "They just said they and KSP would take charge of it. Things being slow in Mounton right now, we had a little time to poke around. There were a large number of questions unanswered and nobody seemed to be following those lines of investigation to our satisfaction."

"What did your *poking around* reveal?"

"The thieves weren't worried about a dog. It's likely they knew the MacDowells didn't have one, despite having a large dog water bowl and dog toys out on the porch to give such an impression. The perpetrators weren't concerned about anyone being home, since they didn't knock or ring the doorbell to check. This implied it was someone who was fairly familiar with the MacDowell family schedule, including knowing Hannah was out, Naomi was in school, and Mac and Jeb were at work. It was somebody who knew them.

"The front doorbell camera captured on video three men breaking into the house without knocking or ringing the bell. They trashed the house, particularly the granddaughter's room. They stole a few things, but not enough to justify a three-way split. We started to ask why. Did they know enough about the MacDowells to know their schedules, but not that they didn't have much in the way of valuables? Doesn't seem likely. Why would someone destroy the home and desecrate the little girl's room?"

"Revenge?" asked Hollister.

"Possibly. There was one thing of extreme value in the house. As the prosecution was extremely eager to verify, Sheriff MacDowell's Colt Peacemaker revolver. Their own experts claimed the pistol may be possibly worth a hundred and fifty thousand dollars. Yet the burglars seemingly avoided his Pelican case."

"Why do you say 'seemingly,' Deputy?" Cummings asked.

"The FBI and the prosecution made a big deal and presented evidence the lone fingerprints and DNA on the Colt's carrying case were Sheriff MacDowell's. But Hannah often cleaned the Colt and moved the case inside the safe to get to hers. Yet her prints were not found on the case at all. This seemed to lead to the case being touched during the break-in and then wiped down. When the sheriff touched it immediately after the break-in, he got his prints on it.

"Now, we know someone messed with the pistol case and theorized they removed the Colt to use it on Adrian. Hannah never touched the actual antique with her bare hands while cleaning it to avoid getting oils from her skin on it." Davis looked at Mac. "The sheriff is not quite as…careful. His prints were on the weapon and shells inside it from when he loaded it. Whoever used it on Adrian must have worn gloves. They got into the case and wiped it down thoroughly. Too thoroughly. They were wearing gloves because they didn't want any trace left they had been in the case. What's important here is the *lack* of prints. They were so worried about fingerprints and DNA, they got rid of too much. Maybe they wanted to get into Mac's gun case and everything else was just to cover it up."

"But what about what they did to Naomi's room?" Hollister asked, looking to see if Jeb was going to explode in court.

"More distraction from the gun case in the safe," Davis explained.

"All you have is Hannah's prints were not on the case and a couple of unproven theories about prints and why someone would break in and wreck their home," Hollister said.

"But wait! There's more," Williams continued in his best late-night commercial voice. "The next morning someone impersonated a security guard and called Mrs. MacDowell to come to her granddaughter's school in order to empty the house. Here are affidavits from the school and the real security guard."

"Objection. These affidavits are not in evidence and we have had no time to look into this," Carpenter interjected as he pushed up from his chair, while staring at the documents Williams tried to hand to Hollister.

"Sustained. Mr. Cummings, presenting new evidence this late in the game is in bad form," the judge said. "The affidavits are excluded from evidence."

Deputy Davis Williams put the affidavits back in the folder as he looked at the prosecutor, "Boy, who didn't see *that* coming?"

#

"Yes, Your Honor. These documents are news to me as well," Hollister mumbled looking down at the folder in Davis Williams's hands.

Looking at the judge, Davis apologized. "I'm sorry, Your Honor, some of this is new evidence and has just come to light."

Hollister, flustered, looked down at the questions listed before him. "Deputy Williams, what else did you find?"

"Objection!" Carpenter interrupted.

"On what grounds now, Mr. Carpenter?"

"The witness is testifying to facts not in evidence and ground not covered in his deposition."

The judge considered for a moment. "I'm sorry, Mr. Carpenter, but you missed and whiffed on this one. You opened up this line of testimony when you questioned Deputy Williams about the MacDowell break-in and his qualifications. I disallowed the affidavits, but Mr. Williams's testimony stands. Continue, Mr. Williams."

"Yes, sir. Now we are theorizing two break-ins. One break-in happened at the front door where a doorbell camera is blatantly evident and made it *look like* a home invasion for revenge and burglary. A fact borne out by the doorbell cam video already shown. We believe the robbery and vandalism were just a cover to inconspicuously steal

Mac's Peacemaker. The perpetrators entered purposefully through the front, knowing about the Ring doorbell cam. Then a second, stealthier break-in was to return the gun back to the safe before anyone noticed its absence. The second break-in wouldn't have been through the front door, but in the back, where there is no security camera, and after they lured Hannah out of the house.

"They called Hannah to get her to leave, broke into the kitchen door without a trace, reopened the safe, replaced the gun in the case, wiped everything down, closed the safe, and exited, relocking the kitchen door all in less time than it would take Hannah to get to and from the school. They *again* meticulously wiped down the case Mac had touched the day before.

"Even with my limited investigation experience, this screams professionalism. In a town of barely 600 people, this is a whole new level of sophistication and eliminates anyone local. The first burglar is most likely looking to be an out-of-towner," Davis said.

"Do you have any proof of a second theoretical break-in?" Hollister asked.

"Actually, we do. Someone called Hannah away to empty the house," Davis said. "But for years, Mac and Hannah always set the combination lock at zero. This way, they would know if Naomi touched the safe. When Hannah came back home, the lock was on 39. The same holds true for the initial break-in. The combination dial sat at 82. We have timestamped photos of this.

"What do we *know* at this point?" Davis asked. "Three masked men got into the house without knocking, ringing, or breaking the front door jamb. The second man was short and slender. He and the third man were nervous and jumpy. The first one looked more confident and surer of himself. The third one was taller and has a bit of a limp. It's someone who knows the MacDowells' schedules, knows they don't really have a dog, and knows items of value to steal, opened the gun safe, but didn't take the valuable Colt case."

Hollister read the next question on his list, "Do you have suspects who may fit these profiles?"

"The two elder Stamper brothers, Syrus and Spencer. The physical descriptions match despite the masks. See how the one limps? Spencer injured his leg in an…incident last year. Their criminal records and history with Sheriff MacDowell made them the likeliest suspects. Their attorneys arranged for their release from incarceration in the week before the break-in."

"But you have no proof it was them?"

"Actually, the youngest brother, Sonny, let Mac into the Stamper…residence and they both saw a recently installed flat-screen TV with a cut cable matching the one stolen from the MacDowell house. He told the sheriff someone hired his brothers to rob Mac's house."

"Objection!" Carpenter appealed. "Hearsay."

"Sustained," the judge said. "Officer William's last statement needs to be disregarded by the jury."

"What about the third man? Do you have any idea who he might be?" Hollister asked.

"Yes, we do, "Davis said. "Prior to the break-in, one of our deputies, Jesse Hendricks, made a traffic stop for excessive speed on a carrier truck hauling vans. Turns out they were stolen vans and the FBI suspects a Markus Grogan, who has records and warrants in Kentucky, Ohio, Georgia, and most recently, Florida, for grand theft auto and breaking and entering. This was the same FBI Mr. Carpenter referenced. The man Jesse pulled over presented a license identifying him as Mark Calhoun. When I approached him after the break-in, Mr. Calhoun refused to identify himself and refused to answer any questions. Once we learned of his location, a circuit court judge granted us a search warrant due to the fact his photo matched Markus Grogan and the vans on the carrier matched the descriptions of stolen vehicles. Markus Grogan has warrants for B&E, so we added tools of the trade to the search warrant. The same search produced lock pick tools, a bag of medical equipment reported stolen from Cincinnati, and an Ohio driver's license for Mark Calhoun and a Florida one for Marc Collier. The bag included white vinyl gloves, sanitizer wipes, and a stethoscope. We also found Mrs. MacDowell's guns and laptop. It seems he didn't trust the Stampers with them and didn't want to fence them as it could point back to him. He must not have wanted the proceeds the stolen goods would produce. Money wasn't the motivation for the break-in."

"Why is medical equipment important?"

"Because the vinyl gloves would let you work without leaving fingerprints. The sanitizer wipes matched the brand, type, and chemical composition of the ones used to wipe down the Pelican case, and the stethoscope's head was the exact dimensions of the circle on the safe on the MacDowells where no glove prints were found. An exact circle with smudges all around it, but not in the circle. Grogan used the stethoscope to listen to the tumblers of the safe."

"It seems like a great deal of circumstantial facts, but hardly concrete evidence of Sheriff MacDowell's innocence," Hollister said.

If Davis didn't know better, he would say Hollister might be doing the prosecutor's work for him.

"Without more, you might be right," Davis continued. "Three men broke in, two of which match a description of the Stamper brothers who have a grudge against the MacDowell family. With the stolen goods found at his place of residence, Grogan was clearly the third man. When arriving to execute a search warrant from a Mounton County judge, the same judge who had moved this trial's venue to Lexington by the way, Officers Patricks and Dawe, as well as the KSP, found the elder Stampers beaten, lying in pools of blood. The KSP bodycams and a separate video by Deputy Carlysle will show their condition when all the officers arrived. Also, because they have been incarcerated before, we already have prior samples of their DNA. Along with their care at the hospital, we procured more than enough DNA matches to Syrus and Spencer Stamper for the defecation and urination in seven-year-old Naomi MacDowell's bedroom." Davis offered Hollister copies of the search and arrest warrants, which he wouldn't touch. "Syrus seemed overly anxious to confess to things we neither knew nor cared about."

"Before you object, Mr. Carpenter," the judge said, "these are public documents and before you get all heated up, I am admitting them into the record. They are not evidentiary of any fact other than the officers obtained the warrants legally."

"Here are copies of the DNA results the FBI provided. I guess since they had missed so much earlier, they felt a little guilty and rushed these through. We got them in days instead of weeks." Davis offered Hollister several printouts from the file folder.

"Objection. Same objection as before."

"Sustained," the judge agreed. "*These* evidentiary results have not been vetted by *either* counsel and excluded from evidence. Nor were they provided by the defense in the proper time frame. Mr. Hollister, I'm going to advise you if your witnesses keep producing inadmissible evidence, we are going to have a little chat about this."

"Yes, Your Honor," Hollister understood. "Deputy, can you continue without more inadmissible evidence?"

"Yes, sir. We found some property stolen from the MacDowells' house at the Stamper shack. We found the necessary equipment in the room of Markus Grogan, wanted for breaking and entering. When apprehended, to avoid first-degree murder charges, which KSP *may* have suggested they were considering, Grogan admitted an unknown third party hired him to break into the MacDowells' house both times to steal and replace the Colt. In fact, he seemed overly eager to name the Stemple kids and the Stampers as co-conspirators. We hadn't gotten a chance to question him about them before he started ratting them out. We don't know why. He seemed to think he owed them a little payback. The unknown party facilitated Grogan's hiring, transactions, and handoffs through emails, burner phones, and dead drops and he never knew who hired him. All he had was a phone number for a burner cell which is no longer working. My guess is if I had copies of his affidavit, interrogation, and signed confession, you wouldn't want them as evidence."

"You're right. Let me ask you, Deputy," Hollister said, ignoring the offered papers, "up until this time, didn't you keep an open mind it could have been the sheriff who got into the safe and staged the break-in?"

"No, sir. First, Sheriff MacDowell would never do something like that in a million years. But personal impressions aside, why would Sheriff MacDowell wear gloves to get into his own safe? He certainly wouldn't need a stethoscope. He already knew the combination."

"Well, Deputy, this looks like a thoroughly packaged investigation."

Davis smiled toward the prosecutor, "It's been an experience, I'll tell you."

#

Leading Lessons Learned

"Hey, Sonny," Mac greeted the big man as he approached the front door of *The Digger's Hole Saloon*. He drove there after court. From Lexington to his house, it was out of his way, but he promised himself he would swing by. It was the first chance he had to get away since hearing about Sonny's hand.

"Hey, Sheriff Mac."

Mac stuck his hand out to shake the big man's hand, but at the last minute noticed the blue cast around Sonny's hand and wrist and switched hands.

"Hurt much?" Mac asked his friend.

"Naw, itches a might," Sonny looked down at his hand. "Ya wanna sign it? Peggy an' Howdy an' everybody at the bar signed where they could. I cain't hardly read 'em, but that one there's Peggy's."

"I'd be proud to sign it."

"I think there's some room here on the bottom," Sonny said, twisting his wrist around for Mac to see.

After Mac signed the cast, he looked at Sonny's face. "Sonny, how did you hurt your hand?"

"Well, when I busted out the winder of your truck, it hurt a bit. I'm powerful sorry about that. You want me to pay for it?"

"No, Sonny," Mac chuckled. "Leave it to you to save my life and Hannah's and then offer to pay for the damage."

"Yeah, I reckon your winder'd probably burnt up no how."

"Probably. Funny how the fracture was on the palm of your hand when you punched my Bronco."

"Sheriff Mac, I gotta tell—" Sonny began.

"Say! Did you hear about your brothers?" Mac interrupted, looking down at Sonny's cast.

"Yeah. Mr. Dawe came by an' tol' me they was busted up pretty good," the big man said as he looked down. "They gonna be all right?"

"I doubt if they were ever 'all right,' but if you mean are they going to heal from the beating, the answer is probably. But it's going to take a long while," Mac told him. "Spencer woke up a day or two later. After a week in Bardstown, courtesy of Mounton County, KSP is transferring them to the Big Sandy hospital, to await trial. When I think about Naomi's room, and Hannah trapped in our burning stable, I believe they had it coming. You were probably here at *The Hole* working, or sleeping upstairs, the night they got beat, and which means you don't know a thing about it, do you? I mean, you work this door most nights at 7:00 P.M., don't you?"

"Uh…yessir, I do."

"Good. That's what I thought. Well, I just wanted to check on you and your hand and let you know the authorities have your brothers safely locked away and are giving them excellent medical care."

The two men shook hands and Mac walked back to his rental truck.

I now know why lawyers use leading questions.

#

Trial: He Got Better

"Mr. Carpenter, would you like to cross-examine?" the judge asked.

Washington Carpenter stood, thinking about the inadmissible stack of affidavits, warrants, and DNA reports. "No, Your Honor, I...reserve the right to cross later, if it pleases the Court."

"Mr. Hollister, you have any more witnesses?"

"Your Honor, I would like to recall Acting Sheriff Jebediah MacDowell to the stand."

The gallery gasped and murmured until the judge slammed his gavel down. "QUIET!"

"Your Honor, we object due to the fact this witness has not been available to us in recent days," Carpenter whined.

"Have you tried to get a hold of him?"

"Well, no."

"May I ask why?" the judge frowned.

"We heard he was dead," Carpenter said sheepishly.

"He certainly looks alive to me. So, you object because you didn't have access to a witness you didn't try to get ahold of...because you thought he might be dead? Did anyone SAY he was dead? Did you see a death certificate?"

"Yes, Your Honor. I mean, no, Your Honor."

"Overruled. Mr. MacDowell, if you please."

As Jeb stepped up to the witness stand, Judge Gibson reminded him he was still under oath and Dayton Hollister addressed him.

"Mr. MacDowell, I, like many others," Hollister said, "am both pleasantly surprised and happy to see you survived your recent accident. I am told you have some information you would like to share with the Court."

At this, Carpenter raised an eyebrow. It sounded like Hollister really didn't know what was coming, just like he mentioned in the sidebar. He seemed just as surprised as Carpenter himself was that Jeb was alive. Up until now, he thought Hollister was feigning ignorance as just a tactic to lead up to a mistrial.

"It wasn't an accident, but thank you. Yes, sir," Jeb began, "As acting sheriff, I initiated a parallel, but unofficial, line of investigation to what the FBI and KSP were following in the murder of Adrian Stemple. While recovering from my misadventures, I was able to focus on the investigation both unimpeded and covertly."

"What did you find?"

"Objection," Carpenter snapped. "Your Honor, we have not deposed this witness about this investigation or this line of questioning."

The judge looked at Carpenter in sheer disgust. "But you *did* depose him. More importantly, we will not penalize the defendant just because when you had him in the hot seat you didn't ask the right questions. Mr. Hollister has already stated he knows no more about this than you do. If this young man has something to say impacting his father's murder trial, I am willing to listen. If you disagree with my decision, I look forward to reading your appeal. Overruled. Acting Sheriff MacDowell?"

"Because of how well we know all the parties concerned, we noticed a number of discrepancies anyone not familiar with the individuals involved would have missed," Jeb said as he looked directly at the prosecutor. "One of the benefits of living in a small town is we all know each other and everyone's little idiosyncrasies. Details people from bigger cities may not know about each other and tend to overlook. When Adrian called for Dad to come to his house, he sounded strange. And he asked for 'Sheriff Jacob MacDowell.' Which he also wrote on the envelope on his door. He signed the envelope *Adrian T. Stemple, Esq.* Dad's known Adrian Stemple going on thirty years and it's been almost as long since they called each other by anything other than their first names. At least as long as I have been alive. I think he was trying to tell Dad something over the phone and with the envelope."

"We think someone had a gun aimed at him," Jeb continued, "most likely Dad's pistol, and someone forced him to make the call and handwrite a will."

"The prosecution thinks the same thing. They just think it was your dad," Hollister said.

Jeb continued. "Then there's the will. It named 'Ginny' as a beneficiary. But Adrian and Dad both knew Ginny's legal name and as an attorney, Adrian would never put a nickname in a will.

"As for the phone call, Dad was at the station and I answered the phone, so how could he have forced Adrian to make the call? No, Adrian was trying to give my dad clues about something strange going on. Holographic wills are commonly challenged. My understanding is the prosecution's own expert witness testified along those lines. But in the big picture, the whole holographic-will-under-duress thing was deliberately set up to fail, to let the estate fall to whoever's next in line."

"Adrian's kids?" Hollister guessed.

"The estate, seemingly, becomes the motive for the killing," Jeb said. "We believed Mandy and Jasper forced their father to call the office and handwrite the will at gunpoint, using the same Colt secretly stolen from my parents' safe earlier. The Stampers assisted in the break-in and the desecration as a coverup to steal the Colt. They, or more likely Markus Grogan, replaced the weapon and framed Dad for it all. With the new will proven as written under duress, they believed the estate defaulted to them. It's pretty ingenious.

"But this is where some irony comes in. The Stemple kids don't know squat about wills, or much of anything is my guess, but the brains behind all this did. They convinced the Stemple kids that when the holographic wills were thrown out, the estate falls to the family.

Actually, the estate falls to whoever is named by the last *legal* will. Through a couple of warrants I obtained while on leave, I found Adrian drew up a new will and trust about six months ago. These notarized and filed documents with the clerk of Mounton courts left one dollar each to his kids in the hope they would grow up if they had to earn a living. Everything else he left to the county of Mounton in a trust, and this is the ironic part: the trustee is my father."

"The under-duress-holographic will was not too far from the truth?" Hollister asked.

"Sort of. It was meant to be a motive to frame Dad for murder, but in the real will and trust, he doesn't get a dime. I have copies here and the warrants, if you would like them."

"Objection," Carpenter called out.

"Yeah, yeah," Judge Gibson said, tired of the constant objections to inadmissible evidence. "Sustained. Mr. Hollister, please advise the witness his testimony is valid, but the deadline for introducing new evidence is long past. The prosecution has not had time to review it or verify it." Looking at the jury, "Please disregard Mr. MacDowell's last statement and offer of documentation."

The jury sat blank-faced, trying to digest the new information.

"You're saying Mandy and Jasper Stemple are behind the break-in and their father's murder?" Hollister asked, anxious to get to the point.

"We have no hard and fast proof of that. Our office," he didn't happen to mention it was *him* or Duncan in a rented silver van, "has been keeping them under surveillance for the last several days. But as far as being the masterminds behind all this, as I said, you could probably put everything the two of them know about holographic wills in a teacup. They do have the multi-million dollar estate as a motive, a murder weapon as the means, and opportunity. They were at the scene. The FBI found their DNA and fingerprints all over Adrian's study."

"All of which could easily be explained. They used to live there," Hollister said.

"That's not how it works. Fingerprints and DNA evidence reside in layers," Jeb explained. "Their prints were the top layers on the furniture around the body, overtop Adrian's, and they haven't lived there, or visited, for over a year. Plus, Adrian had a housekeeper come in twice a week to do a thorough cleaning."

"Surely cleaning isn't enough," Hollister said. "My understanding is there were no prints on the will but Adrian's."

"True," Jeb smiled, "but Mandy's DNA was on the gum inside the envelope flap the holographic will was in. The FBI was happy to let us know about their findings." Jeb held out a manila folder for Hollister to accept, but instead he backed away from it as if Jeb was handing him a poisonous snake.

"Objection!" Carpenter was on his feet for this one.

"Mr. Hollister, I've had enough," the judge barked. "I've given you some leeway based on the sidebar earlier, but foreknowledge or not, you let one more piece of inadmissible evidence pop up, and I will empty the courtroom and have a rather stern chat with everyone involved. Objection sustained. Let's wrap this up without any more pissing contests."

Hollister looked thoroughly flustered by all the surprises in court. He didn't think to go off script and ask questions not on the legal sheet. Jeb could see Hollister's mind racing a million miles per hour. He was just grateful the lawyer didn't ask about his ghostly appearances to shake Grogan and the kids, or the Polaroid photos he and his dad had sent to the various players, plus Douvez, to do the same. Spooked people make mistakes, and this group was no different. All of them immediately jumped on a phone, suspecting each other of blackmail, a double cross, and awaiting instructions. During his "absence," one of Jeb's tasks was to get warrants to tap Grogan's and the motel phones, where he heard how spooked they all were. He had to remember to thank the antique firearms dealer in Louisville for loaning him the old Colt. He used it for the photos he sent out.

No one had actually *said* Jeb was dead. His parents had told Naomi the truth, but she wasn't assured until he had snuck into the house at night to convince her. His mom and dad had sworn her and Sonny to secrecy, but to keep her away from questions, they home-schooled her for a while. They trusted her, but they had taught her not to lie. Better to be safe than sorry. They just let everyone draw their own conclusions and let the town gossip mill do the rest. They had spotted a tail on him for several days prior. His dad figured Jeb could be more effective if the opposing side couldn't keep track of him and throw curves and false alarms at him. He needed the freedom to watch the Stemple kids, follow leads, get warrants, and handle the "blackmail" photos. Plus, it was fun to rattle Grogan's and the kids' cages. It was the least he could do to the people who had tried to kill him.

#

Trial: Phone Tagged

"Mr. Carpenter, would you like to cross-examine?" the judge asked.

Washington Carpenter stood, thinking about the inadmissible mountain of affidavits, warrants, and DNA reports. "No, Your Honor, I…would like to reserve the right to cross later, if I may."

"Any other witnesses, Mr. Hollister?"

After looking down at the yellow legal pad in his hands, Hollister answered, "We call Deputy Joseph Dawe to the stand."

"Objection. We have not had a chance to depose this witness," Carpenter bleated.

The judge looked at several documents before looking up.

"But you do have him listed as a witness from the beginning I see," the judge said. "So, you've had a chance to depose him, but you just chose not to."

"We didn't believe Deputy Dawe had anything relevant to add to the case, Your Honor."

"Then why did you list him as a witness?" The judge smiled. "I know it couldn't have possibly been a smoke screen to deluge the defense with possible witnesses or to keep them out of the courtroom. I assume you must have thought Officer Dawe has some relevant testimony to give. In case you haven't figured it out, objection overruled."

Looking at Mac's attorney, "Mr. Hollister, just because Mr. Carpenter dropped the ball here doesn't mean you get free rein. I don't like surprises, and though he's listed as a witness, tread lightly. The ice under your feet is quite thin."

After the bailiff swore Dawe in, the deputy stepped around and sat in the witness chair.

"Deputy Dawe," Hollister looked again at his notepad. "Let's get right to it. What testimony do you bring to this trial about Adrian Stemple's murder?"

"Acting Sheriff MacDowell asked me, secondary to my regular duties as the night shift officer, to call the KSP, Lexington, and Louisville detectives to find any possible pawn shops who might fence stolen goods. They were overjoyed to give me the information and save them one more tedious task they would have to do."

"What relevance does this have with Mr. Stemple's untimely death?"

"None. There is no connection. Not one single pawn shop has seen or heard of anything anywhere closely related to the MacDowells' stolen goods. The detectives in those cities, who eventually followed up on the pawn shops, confirmed as much in their investigations. It was a total dead end."

"You have nothing related to the murder?"

"I didn't say I had *nothing*," Dawe continued. "It appears as though the robbery was not motivated by greed, since no one ever fenced or pawned any of the stolen articles. Why break into the MacDowell home if not to steal stuff and sell it? Why go to all the trouble if not for money? Revenge? No. One guy gets angry enough to retaliate. Maybe two. But three? No. Three guys take planning and organization. Clearly, it wasn't for the money or revenge. There weren't enough valuables stolen to pay for the risk for three guys. These conclusions brought us to the one valuable item in the house seemingly untouched."

"So, all you bring to the party is a lack of finding a fence and some speculation about the break-in? What does this have to do with Adrian Stemple?" Hollister asked, clearly annoyed he hadn't had a chance to depose Dawe and didn't know what came next.

"Actually, I have a few more pieces, but by themselves they are not enough to exonerate Sheriff MacDowell," Dawe stated. "Through some…personal connections, I was able to obtain the call records of the phone booth in Mounton. It's the lone working one in town and Acting Sheriff MacDowell, while on leave, spotted Markus Grogan frantically making a phone call. Since it's a public phone, we didn't need a warrant, we just needed permission from the phone company who were happy to help. It seems at the exact date and time Mr. Grogan made a phone call to a burner cell phone. Because it was a burner, we don't know exactly who answered the call, but we do know it was through a cell tower servicing a two-block diameter in Lexington relayed the call."

"There must be millions of calls handled in that Lexington area all the time," Hollister stammered.

"Not quite millions, but yes, a lot," Dawe said. "Another piece of the puzzle was our connection in the phone company provided us with the outgoing inmate calls from Big Sandy penitentiary. Being convicts, we didn't have to worry about warrants to get the phone records and the correctional officers and warden at Big Sandy obliged us happily. A thing most people don't know is: convicts have no rights by law. You don't need warrants for just about anything. Now, the law cannot *record* the one phone call a suspect makes, but the phone company does record the number they call. The phone records include the time, length, and destination of the call. I was able to confirm it with my contacts in the phone company. The only phone calls inmate Devin Douvez made were to his lawyers. By coincidence, the same firm who got the Stampers released. By further coincidence, it's the same exact firm heading the unlawful death lawsuit by Mandy and Jasper Stemple against Sheriff MacDowell and Ginny Starcher.

"According to public court records, those attorneys are Beacon, Hill, and Hollister. Why…your name is Hollister, isn't it, Mr. Hollister?"

#

Trial: Evidently Inadmissible

Mr. Carpenter looked as engrossed in the testimony as the gallery. He declined to cross-examine at this time, citing he needed time to investigate the phone records.

"Any other witnesses, Mr. Hollister?"

"Yes, Your Honor. For my final witness, I would like to call Jacob MacDowell."

"Objection, Your Honor!" Carpenter stood. "The defense did not inform us of this witness's testimony and we have had no time to prepare for it."

"And there goes 'the no more pissing contest' concept. Mr. Carpenter," the judge began, "let me get this straight, you are objecting to a defendant on trial for his life testifying on his own behalf? You did *graduate* from law school, correct? Him being the suspect, I imagine you did depose him. You had your shot. I'm simply overruling this for the trial transcript because otherwise, it would be too ridiculous to dignify with a response."

"Yes, Your Honor."

The bailiff swore Mac in. Mac turned and sat in the most important chair of his life.

"Mr. MacDowell, can I call you Mac?" Hollister began, trying to get the jury to humanize Mac. "We've heard the timeline of events and the testimony of others. Can you tell us your side of the story?"

"No, sir," Mac said. "I can tell you the truth, there is no 'side.' During the course of this trial, I began to see that the truth was not as important as agendas. Not by far."

"Okay, Mac, tell us the truth."

"First of all, I am not disputing any of the *facts*. I had my disagreements with Judge Stemple, especially just before he died. More recently, someone broke into my house. Adrian Stemple and I had lunch and discussed his kids' lawsuit against me. Not much later, Adrian was shot with my Colt." An audible gasp emitted from the gallery. "Adrian both made the phone call inviting me to his house and wrote the holographic made under duress. I was at his house about the time he was shot. The killing slug came from my gun and had my prints on it."

#

"Mac, you seem to be making the prosecution's case for them," Hollister stammered.

Indeed, Washington Carpenter was leaning back in his chair comfortably, watching the testimony intently.

"Well, Mr. Hollister," Mac turned toward the jury, "those are just facts, but I decided I needed to dig a little deeper to find out the whys, the context, and who was really behind all of this, since I knew it wasn't me."

"What did you find?"

"First of all, Judge Stemple and I didn't see eye to eye because his criminal activity was going to get my granddaughter killed. Then he tried to shoot me but Ginny shot him dead first. That put a bit of a damper on my friendship with the Judge. The grand jury transcripts from last year document and exonerate both Ginny and myself as they declared the shooting as self-defense.

"Secondly, Adrian and I did have a conversation in the diner about the lawsuit his kids are bringing against Ginny and me. Ginny just didn't hear all of it. Adrian was saying he cut off his kids from their allowance once he heard they were suing and they, not he, blamed me for everything bad in their world."

"You said 'secondly,'" Hollister said, still nervous over testimony he didn't know where would go. "What else?"

"Deputy Williams looked more into the break-in. Dawe checked out the fences in this part of state as well as the phone records between the prison, jails, phone booths, and various parties, and Jeb investigated the murder. I looked into the bigger picture."

At this point, Mac looked at the judge. "Sir, I believe no one can sue me for anything I say in court, is that correct?"

"Yes, sir," the judge confirmed. "Everything you say in the witness chair the law considers privileged, and you are protected from slander or libel."

"Thank you," Mac said. "I asked because, frankly, Mandy and Jasper don't have the brains, ability, or ambition to mastermind something this devious. They're essentially spoiled brats. The two of them were too lazy to look outside their own family for someone to date. If it wasn't for their family's money, I have no doubt they would be homeless right now. So, if not them, who?"

"Indeed?" Hollister asked. "It sounds like you don't think Mandy and Jasper Stemple had anything to do with this, despite your own son's testimony."

"Oh, they were involved. They were the ones who gained financially from the murder of their father and Mandy's DNA clinched it. Phone records from their motel room verified their involvement. They just weren't smart enough to come up with this scheme. But some of it seemed eerily familiar.

"As some of you may know," Mac addressed the jury, "we had a catastrophic fire at my farm this month. My wife nearly died. Several of our horses and those we board did burn in the fire. Horrible, painful deaths. My granddaughter's pony was among those who perished. Our barn and stable burned to the ground as well as all of our farm equipment.

"It was definitely arson, and before the prosecutor can start blaming me for it, I was just getting out of court. He, himself, can testify we were having a little conversation not related to the case. I have a bit of an alibi.

"The fire got our insurance canceled, crippled our income, all but burned my wife's ancestral home, destroyed all our equipment, and severely impacted our line of credit. We used the house, farm, equipment, and buildings as collateral to fight this murder charge and the unlawful death suit the Stemple kids are bringing against us. It may have ruined us financially."

"Who *did* start the fire?" Hollister asked.

"Oh, that's easy. It was the Stampers. KSP right this moment is executing additional arrest warrants in the Stampers' hospital rooms, where KSP is holding them for the break-in at my house. They are singing like birds. Well, not actually singing. Spencer just regained consciousness and the doctors had to wire Syrus's jaw shut. Someone tuned them up pretty good a few hours before law enforcement showed up to arrest them. They waived their rights to an attorney in exchange for some much-needed medical attention at the prison hospital. You would think as many times as they've run up against the law, they would know better than to admit to anything without a lawyer. It wasn't until after they signed the confessions right away and admitted everything that they tried to call one. Before their lawyer could get back to them, Syrus tried to get a plea deal on the break-in, which was just sad since they had no information to trade on. Grogan had already confessed and threw the Stampers and the Stemple kids under the bus. The arson charge is a slam dunk as the moonshine used as an accelerant chemically matches what the Stampers produce in their still as well as the Mason jars used in the fire.

"While they were in a giving mood and scared stiff, but before they called their attorney, Syrus confessed to destroying our tractor last year. The KSP may have hinted around having evidence of as much last year, before their confession, but the law actually allows them to stretch the truth. Funny how it works, the law can lie to a suspect, but the suspect can't lie to the law. If it wasn't inadmissible, KSP would be happy to provide their confessions, both written and videotaped, for your viewing enjoyment."

"Did you find out anything else?" Hollister inquired.

"Well, yes. This whole thing of 'getting me in trouble with the law while destroying my reputation and putting on enormous financial pressure' all had a familiar ring to it. Like I'd been there before. Turns out I was. Last year when Devin Douvez tried to destroy me and my family, he used similar tactics."

"But isn't he incarcerated now?"

"Yes, he is, but there are a number of issues there. He swore he'd get revenge and he had a truckload of money stashed somewhere the feds couldn't dig up."

"But he's rotting in prison," Hollister countered.

"The one thing about prisons most people don't think about," Mac began, "prisons not only keep criminals in, but protect them from the outside world. Devin Douvez is not so much rotting as sitting protected in prison, with a concrete and steel alibi."

#

"You believe Devin Douvez is behind all this?" Hollister asked incredulously.

"No, sir. I *know* it," Mac said definitively.

"How could he?" Hollister asked, floundering in his ignorance of Mac's testimony.

"Douvez has the means—the missing money he hid. His motive was simple revenge. Nothing would have delighted him more than me being convicted guilty of murder charges and my family destitute while trying to save me."

"What about opportunity?" Hollister asked. "The man is in prison over two hundred miles away. Surely you don't think he could orchestrate such a complex scheme from hundreds of miles away, locked in a prison cell?"

"You see, Dayton—may I call you Dayton? Douvez was the piece that didn't quite fit until we started looking behind the scenes. Dawe's research into the phone records cleared it all up. The lawyer bringing the suit against Ginny and me was Edward Beacon. That's the name of your partner, if I am not mistaken. By itself doesn't mean anything.

Could be a coincidence. But the lawyer the Stampers called, after they confessed, but before KSP charged them with arson, was Morgan Hill. Again, they may have heard the name in connection to my trial, know he's a high-priced criminal attorney, and probably the one attorney they've ever heard of. Except for the fact the Stampers don't have any money. How can they afford a high-priced attorney?

"They can't. But maybe the same someone who paid your firm to get them off the kidnapping charges recently would pay for them again." Mac nodded at Jeb, sitting in the courtroom, who stepped outside. Carpenter noticed the movement and was sitting straight up now. Jeb stepped back into the courtroom with an elderly gentleman in handcuffs and two Kentucky State Patrol officers.

"There are a couple of other little links pulling it all together. As I said, the attorney who filed suit against Ginny and myself is Edward Beacon. He's right back there with my son. Say hi, Ed." Dayton Hollister looked to the entrance of the courtroom to see his taller partner in cuffs. His mustache matched his silver hair perfectly.

"It wasn't obvious who was paying for his services, but someone was because it was such a loser. Adrian, himself, told me no firm would take it on contingency. Until you listen to Douvez's cellmate snitch. He says Douvez's sole contact with anyone was his attorney. If you take the time to look it up, it's also Morgan Hill. Isn't he your other partner? I was at Douvez's trial and I can tell you for a fact it was him. Strange, but despite the numerous phone calls from Big Sandy, he never filed an appeal. Wonder what they were talking about all those times?"

Jeb, the deputies, and Edward Beacon stepped back into the hall.

"Your Honor, with all this objectionable evidence declined, I bet if I could produce a signed confession from Mr. Beacon about his knowledge and firm's involvement in this conspiracy, my guess is, it would be inadmissible."

"You would be correct, Mr. MacDowell," the judge said.

"Objection! Mr. MacDowell is trying to introduce materials not in evidence we have had no opportunity to vet," Carpenter said as he stood, a little less adamant than he had been.

"Sustained. The jury will disregard the witness's last statement," the judge directed. Mac grinned. *But like the jury, Hollister and Carpenter can't un-hear it.* "Mr. MacDowell, do you have anything else?" Even the judge had dispensed with the illusion Hollister was running the defense.

"Yes, Your Honor. Here's how I see it: Devin issued instructions through Dayton or Mr. Hill and paid for all of this through his hidden offshore accounts. I imagine he paid them quite handsomely. He loans money to the Stemple kids to pay Beacon knowing as soon as the new will fails, they can pay him back. Beacon met the Stemple kids at *Motel 44* and…" looking at Carpenter, "…based on some friendly intel, they may still be there. And very likely willing to discuss Mr. Grogan's part in all this. Douvez gave them instructions on how to kill Adrian and frame me. He paid Hollister to get the Stampers out of jail and to contract Grogan. Besides attempting to kill my son in his truck, Grogan does the initial break-in and comes back to make the swap. He didn't know the Stampers were stupid enough to use their own moonshine and Mason jars in the arson, leave DNA at the break-in, or call your firm directly when they got caught. Score one for lack of public education. Or cable TV. He obviously doesn't know them as well as some of us do."

Mac looked back up at the judge.

"I'm guessing a signed confession from Devin Douvez would be inadmissible as well? Yeah, never mind."

"Mr. Carpenter, if you will?" the judge asked with a smile in his voice.

"Objection. Same grounds, Your Honor," Carpenter said.

"There it is. Sustained." Rolling his eyes toward the jury, the judge said, "You know how this works by now, people. Please disregard Mr. MacDowell's last question."

"When did you know—" Hollister asked, his tan face paled.

"When did I figure your involvement? Not long after you pushed your way into my cell when I got arrested, I got a mental itch I couldn't quite scratch," Mac said. "I didn't recognize you right off as one of Douvez's lawyers, because of all the weight you lost, the dark beard, the shaved head, the spray-on tan, and all. Looks like you mighta had your teeth fixed and probably wearing contacts instead of those Coke-bottle glasses you used to wear. I only saw you for a quick moment over a year ago. But Hollister is a fairly uncommon name hereabouts and Ginny had just told me about the high-priced firm who got the Stampers out. Last time I saw you, you looked completely different. A friend of mine mentioned shaving one's head might make one a new person. Took me a while to remember you though I had spent a lot of time in the witness chair facing your partner during Douvez's trial. You've transformed into a different person now. I imagine it wasn't an accident.

"During the trial, you let Mr. Carpenter lead the witnesses around by the nose and barely objected. It looked like to me everyone including his Honor noticed it. It was like you *wanted* me convicted. You're not a *bad* attorney, Dayton, but I don't think you're a *good* one either. I think you're *both*."

"I played along but notified my buddy Dave at the FBI and it was both easy and his pleasure to track any connections to or from you or Douvez to offshore accounts. They are exceptionally happy they can stop looking for Douvez's hidden funds. Dave may get another promotion. If it was admissible in court, he could, hypothetically, provide you with the warrants, paper trail, and seizure documents." Dave Smathers of the FBI smiled and waggled his fingers at Hollister in a playful wave from the gallery.

"The Stampers and Grogan are already in custody and eager to be turning state's evidence. Douvez is in Big Sandy, but facing new charges of conspiracy to commit murder, insurance fraud, arson, breaking and entering, and a few others as we speak," with a look at Carpenter, "by a federal prosecutor. Oh, yeah, the overseas money makes this a federal case now. KSP and the FBI have filed similar charges, plus murder one, against the Stemple siblings and attempted murder for Grogan. Guess who else is getting the prize package?"

Washington Carpenter thought about the pile of search and arrest warrants, FBI documentation, DNA results, and signed confessions mentioned in the last two hours. It may be inadmissible in *this* trial, but it doesn't mean they don't exist. After a moment's pause, he stood up.

"Your Honor, at this time, the Commonwealth of Kentucky would like to drop all charges against Sheriff MacDowell. We will be issuing an immediate warrant for Dayton Hollister, Morgan Hill, and Edward Beacon for questioning."

"Case dismissed. Will the Fayette County deputies please detain Mr. Hollister until Mr. Carpenter can issue his warrant."

"Uh, there's no need, sir," Mac said still in the witness chair. "They can detain him, but the federal prosecutor has already issued warrants for his arrest. Mr. Smathers would like to take him, if it's okay with you."

"It is. The sooner I can be rid of this silliness, the better. Sheriff MacDowell, you are free to go," the judge said with a rap of his gavel. After thanking the jury for their service, he immediately stood and exited the courtroom.

Hannah rushed from gallery and swerved around the podium to greet Mac coming down from the witness stand. Jeb stepped out and whispered to the two KSP troopers holding Edward Beacon and they handed him over to the FBI. Dave Smathers grinned from ear to ear at Mac as he cuffed Dayton Hollister. He mouthed the words, "Pay bump."

"I have never witnessed you expound in such abundance in your entire life," Ginny said as he shook Mac's hand. "I guess the imminent threat of lethal injection loosens the tongue, eh?"

"Yepper."

#

Washington Carpenter's assistant was putting away all the documents from the trial into his briefcase while her boss walked up to

Mac.

"Sheriff, I would like to see those confessions you extracted from Beacon and Douvez," Carpenter insisted.

"And I surely would like to give them to you, but I don't have them."

"But in court you said—"

"I said, '*IF* I could produce them, they would likely be inadmissible.' I didn't say I had them, I just asked a hypothetical '*if I could*,'" Mac smiled. "You gave me that idea, by the way. The Fayette County Sheriff's Department detained Mr. Beacon for a broken taillight and an unpaid traffic ticket. It's sheer coincidence Jeb stepped in and out of the courtroom at the same time those deputies brought Mr. Beacon into the wrong room."

"Bullshit!" Carpenter grinned. "I objected, like you knew I would, preventing you from producing Beacon's confession, which you didn't have, but Hollister couldn't *un-hear* it! He looked back and saw Beacon in cuffs and…damn! The same with the confession from Douvez. You bluffed us all and played the system. You are one crafty sonnuva—"

"Gun. Speaking of which," Jeb interrupted, looking at his mom. "When do you think Dad will be able to get his Colt back?"

"I'll get it expedited and sent over. And you! With the fake death. My guess is you were scaring Grogan and the kids into making some rash moves. You know, Sheriff, I'm just going say it, I was wrong about you."

"Yepper," Mac said.

"Don't let it trouble you, Mr. Carpenter," Jeb said, coming up from the back of the courtroom. "Dad said all along you were just doing your job, trying to put what you thought was a guilty man away."

"No. It was more than that," Carpenter admitted, looking at his shoes momentarily and then directly at Mac. "I took it too personally. I really thought you had killed a judge, railroaded my friend and boss, and were playing on the wrong side of the law. I felt like you were spitting in the face of everything I had lived my life for, and it gave me tunnel vision. I should have made sure the police had investigated every possible avenue. But I was sure it was you and I didn't. If there's anything I can do…well, I'm sorry."

"Don't give it a thought Mr. Carp—" Mac started.

"Actually," Hannah interrupted, "there IS something you can do."

Mac looked at his good Baptist wife. For the first time today, he wasn't sure what was going to come out next. Hannah cherished and protected her family more than anything in this world. She had taken Carpenter's attacks on her husband to heart. Despite her personal relationship with her Lord and Savior, Jesus Christ, she wasn't above verbally castrating the state prosecutor. He'd seen it before and it wasn't pretty. It was the first time Mac felt sorry for the man since the whole trial started.

"Mr. Carpenter," Hannah asked with a smile, "how's your phone voice?"

#

No Allowance For Crime

"Deputy!" Reginald Dalton greeted Jeb as he opened the great carved front door of his house. "What a surprise. I didn't know you were coming."

"I kind of drove down unannounced on purpose, Mr. Dalton," Jeb said as he stepped into the marble foyer. "I didn't call ahead because I wanted to be sure I caught Denton at home. You know how it is."

"Denton?" Mrs. Dalton quavered from the sitting room entrance. Her son stood behind her, with a stricken look on his face.

Jeb turned toward the boy as he spoke to the parents.

"I'm sorry it took me this long to get back to you, but I think I may have some alarming news for you. In my recent 'downtime,' I have looked into this case and done some poking around and speaking to a few folks. It seems as if Denton may have committed the robberies of the tire store and the liquor store in Harrodsburg, as well as the Texaco station in Mounton."

"Our son?" Mrs. Dalton held her left hand protectively in front of her teenage boy.

"I'm afraid so," Jeb said. "The first robbery was at the Texaco in Mounton and involved some energy drinks, candy, and two-stroke motor oil. The window they climbed through was too small for a man, but your son there could fit through easily. After we went back and checked, there were tire tracks leading from the station. Tire tracks matching two 143cc TM MX 144 2Ts. The exact make and model of your son and Chaz's bikes, is it not?"

"Denton?" Dalton looked at his son with new eyes.

"The chainsaw noise the witnesses heard at the Harrodsburg robberies was from the whine of the two-stroke engines on the trail bikes," Jeb explained. "I thought of it because I had a much cheaper one when I was a kid. They sound like a cross between a bees' nest and a chainsaw. Unmistakable. When the witnesses listened to a recording of two bikes, they positively identified the sound. And 143cc motocross bikes use two-stroke oil."

Knowing he was found out, Denton exclaimed, "It was all Chaz's idea!"

"Seems unlikely," Jeb continued, turning to Denton. "You were at both the liquor store and tire shop with your parents in Harrodsburg prior to the break-ins and were likely casing the place for alarms and cameras. You avoided the floor safe because you knew the store locked it. Pretty smart for a fourteen-year-old. But like a typical fourteen-year-old, you didn't realize most high-end purchases would be through a credit card and not cash. Tire tracks through the fields leading from the stores confirm two motocross bikes. My guess is since your dad is 'garnishing' your allowance, you and Chaz are supplementing your incomes through extra-curricular activities."

"Oh, my God!" Mrs. Dalton stepped away from her son.

"It's true, isn't it, Denton?" Dalton said. "You and Chaz robbed those places...*because I took your allowance?*"

"It wasn't fair!" Denton screamed. "You spent more on tires on your fancy car than my motorcycle cost! You've got boatloads of money and yet you're keeping mine!"

Dalton turned toward Jeb. "I am sorry, Deputy. We had no idea. What is going to happen now?" He knew enough about criminal justice to know his son would face serious juvenile charges.

Jeb looked at the family. *All this money and they're as messed up as everyone else.*

"I'll tell you what, Mr. Dalton. I've spoken with the store owners and the Mercer County Sheriff's Department. If you and Chaz's parents make restitution of the damages and stolen property, and the boys do some mandatory, but unofficial, community service overseen by the Mercer County Sheriff, they won't press charges against the boys. We can keep them from arrest and trial, but they will need to do whatever the sheriff says, until Mercer County is satisfied they learned their lesson."

"I'm not going to be some pig's slave!" Denton snapped.

"Son, you ARE going to do whatever the sheriff says and I don't care if he holds you until you are eighteen," his father said quietly. "You have no idea what a favor Deputy MacDowell and the sheriff are doing for you. Since your attitude is as much our fault as it is yours, your mother and I are going to volunteer for community service as well."

"What?" Mrs. Dalton demanded.

"Damn right," Dalton told his wife. "A little roadside cleanup or washing police cars might do this family some good. You're just going to have to get your mani-pedi a little dirty. Our son has screwed up and we are partially to blame." He turned toward Jeb. "Deputy, I apologize on behalf of my family. We'll do whatever we need to to make this right."

"Don't worry about it," Jeb said as he stepped out the door. "Just make sure Denton learns wrong from right."

Dalton walked Jeb to his SUV, closing the carved door behind him.

"Deputy, a word?"

"Sure."

"If I'm out of line, please tell me. I have been following your father's recent troubles," Dalton said quietly and handed Jeb a business card. "It would be impossible not to. But as an attorney and somewhat familiar with Dayton Hollister, I took a special interest in the case. Now that the Court has acquitted him, I believe your father may have an exceptionally strong case against Devin Douvez for the physical damages, defamation, and a few other items. Come to think of it, you have a pretty strong wrongful death suit against him. The insurance company will help pursue this. Plus, your dad can file against Dayton Hollister for conspiring and for how he handled his case. For what you've done for my family, I would be happy to handle all of those gratis."

Jeb looked at the business card.

"I'll pass your info on to my dad and see what he says. You know you don't have to do this right? The offer to your son had nothing to do with this."

"I know," Dalton said. "My son was going down a dark path and hopefully, now, because of you, we may be able to save him. We can never repay you."

"Sure you can. Get Denton on the right track. Then we're square."

#

Phones, Faults, And Follow-Up

Several days later, Mac supplied Carpenter and the federal prosecutors with the digital photos taken by Duncan at *Motel 44*. Duncan provided his written affidavit of the events he witnessed there, including the hand-off of what was no doubt Mac's Colt before and after Adrian's shooting. After further investigation, the FBI provided the DNA reports, phone records at the Fayette County Jail and Big Sandy prison, warrants, and the results of the search at Grogan's room. The Kentucky State Police provided both prosecutors with digital copies of the Grogan and Stamper confessions, copies of the attempted plea bargains, the Stampers' arrest warrants, and copies of their body-cam footage to Carpenter and the Federal prosecutors. All in all, both Carpenter and the feds had enough to convict the Stampers, Grogan, the Stemple kids, and Douvez and keep them in prison for a long, long time. None of them should ever see the outside of a chain-link fence again.

"The Lexington detectives found Mandy and Jasper Stemple right where you said they would be. Mandy has been especially cooperative. She essentially threw her brother under the bus for shooting their father, claimed to be a victim of the scheme, and admitted Douvez initiated the whole sexual abuse rumor. It's amazing what someone will do to avoid the death penalty."

"Tell me about it," Mac sympathized.

"And that last call about did it," Carpenter grinned. The MacDowells sat in his office in Frankfort. "I just got off the phone with Midwestern Fidelity. Stotts is on board. I spoke with his boss's boss. Instead of your insurance company canceling your policy, they have decided to pay your claims as soon as possible as it is preferable to an investigation launched by the Commonwealth of Kentucky. Since the Stampers admitted to destroying your tractor last year, the insurance company agreed to not raise your rates. They are retroactively reducing your payments until the raised amount they charged you is negated. They are also making good on all of your customers' horses and damages since you had a separate policy for that."

"Mighty kinda you, sir," Mac said.

"Well, it's the least you could do since you—" Hannah started.

"Honey. Mr. Carpenter was just doing his job," Mac chided his wife.

"No, she's right, Sheriff. It was the least I could do," Carpenter confessed. "I went too far and half-blinded by revenge for what the Douvez case did to the Kentucky justice system, I took it personally. Totally not your fault. It was his. I know that now and if there is ever anything else I can do to help make it up, don't hesitate to ask."

Mac looked over at his wife. She smiled.

"Do not judge, and you will not be judged. Do not condemn, and you will not be condemned. Forgive, and you will be forgiven. Luke 6:37"

Mac looked at Carpenter. "What she said."

#

Reginald Dalton was as good as his word. After Jeb spoke with his father, the newly reinstated sheriff called the attorney and after the meeting, Dalton began the paperwork to file suit against everyone involved in troubles plaguing the MacDowell family over the last year or so. Dalton didn't mind when Mac told him he had checked out the attorney's background quite thoroughly.

"I've had some issues with less-than-reputable lawyers lately."

Mac looked back at the last few months and began to believe you could find real justice in a courtroom. He realized that maybe all lawyers weren't scumbags. Currently, the score was Bad Ones: 3, Good Ones: 2.

The FBI had the Marshall's Service confiscate all of Devin Douvez's assets, but Dalton plead a successful motion proving a large portion of the estate Douvez was gained legally, inherited from his family. This looked like a win for Douvez until Dalton sued him for all of it. Between the forfeiture of his ill-gotten gains and the suit filed against his legal assets, Douvez was now penniless and powerless to fight the new criminal charges against him. The remaining question left was which MacDowell would end up with the lion's share of Douvez's personal wealth: Mac for the defamation, personal attacks, and damages, or Jeb for the wrongful death of his wife and unborn son. Mac's bet was Jeb.

Dalton filed various suits against Mandy and Jasper Stemple; Beacon, Hill, and Hollister; Dayton Hollister as an individual; and everyone involved in the kidnapping and subsequent murder of Beth. Between the insurance company making them whole for the barn, stable, horses, customer damages, vehicles, medical bills, being debt-free to begin with, and according to Dalton, "if you win half your suits, you will never have to worry about money again. You aren't going to be 'Papa John-rich,' but Naomi won't have to worry about college tuition."

Mac smiled. Everybody in Kentucky was familiar with John Schnatter, who founded Papa John's Pizza and lives in a suburb of Louisville. Papa John is one of the richest men in Kentucky.

Jeb followed up with the Mercer Sheriffs and as promised, the Dalton family appeared on the weekends for community service. Some less happy about it than others. After it was clear Reginald Dalton was truly sorry for fostering Davis's sense of entitlement, Mercer County promoted him from road cleanup to working as a public defender on weekends and evenings, pro bono. His wife and their son were somewhere along Highway 55 picking up garbage.

#

Epilogue

Mac had invited everyone to Ginny's for a celebratory party. Ginny had closed the diner for the afternoon for the special occasion. Hannah, Jeb, and Naomi sat at Mac's usual booth. Howdy and Sonny had their own booth right next to the one with Peggy's two boys and her mother. Sonny would have sat with them, but he barely squeezed in one whole side of his booth with Howdy sitting across from him. Darlene and Mr. Darlene sat in the booth behind Mac's while Duncan, Patricks, Heaven, and Jesse sat at the counter, except for Davis, who was sitting at a booth in shorts and an old Washington Redskins jersey, along with Felicity and Gabe. The night deputy, Joseph Dawe, his wife, Patty-Jane, and their two boys, took up a whole booth on their own. Ginny and his waitress, Peggy Clay, ran around keeping everyone's sweet tea and coffee filled. Sonny wasn't aware he was watching like a love-sick puppy as Peggy move about the room.

"I don't know where to start" Mac began but looked at Jeb.

"What Dad's trying to say is: he used up all his words in his testimony." Jeb paused waiting for the giggles to subside. "He—no, WE all are thankful for the help from everyone. The county reinstated Dad and I can now go back to just being a deputy, and Dawe can quit working overtime again. I'm sorry I had to pull a disappearing act for a while. I hope you'll forgive me. But Mom made sure Dad never really lied to anyone. He just sort-of implied my passing.

"As for all the damages, Mom got her weapons back and the insurance company is going to pay for everything we lost, including my truck. Mom and Dad repaid what little they had used of the line of credit from the bank and cleared the mortgage on the farm. Due to the indictments against the Stemple kids, the lawsuit against Ginny and Dad died on the vine. Just goes to show if someone messes with somebody in Mounton, they mess with us all."

Mac looked at his friends and family, held up his glass, and agreed, "What he said. Here's to Mounton."

The group laughed and cheered.

"Daddy, can I say something?" Naomi asked Jeb.

"Sure, baby," nervous about what that might be. She had spent a year living with her Pappaw, and who knows what might come out of her mouth.

Naomi stood up in her booth and picked up her small glass of sweet tea.

"Here's to Bob."

"To Bob," everyone echoed.

When everyone settled down to their conversations and pie, Hannah leaned in toward Naomi.

"SweetPea, where did you learn how to toast?"

"I seen it on TB and watching Pappaw. Did I do it wrong?"

"No, baby, you did it just right."

"Sheriff Mac? Could I bend yore ear a minute?"

"Sure, Sonny," Mac said. "Let's step outside where it's a bit quieter. What's on your mind, son?"

"I gotta ask ya a question. I ain't got no family to ask and yore 'bout the smartest man I know," Sonny began.

"Sonny, to paraphrase my daughter-in-law, Beth, if I am the smartest man you know, we have GOT to get you more friends," Mac joked. When the big man stared back at him blankly, Mac asked, "How can I help?"

"Well, it's about girls, sir."

Oh, crap! I thought it was gonna be about something easy, like nuclear physics. Howdy mentioned Sonny and Peggy been kinda makin' eyes at each other.

"What about 'em, Sonny?"

"Reckon when you know if one likes you?"

"That's easy. Let me tell you something my dad told me and I told Jeb. If a woman likes you, she will let you know. Women are much smarter than men."

"She shore is smarter'n me, ain't no doubt 'bout it," Sonny said.

"Sonny. She's a woman. Means she's already smarter than any man who ever lived. If she sees what a good man you are, she's smarter than most women too. You just wait for her to let you know. She will."

"When will I know when to kiss her?" Sonny's voice cracked with the pain of never having a real male role model.

And there it is.

"Sonny, we have now concluded the part of this conversation where I have a clue as to what I am talking about. But you sit right here. I'm going to go get an expert to talk to you. She can help you with everything you need to know."

Ten minutes later, Sonny relayed everything to Hannah. Hannah couldn't believe how her husband had quickly dumped something this important in her lap. She could practically see the bus roll over her.

"I'll tell you, Sonny, Mac is about the smartest man I know."

"That's what I said!"

"All right, tell me about this girl…"

Mac and Hannah stayed after to help Ginny clean and to let Peggy get back to her boys. Jeb had taken Naomi home to put her to bed. Afterward, the MacDowells stepped out of the diner and Mac stretched before they started walking toward her Jeep. Mac had come to realize his job *was* to take care of this town, but also to take care of his own life and needs. He heard a comedian once say, "In the event of an aircraft emergency, first affix the breathing apparatus to your own face and then take care of the child with the most earning potential." It thrilled him to realize he did not have to do it alone. *The whole town of Mounton had potential. Well, maybe not Mrs. Fisher.*

With those thoughts still bouncing around his brain, Hannah reached up and snatched the cigar from his shirt pocket.

Damn. She caught me again.

"Here you go," his wife announced as she handed him the cigar. "You deserve this one. You put a whole bunch of bad people in jail, beat a murder rap, and made us whole again. I guess one cigar won't kill you."

Mac's shocked quickly subsided as he clipped the end and lit it before she could change her mind. Hannah had been against his occasional cigar for years.

"Nope! Changed my mind," as she snatched the cigar from between his teeth. Mac knew it was too good to be true. Hannah smiled up at him. "I deserve it. I saved some horses, got nearly burned up, kept the farm running, mortgaged the family home, and raised a smart granddaughter. Plus, I taught Sonny about girls." She brought the cigar to her mouth and puffed on it like she had been doing it for years.

"Baby, you may want to take it a bit slower," Mac cautioned. "It takes a bit of getting used to."

"Jacob MacDowell, I married you just a hair shy of thirty years ago. Do you think I don't know what a cigar tastes like? Who do you think I've been kissin' all these years?"

"I thought *I* was kissin' *you*."

"You would."

#

Special Thanks

Special Thanks to Brad Witherell of the Antiques Road Show for his help with details about Sheriff MacDowell's 1873 Colt Peacemaker Single Action Army revolver. Brad Witherell has been a gun collector since childhood and established Witherell's (http://witherells.com) in 1969. Over the past 32 years, he has worked for many of the country's leading museums and collectors as a dealer, auctioneer, consultant, and appraiser. Brad is a life member of the Colt Collectors Association, Texas Gun Collectors Association, Antique Bowie Knife Association, and the National Rifle Association.

Thank you to the men and women of law enforcement who keep us safe day in and day out.

Many thanks go to Karen T. Newman, and her company, Newmanuscripts, for her hours of dedicated editing and insight. And special thanks go out to my loving wife for making the writing of this possible…without divorcing me.

To the readers who purchased this book, thank you.

More from Paul K. Metheney

- *Concepts for Texas Hold'em* - making more money at Texas Hold'em Poker tables in casinos
- *Posse Whipped* - a Southern sheriff struggling to save his town, all while protecting his most valuable law-enforcement assets... his family and friends.
- *Escape Claws* – What if werewolves were real? What if you were one?
- *That Boy Ain't Write in the Head* - the greatest hits of mixed genre stories: Sci-Fi, Alternate Universes, Time Travel, Supernatural, and More
- *Two Minds, No Waiting* - a collection of stories involving science fiction, time travel, alternate universes, and worlds beyond imagining by Steve Rouse and Paul K. Metheney
- *Beautiful Lies, Painful Truths Vol. I* - a Left Hand Publishers anthology of short stories focusing on the ironic beauty between humanity's love of Life and fear of Death, featuring two interconnected short stories by Paul K. Metheney.
- **Beautiful Lies, Painful Truths Vol. II** - a sequel to Left Hand Publishers anthology of short stories. Life seemingly brings joy, happiness, hope, and love. Death can end sadness, illness, suffering, and pain featuring a double short story by Paul K. Metheney.
- *Classics ReMixed Vol. I* - An anthology from Left Hand Publishers of short stories twisting classic stories and your imagination in all new ways. One story includes a Paul K. Metheney twisted version of Rapunzel.
- *Classics ReMixed Vol. II* - The sequel to the anthology from Left Hand Publishers' short stories warping classic stories with all new twists. Paul K. Metheney takes on Pinocchio and the Dark Knight in disturbing new ways.

Posse Whipped
By Paul K. Metheney

A Southern sheriff struggling to save his town from corruption, drug trafficking, moonshiners, and the economy, all while protecting his most valuable law-enforcement assets... his family and friends. As the sheriff protects his town and loved ones, a villain from his family's past assembles his own eclectic posse of criminals to destroy Sheriff MacDowell and everything he holds dear.

A down-home journey into the hills of Kentucky brings you a sometimes humorous novel set in a modern-day western fight for survival, justice, and family. The spirit of the Wild West meets the 21st century in an adventure for the John Wayne in us all.
LHP http://tinyurl.com/y7b8dawj
Amazon http://tinyurl.com/st9x4rkt

***

Concepts for Texas Hold'em
By Paul K. Metheney

An easy-to-read pocket guide of concepts, notes, thoughts, and strategies on making more money at Texas Hold'em Poker tables in casinos. From tactics to use at the table, to money management, to etiquette and terminology, Concepts for Texas Hold'em will steer you toward bigger profits from your poker sessions. Aimed at intermediate to advanced players, we skip over the basics of the game to tricks, tips, and thoughts on how to make the most from your play.

Maximize your wins in your casino cash games of Texas Hold'em Poker. Minimize your losses.
LHP https://bit.ly/3r39YDF **Amazon** https://amzn.to/3AVTj7v

***

That Boy Ain't Write in the Head
By Paul K. Metheney

Mixed Genre Stories: Sci-Fi, Alternate Universes, Time Travel, Supernatural

A science-fiction author tries to save the world from an alien attack, extraterrestrial visitors that only eat cancer, a man travels back to his past, and a Secret Service Agent must protect the President from destroying the White House. These are just a few of the fantastic tales that await you inside.

This collection serves up Paul's best stories and an all-new menu of fresh tales to stimulate your literary palate.

The title of the book derives from a strip bar bouncer taking one look at Paul and saying
"That boy ain't right in the head."
LHP https://bit.ly/3r0TAnn **Amazon** https://amzn.to/3AVTj7v

***

Two Minds, No Waiting
By Steve Rouse & Paul Metheney

Take two very disturbed minds. Add the ability to create any worlds or situations they like. And you have the recipe for a collection of science fiction stories like none you have ever tasted.

From alien saviors and attackers, to time travel, to fantastic tales that include unique teachers and hunted mammals. This collection contains alternate universes and superheroes. If you're ready to set aside your beliefs in what is or isn't possible, it's time to get your imagination rewired by ...

Two Minds, No Waiting!

LHP - https://bit.ly/3R9q5dI   Amazon - https://amzn.to/39jAjFm

***

Please Review Paul's Books

It's free to leave reviews at Amazon or Goodreads.com.

Beautiful Lies, Painful Truths I Amazon: http://amzn.to/2reSyIe Goodreads: http://bit.ly/2BobVCi	**Beautiful Lies, Painful Truths II** Amazon: http://amzn.to/2ngBq0i Goodreads: http://bit.ly/2sIkBpP
That Boy Ain't Write in the Head By Paul K. Metheney Amazon - https://amzn.to/3AVTj7v Youtube - https://youtu.be/zpDkfvbzimw Goodreads - https://bit.ly/3E02x4z	**Classics ReMixed Vol. II** Amazon - https://amzn.to/3aC5aeh Goodreads - https://bit.ly/2vMBMDm
Two Minds, No Waiting by Paul K. Metheney & Steve Rouse Amazon - https://amzn.to/39jAjFm Goodreads - https://bit.ly/3pkLzH9	**Classics ReMixed Vol. I** Amazon - https://amzn.to/2M0qRLx Goodreads - https://bit.ly/2LZsIQl
Concepts of Texas Hold'em By Paul K. Metheney Amazon - https://amzn.to/3AVTj7v Youtube - https://youtu.be/zpDkfvbzimw Goodreads - https://bit.ly/3E02x4z	**Posse Whipped** By Paul K. Metheney Amazon - https://bit.ly/3Gl5a5w Barnes & Noble - https://bit.ly/3Hpsqyc Goodreads - http://bit.ly/3HX8rZk